The Arsenic Eater's Wife

Tonya Mitchell

BLOODHOUND
— BOOKS —

www.bloodhoundbooks.com

Print ISBN: 978-1-916978-26-3

Praise for the author

Tonya Mitchell has crafted a gorgeously gothic and atmospheric whodunit filled with surprising twists and memorable characters that I tore through in a single sitting. Inspired by a true-life crime, *The Arsenic Eater's Wife* offers proof that the darkest mystery remains the human heart.
— Kris Waldherr, author of *Unnatural Creatures: A Novel of the Frankenstein Women* and *The Lost History of Dreams*

A provocative, suspenseful Gothic treat of a novel, inspired by real events. Mitchell's atmospheric prose carries readers into the past as a woman accused of murder desperately tries to reclaim her innocence and survive a harrowing betrayal. Rife with secrets, intrigue, and serpentine twists. You won't be able to put it down!
—Paulette Kennedy, bestselling author of *Parting the Veil*

Tonya Mitchell's *The Arsenic Eater's Wife* renders a dark and intricately brushed portrait of the dichotomous business of human nature. Set against the scintillating murk of 19th century

Liverpool England, Mitchell's novel simmers good, and hot, and glorious with atmosphere, arsenic, intrigue, and lies.
—Robert Gwaltney, award winning author of *The Cicada Tree* and Georgia Author of the Year.

Based on a true story, *The Arsenic Eater's Wife* is a carefully plotted, suspenseful novel. Mitchell excels at fictionalizing historical figures. Brimming with rich details and unexpected twists.
—Kate Belli, author of The Gilded Gotham Mystery series

Mystery, death, and intrigue wrapped up in a Gothic tale.
—Pam Lecky, author of The Lucy Lawrence Mysteries

When a young wife is falsely accused of murder, how far will she go to clear her name? Inspired by an infamous real-life trial, *The Arsenic Eater's Wife* is a masterclass in historical suspense, brimming with intrigue, family secrets, betrayals--and a final quest for revenge.
—Elizabeth Blackwell, author of *On A Cold Dark Sea* and *Red Mistress*

Impeccably researched and rich with historical detail, *The Arsenic Eater's Wife* is a fictional mystery based on the true story of a woman wrongly convicted of her husband's murder. With more than a hint of the Gothic, Tonya Mitchell masterfully builds a palpable sense of dread throughout, but manages also to offer her characters grace even when their actions and feelings are deeply flawed. This is historical fiction at its best, offering justice in the form of story to a real woman who did not receive her due in life.
—Molly Greeley, author of *Marvelous*

Gothic author Tonya Mitchell spins a masterful tale of doomed romance and treachery in *The Arsenic Eater's Wife*, a grim, gripping historical mystery "reimagining" of a salacious, pulled-from-the-headlines murder in 1880's England. Mitchell weaves an emotional tale that perfectly captures the agony of a well-bred "fallen" woman falsely accused. The courtroom scenes are especially affecting. I couldn't stop reading this until the bittersweet conclusion. Kudos to Mitchell for a story well told.
—PJ McIlvaine, author of *A Good Man*

Mitchell's sophomore novel is enthralling from beginning to end —a twisted tale of love, betrayal, and revenge. I couldn't put it down!
—Stacie Murphy, author of *The Witch's Secret* and the Amelia Matthew mysteries

A genuinely gripping story of a young woman trapped. Mitchell brings depth and authenticity to her characters and setting, while expertly recreating Victorian trials of murder by poison. A compelling tale that will have you wondering who did it right to the end. A must read for fans of historical fiction.
—Kerry Cathers, author of *A Writer's Guide to Nineteenth-century Murder by Arsenic*

This Victorian-era mystery had me in its grip from the first page to the last. The story is laced with suspense and shocking twists, and depicts a time when a troubled marriage left women tragically few options. A first-rate page-turner.
—Nancy Bilyeau, author of *The Orchid Hour*

arsenic-eater *n.* a person who deliberately (and often habitually) eats small quantities of arsenic compounds in the belief that this will improve their health, appearance, or sexual potency.

–Oxford English Dictionary

Now, arsenic is a white powder. I have placed as I write one grain of this white powder in this space.

The smallest dose of arsenic ever known to destroy human life is two grains, and that was in the case of a woman; and certainly no smaller dose has ever been known to destroy the life of a man.

–Alexander William Macdougall, *The Maybrick Case*

For my sister, Connie
A hard act to follow

Part One

All human beings, as we meet them,
are commingled out of good and evil.

—Robert Louis Stevenson, *The Strange Case
of Dr. Jekyll and Mr. Hyde*

Chapter 1

Torrence House

Liverpool, England

May 18, 1889

The day they come for her, Constance Sullivan is lying still on the bed. She opens her eyes to a dim room with shuttered windows. Ribbons of light reach through the slats, fingering the burled wood of the dresser, the rough brick of the fireplace, the burgundy fleurs-de-lis of the wallpaper. The spare bedroom, not her own. The wrongness of it—that she should be lying here—confounds her, but only for an instant.

Jarring pain knocks at her temple, and then she remembers: William is dead.

She sits up and gulps air. *If you go back to sleep you needn't face it*, a voice inside her says, but the absurdity that these last few days can be avoided, slept away, is too much.

Memories split open: Edward's grip on her upper arms as he shook her; Ingrid's sly grin as she handed Constance's note to the police; little Billy's lips, white and puckered, as he looked down at his father lying prone. "Must he go to the angels, Mummy? Can't he stay here with us?"

Constance had been too overcome to speak. William might still have been breathing, but he was already gone. Death had crouched in the bedroom for days, its cloven hoofs creeping ever closer.

A whiff of sour air—putrid breath and body odor. Her own. Vomit has congealed in the bedpan on the floor. How many days have they shut her away?

She feels it then, the scrutiny of the air, the leaded weight of it: the house waiting for her next move. It is malevolent, Torrence House. She'd known it the first time she'd stepped across its threshold and felt it taking her in, appraising her weaknesses, testing her senses. She'd shivered and walked its empty rooms, listened to William prattle on about what they could make it when she knew full well the decrepit house had already made itself: its murky cells of rooms, its long corridors that fled into darkness. It was unchangeable, shrouded in a perpetual gloom that no amount of money spent on lavish decor could lift. That day they'd stirred the dust in the front hall into eddies as they left to explore the grounds, and her throat had constricted when William saw the orchard, the hothouse, the pond. "We must have it," he'd said, and she knew she had lost.

A floorboard moans outside the door. She comes to herself and stands. The contents of the room pitch, and she sags against the bed. She brings up a hand to smooth her hair and winces. Her body feels as if it's been wrung through a mangle. In all her twenty-six years, she's never felt so bone-weary. So used up. Her head has just hit the pillow when the door is thrown open. Dr.

Hendrickson strides in. He finds her wrist among the bedclothes and doesn't meet her eyes.

"I—"

"Be still," he says, his thumb on her pulse. His lips are a scowl. The smell of carbolic soap wafts off him.

She's about to speak again when Nurse Hawker enters the room and casts the shutters wide. Daylight splashes into the room. Constance feels as if she might be sick.

Male voices downstairs. She has no idea who is in the house.

The thoughts in her head are too crowded, wrestling for space. There's too much to take in, too much to remember.

A shadow at the threshold. Ingrid, clothed in full mourning. As if she is the widow. For a moment, their eyes catch and hold.

Footsteps on the stairs. The men are coming up.

"You must let me go too," Constance's mother shouts from below. "You cannot keep me from her!"

Dr. Hendrickson steps away from the bed, as if his proximity to her will taint him. Nurse Hawker sniffs at Constance before she looks to the doorway.

A policeman is the first to enter. Constance doesn't stir for fear of vomiting, yet panic shoots through her, swift and stinging. Following him is the superintendent of police. He came before—two days ago, four? She can't recall his name, what he told her. She'd been too exhausted to listen.

Her solicitor, Mr. Seaver, enters but doesn't meet her gaze. A fourth man, with heavy jowls and gray whiskers, is next. His eyes dart to her and away. She almost misses Dr. Hendrickson's deferential nod in his direction, his murmur of "magistrate."

The superintendent positions himself at the foot of the bed. He still wears his bowler. "This is Mrs. Sullivan, wife of the late William Sullivan," he calls out, as if on stage. "I understand Mr. Seaver has requested a delay and therefore I need not give evidence."

"That is correct," Mr. Seaver says. "I appear for the prisoner and suggest a remand of eight days."

Prisoner. The room sways and the house waits. Constance's heartbeat thrashes in her ears. She clutches her stomach, swallows down bile. Vomit has dried in the folds of her dress. There is a bruise on her finger where her wedding ring used to be.

"Eight days?" the magistrate inquires. He can't bring himself to look at her.

"Mrs. Sullivan is ill," Seaver says, gesturing to the bed. "She must get her footing. She is in accord with the delay."

Constance can't remember when she'd last seen Seaver. Has she, in the days she's passed ill in this room, agreed to any such thing?

The magistrate nods. "Very well; I consent to a delay in the proceedings."

The men shuffle out, requiring nothing of her. Downstairs her mother's voice is shrill, her words so rushed Constance can't make out their meaning.

Nurse Hawker shuts the door and approaches the bed. "Get dressed."

Constance pulls in her chin. "I will not. Can't you see I'm ill?"

"They are waiting." The nurse's eyes are hard black stones.

A spike of dread claws at her. "Who?"

"The superintendent and the others. You must go. You can't stay here."

Her mouth works but no words come. She begins to tremble. *Timothy. He must have received my letter by now. He'll come. He won't abandon me like all the rest.*

Nurse Hawker sets her shoes on the bed and pulls a wrap from the chair in the corner.

"I can't go like this. I must pack. I must bathe."

Hawker's only reply is to work Constance's feet into her shoes. Then she's yanking her from the bed, pulling her to the door like a wayward child. A policeman waits in the hall. He grabs her other arm, and the two force her down the stairs.

It's all happening too quickly. She must *think*. She is mistress of this house; they can't handle her so. But they are down the steps, each turn a dizzying spin, before she can gather words.

A knot of men awaits her at the bottom. Behind them, the servants—the cook, the parlor maid, the butler—are round-eyed and wary. Anne, the children's nanny, isn't among them. She stands next to Ingrid, a woman she believed was her truest friend not so long ago.

"What have you done with the children?" she says to no one in particular, her voice raw and tremulous. "I must see them." *I must say goodbye.*

No one breathes and then there is movement between the superintendent and Seaver. It's her mother, pushing her way past them. Her light blond hair has tumbled from its chignon. Her eyes are red welts, her skin so pale Constance can see a blue vein at her temple. Her mother tries to approach her, but the superintendent clamps a hand around her wrist.

"Now, now," he says, low. "There'll be none of that."

Her mother ignores him. "They've taken them away, Connie. I'll get them back. I will see all this put right."

Constance sinks at the knees like a marionette. The policeman and Nurse Hawker release her, and she is swept from the floor and whisked to the front hall. Her eyes graze the photographs on the table there. The ones of William lie face down. "So the master's spirit can't possess those of us left," Molly, her maid, had said. She wants to scream at the absurdity of it.

Someone opens the front door. A wreath of laurel draped with black crepe hangs upon it, declaring Torrence House a place of death. She's passing through it when she realizes, looking up, it is Edward Sullivan who carries her. Edward, her brother-in-law, whom she had trusted. Edward, who would have done anything for her weeks ago. She kicks and writhes in his arms. She cannot bear the touch of him.

Then she lurches forward and is sick.

For all the shame of it, it has the desired effect. Edward sets her down abruptly before a waiting carriage, cursing as he looks down the length of himself. When he glances up, his eyes, the same dove gray as William's, spark with contempt.

Behind him, the others are coming from the house. Her mother shouts from within, throwing insults at the policeman guarding the door. He has barred her from exiting the house. She shifts to French, her curses threading the air with bitterness, lacing it with vitriol.

Constance will not give them a spectacle. With the tip of her shawl, she cleans the front of her dress as Nurse Hawker climbs into the cab. The superintendent approaches, lifting his chin to the vehicle in a signal for her to follow. With the help of his arm, she clambers in, landing in a pile of soiled skirts. Dr. Hendrickson waits inside. The superintendent steps up, and in another minute, they pull away.

At the end of the drive, she turns and looks at the house. It leers back: the stone exterior the color of a corpse gone cold, hooded windows slit into the roof the squint of canny eyes. A swish of the curtains in an upstairs window. Her mother, palms flat against the glass, face white as the moon, watches her go.

She turns her attention to the dark, cold interior of the carriage. Dr. Hendrickson pretends to take an interest out the window.

Panic kindles in her. She'd trusted them, all of them, and

they betrayed her. Even William. Especially William. "I...I cannot go to prison."

Nurse Hawker raises her chin, the accusation in her eyes sharp as a slap. "You should have thought of that before you poisoned your husband."

Chapter 2

Walton Jail

Liverpool, England

July 24, 1889

Constance picks at a scab on her wrist. Dirt has settled in the creases of her body—the bend in her arms, between her toes. She wants to crawl out of the squalid skin that entombs her and start fresh, start clean. Begin a day that does not dawn with the memory of William vomiting and soiling himself, of William lying pasty and wasted until he breathed no more.

She is securely and wholly fastened in. The walls are stone, the cell door encased in heavy sheet iron. When it boomed closed the first day, it was like a shot going off. She has, in all but name, been stuffed in a coffin with the lid screwed tight.

She's learned to tell time by the passing of the sun. Yet the barred window through which it shines is so small, what little light it casts is meager. At night only a modest gas jet sputters a sickly glow. It's just as well. There's little enough to see: a small chair and table, an iron bed with a thin, musty mattress.

These amenities were arranged by Mr. Seaver for the cost of five shillings weekly. Convicted prisoners have no such luxuries and have only a plank board for a bed. But not even five shillings a week induces the warders to empty Constance's chamber pot more than once a day. The constant mopping of the halls with chloride of lime does little to keep the stench of urine and feces at bay.

Two hours each day she is allowed from her cell: one for morning chapel, the other for exercise in the yard. The Lord's Prayer tumbling from her lips and the sun warming her face are the only pleasures within Walton's dank walls.

The plate before her is licked clean. Her appetite, after a string of days in the infirmary, has returned. The preparation of her food by a nearby hotel is another luxury Mr. Seaver managed. The matron who delivers her meals is none too pleased to see her given such treatment. More than once, the old woman banged her tin plate and cup down with such force on the table, the contents spilled from their vessels. The foulness issuing from the matron's mouth is no less appalling than the cobwebs in the corners, the dry husks of roaches under the bed.

"Sooner or later, you'll swing by the neck. No fancy food will come to your aid then, eh?"

"Fill your gullet now, for it's the gallows for you, you bloody murderer."

She's received not a word from Timothy. She doesn't understand his silence. He must have heard she's here. Why hasn't he written?

The letters from her mother arrive every day or two. They are a temporary reprieve from her feelings of abandonment, yet the news is alarming. Her mother was barred from Torrence House the day Constance left, forced to stay in a hotel. The newspapers are rife with vicious rumors regarding her reputation as wife and mother. The coroner's inquest was temporarily adjourned for William's exhumation.

But these pale in comparison to the situation regarding her children. How frightened Billy, seven years of age, and little Janie, three, must be away from home, away from all they know. Her mother has yet to discover where Ingrid has squirreled them away. How can they deal with the death of their father and the desertion of their mother? They can't possibly comprehend it.

At night, huddled into herself and hollowed out with grief, the loss of her children feels like her heart has been wrenched from her chest. Her rage is what saves her. Without it, she would succumb to hysteria. It's all she can do to bite her fist to keep back her screams.

A metallic bang startles her into the present. Footsteps approach. The small circular hole in the door fills with a rheumy eye.

"Stand back," a voice barks.

The clank of keys, the twist of the lock. The door yawns open and admits the warden. "On your feet." His frock coat is threadbare at the cuffs, his cravat flecked with spots of blood or gravy. "Barrister's here for you."

"There is this business of a nurse who claims she saw you tamper with your husband's bottle of Valentine's Meat Juice the day before he died."

Sir Charles Kent does not look up from his notes. Papers litter the table. They sit in a filthy room reserved for prisoners to meet with their legal counsel, twice as large as a cell but lacking windows. Behind the walls, rats shuffle from one cell to the next. A distant scream down the hall sets Constance's teeth on edge.

At her silence, Sir Charles looks up. He's intelligent, this Irishman her mother is paying a king's ransom to represent her. And he is kind; she can see it in his eyes and the soft curve of his lips. There is no guile, only a shrewd quest for the truth. He's past his middle years, his posture slightly stooped. Yet his presence is commanding. Her mother has chosen well.

And now she must trust him with her life. Surely, this honorable man of the law will see her acquitted.

"I believe you are innocent, Mrs. Sullivan. I've believed in your innocence from the first stirrings in the papers, before your mother even came to me. You have been vilified in the press, convicted by the citizens of this city. I will see this charge expunged, but you must trust me. You must tell me what you know."

"It isn't true. What the nurse said about the meat juice. I merely picked it up on the landing and she saw."

"A far cry from tampering," Sir Charles muses, rubbing his chin. "Seems the good nurse drew a conclusion based on what was discovered in that bottle later. Do you know why she would invent such a tale?"

"They were all against me in that house." She's too ashamed to go on. She, the mistress, treated like a conniver, an exile in her own home. Anger simmers in her throat.

"Yes," Sir Charles says, his eyes moving across her face. "I expected as much."

The air in the room shifts and she breathes again. That he supports her, a stranger, when family and friends do not, makes her eyes smart with tears.

"The fly papers," the barrister says. "Your maid claims she found them soaking in your room. You are aware—"

"I know what she claims. I was leaching them of arsenic, but not for my husband. For a face wash..." She trails off. Even to her own ears it sounds like a weak excuse, thin as air. She begins again, tamping down on her temper. "I have a home remedy for whitening of the skin in which arsenic is an ingredient."

Sir Charles makes a note, sets down his pen, and entwines his fingers together on the table. "I must make it clear to you, Mrs. Sullivan, that much will be made of your trip to London. Your 'meeting,' shall we say, with Timothy Worth. You do not dispute it took place?"

"No."

"There were conjugal relations?"

Her cheeks burn. "Yes."

"The prosecution will use this...meeting to stain your character and paint you a fallen woman. A woman who would do such a thing, they will argue, would also take the life of her husband."

Her thoughts flash—Timothy in bed drinking tea, his tousled hair, his "You do have a way of depleting me."

"It's not the point of the case, of course," Sir Charles says. "The Crown must prove that your husband died of arsenic poisoning first and foremost. A matter I find rather ironic. He was a known arsenic eater, was he not?"

"Yes."

"For many years?"

"Well before we were married."

"And you were married for?"

"Eight years."

"You are American. How is it the two of you met?"

"We were introduced on an ocean liner bound for Liverpool. I was traveling with my mother to Paris. William was returning home after the cotton season. He had a brokerage office in Norfolk, Virginia."

"I see. Well then, regarding the matter of Worth. Mr. Seaver informed me that the Crown has in their possession a letter you wrote him."

"The note, yes. When I was placed in custody at Torrence House, I wrote asking him for help. Ingrid Berkshire gave it to the police." *That insufferable woman.*

"No, not the note. The letter. Dated May 8th. A few days before your husband expired."

A stab pricks her heart, and her mouth goes dry. *No.* "I..." *It cannot be.*

"It was opened by the nanny."

Anne. She closes her eyes, tries to puzzle it out. Her mind plays back the scene. She'd handed the envelope to the nanny in the yard as the children played. "Please mail this straightaway. You can take the children with you to the post box." Anne had smiled. "Of course, Mrs. Sullivan. Consider it done." And Constance believed it because Anne was devoted to her. Dependable as the tide.

"I'm afraid it was revealed at the inquest," Sir Charles says. "It's unfortunate you were too ill to attend the proceedings. And, if I may, a travesty that not a soul in the house had the courage to inform you Anne Yardley read the letter and gave it to Ingrid Berkshire."

Her private letter, for Timothy's eyes only. Opened and read. Revealed at the inquest before reporters. All of Liverpool must know by now.

"Mr. Seaver should have told you," Sir Charles says. "It is unconscionable for him not to have done. But you know now."

She covers her face with her hands. *Oh, Timothy.* It's enough that the police know of their tryst in London, for she foolishly kept the hotel receipt with his letters. And the letters—all of them—were found in the search after William's death. And now the letter to him while William lay ill. No wonder Edward has been so cruel.

"I understand there was another woman, Mrs. Sullivan. That there was, in fact, infidelity on both sides?"

She flinches and takes her hands from her face.

Sir Charles' brows shoot up. "Forgive me. I was under the impression—"

"I knew. I knew William had a mistress."

Sir Charles frowns. "What of her? Tell me."

"I was unaware of this woman—Sandra—until last year." White-hot fury pushes through her and memories bubble to the surface. A flash of pale skin, a tall woman with bright-red hair on a doorstep. "They had a long relationship. It started well before William and I met. It continued after we wed. For years." There is more, but why tell it? Men were always excused for such weaknesses of character, but never women.

"The matter came up in the magisterial hearing," Sir Charles says. "Edward Sullivan was asked if he was aware of any marital indiscretions on the part of your husband and he said yes. I believe the way he put it was 'another woman existed in the case.' The matter was then dropped."

So Edward had known all along. She leans forward, starts to touch Sir Charles' sleeve, but thinks better of it. "I beg you, spare William's memory as much as possible. He did many foolish things, but he's dead now. I would be devastated if this part of his life were made public. You mustn't mention her. You mustn't speak a word."

Sir Charles is silent for a moment. He scratches absently at his chin, considering her. "Need I remind you, Mrs. Sullivan, that your life is at stake? I think you are being too good."

She pushes away from the table, bitterness blooming in her chest like a cancer. "You think me noble, sir? My request to stay quiet about my husband's duplicity has nothing to do with goodness—his or mine. It's for the sake of our children. They must never know. I will not have William's reputation—and by extension the children's—sullied in such a way. Connected with that..." *Whore.* "Woman."

"I'm inclined to agree, albeit for different reasons. If I do touch on it—your husband's keeping of a mistress—it will only be to even the sides. Edward Sullivan can't very well deny it if I put the question to him. It's a matter of record. As I say, the prosecution will make a great deal of your own liaison with Timothy Worth. It can't hurt to mention that your husband was not himself a paragon of virtue." Sir Charles' eyes narrow. "Was there ever any confrontation between you and this woman? Anything to tie you to knowing of her?"

"No."

"Good. Your knowledge of her gives you a strong motive for murder. That is most assuredly how the prosecution will paint it. Let's hope Queen's Council, out of respect for the family, doesn't mention the matter at trial."

Sir Charles collects his papers while she works to bridle her rage. Sandra's mere existence has given the prosecution fuel to hang her. She didn't believe her hatred for William's mistress could be exceeded, but she was wrong. She hopes Sandra suffers now: poor, pathetic, and ugly in her grief.

"Is there anything else leading up to the days of your husband's death you wish to tell me? Anything I need be aware of that might reflect favorably on your case?"

"No." Everyone is blind to her story. Her side.

No one sees her at all.

Chapter 3

Torrence House

April 28, 1889

Constance sits in her slipper chair in the bedroom. Morning sun pours into the room, gilding the bottles, pots, and jars on her dressing table. She pulls on her shoes and approaches the table at the window. A fat robin sings on the sill, and she watches it for a moment, transfixed. When she places a fingertip to the glass, the bird wings away and she sighs. Before her rests a white bowl. She lifts the dry hand towel folded on top. The fly papers float in their water bath, the scent of elderflower wafting to her nose. She stirs the mixture with a finger, replaces the towel, and carefully wipes her hands.

Behind the dressing-room door, William stirs like a bear coming out of hibernation. The cot creaks, a drawer slams shut, something thuds against the wall. The door opens and he shuffles out. He's dressed in a nightshirt over which he's flung a robe of navy silk. He hasn't bothered to cinch it; the belt drags along the ground as he steps to the bed, his movements off.

"Well, well," she says, her tone dry as toast. William's hair stands on end, fixing him with a look of permanent astonishment. His skin is ashen, his eyes rheumy from drink.

He sinks down on the bed and scrubs a hand over his face. He's in need of a shave. "I had a ghastly ride home after the race last night. Rained cats and dogs the whole way back. I just pitched into the wall." He gestures to the dressing room. "I can't understand why the devil I'm so dizzy."

The musty odor of damp clothing wafts to her from the dressing room. William insisted on riding horseback to the Wirral Race in Parkgate and spent the day, and a late night from the looks of it, enjoying the steeplechase.

"It was the strangest thing, Connie. I felt so odd yesterday. My legs were stiff as boards. I spent much of the day..." He stops, his eyes far away.

She stares at him, and recollections unspool: William's face bloated with rage, his hands around her neck, the force of his punch as his fist smacked her eye.

"I need a doctor, Connie." His hands tremble.

And I need to be free of you. The bell rings downstairs and she hears Mary in the hall. "I'll see who it is."

The shadows are thick on the landing. There's never enough gaslight there. It's a wonder no one has plunged to their death. She shivers and takes the stairs. William's brother, Edward, waits at the bottom.

"Welcome back," she says. "Did you just get in?"

"Yesterday, as a matter of fact. I saw William at the race yesterday. Didn't he tell you?"

"No, he didn't." *We barely speak these days, Edward. We are different creatures now.* "Will you stay for dinner? I can't promise William will be down. He's not feeling well. I'm to send for a doctor."

Edward follows her into the drawing room. "Oh?"

Constance pulls the bell. "You might have cautioned him against riding home on horseback in the rain."

"You say that like he'd listen."

Mary steps into the drawing room. "Mistress?"

"Set an extra plate for Edward, Mary. And Master Sullivan isn't feeling well. Please see if Dr. Hendrickson is available straightaway for a house call. If not, leave a note and tell him to stop in at his earliest convenience."

"Yes, mistress," Mary says with a nod. "Mr. Sullivan, sir, if I may, it's lovely to see you. Welcome home. I hope your voyage wasn't too difficult."

"It was ghastly, Mary, perfectly ghastly. Like being tossed about like a toy boat in a bathtub. But I appreciate the kind words." Edward flashes a smile and winks. He's a favorite among the young maids who, judging by their pink cheeks whenever he speaks to them, find him irresistible.

When Mary has gone, Edward steps to the fire and says, low, "At least someone from Torrence House missed me."

"Of course. I'm sure William was too occupied yesterday for you to fill him in at the race. He's always anxious to hear how the cotton season fared in Norfolk. He'll be dying to see you."

Edward turns from the fire. "That's not what I meant."

He's missed her; she can see it in his eyes. Edward would be satisfied to tell William everything at the office tomorrow. He's come to see *her*.

His brows knit and his eyes worry over her. "Something's happened while I've been away. What is it? You're...different."

She looks away, afraid he'll guess what she's done, that he'll see the ugliness of what she and William have become. "Please stay for dinner, Edward. I'm sure William will be more himself after he sees the doctor. He won't like that he's missed you. He'll want to talk business."

"He's had letters aplenty from me."

"Still, he'll have a thousand questions."

The words seem to wound him, and he pulls his eyes away and looks to the fire. "You know him well."

———

"You should have hired a carriage, William," Constance says an hour later.

William grunts. He's propped against pillows in her bed where he hasn't lain for months. "It wasn't the rain that worried me. It was the strange feeling I had in my limbs."

"What sort of feeling?" Dr. Hendrickson says. He's a large, long-limbed man with hands as big as paddles. He sits on Constance's dressing-table chair that he's pulled to the bed, a bear in Goldilocks' chair. He leans over, tugs at William's eyelid, and stares into his pupil.

"It was quite unusual. My legs felt stiff and rather numb, almost like they'd fallen asleep. I managed to sit a horse, but the stiffness came and went."

The doctor frowns and grabs William's wrist to take his pulse. "Had you been drinking?"

William waves an impatient hand. "Yes, but it wasn't that."

"How can you be so sure?"

William shoots Hendrickson a dark look. Though the doctor has seen the children and Constance before, he's never attended William. "Because neither brandy nor wine make me stiff, doctor. Never have. After the race, I had dinner with friends. My hands were so unsteady, I overturned a glass of wine. I was quite embarrassed."

"Have you felt this rigidity in your limbs or the unsteadiness in your hands before?"

"No. My friends thought I'd had too much drink. I played it

21

off well enough, but the truth is, I wasn't drunk. I remember it all quite clearly. And something else. My heart was fluttering oddly. I felt, at times, I was on the verge of paralysis."

Dr. Hendrickson raises woolly brows. "After having strange symptoms you'd never experienced before, you rode home in the rain."

"I see the folly of it now, looking back," William says hotly. "I was shivering when I got home. I removed my clothes straightaway, rubbed the chill from my limbs, and went to bed."

"You might have been more careful, William," Constance says, but there's no teeth in it.

William winces and places a palm against his stomach. "I also have stomach pain."

Dr. Hendrickson listens to William's heart with his stethoscope. When he's finished, he removes the prongs from his ears. "Severe?"

"At times. And my mouth is dry. I can't seem to quench my thirst."

The doctor uses the flat of his hand to press on William's stomach. "Any pain when I do this?"

"No."

"How about here, or here?"

"A little. It hurt worse yesterday."

"Open for me." Hendrickson places a tongue depressor in William's mouth. "Your tongue is furred. Any diarrhea or vomiting?"

"No."

"He's no stranger to stomach upset, Doctor," she says. "He often complains of feeling ill after eating."

"Is that so?" Hendrickson leans forward in his chair and considers his patient. "Do you have heartburn after meals? Nausea?"

"From time to time. Have on and off for years, actually."

"In that case, I suspect you have chronic dyspepsia. It's quite common. The typical symptoms are bloating, loss of appetite, heartburn, nausea. It isn't serious, though it can be taxing."

Dr. Hendrickson stands and removes from his bag a small, stoppered bottle. He dispenses a few drops of clear liquid into a glass of water and hands it to William. "Drink this. It will ease your stomach. Stay in bed for the remainder of the day. I think you most likely ingested some sort of irritant and that, combined with the poor weather and the dyspepsia, has brought you low. The irritant, whatever it is, will evacuate the body soon enough. You should feel better on the morrow. I'll stop again in the morning and have a look."

He turns to Constance. "In the meantime, he's to limit his meals to bread and milk. No meat and nothing spicy." At the door, he pointedly looks back at William. "And no alcohol of any kind, Mr. Sullivan. You'll feel better tomorrow I'm certain, but you must be mindful of what you ingest until then."

She escorts the doctor down the stairs to the front hall. While he shrugs on his coat, she says, "There's something else. William has a habit of taking powder, a white powder, that seems to have an adverse effect on his health. He's taken it as long as I've known him, and the frequency of his doses has increased."

The pupils of the doctor's eyes dilate. She has his attention now. "What sort of powder?"

"He won't tell me. He dislikes me bringing it up. I mentioned the same to another doctor he was seeing last year. He spoke to William, but nothing came of it. My husband told him he wasn't taking anything that wasn't good for him, and he wasn't to worry."

"But you're worried. About his self-dosing."

"Yes. He's irritable when he takes it, and it gives him the ghastliest pallor. I think his stomach upset is related. I think...I think it may be strychnine or arsenic. Perhaps both."

"What gives you this impression?"

A flicker of the winter beds at the botanical gardens, the sharp green of Timothy's eyes. "Just a hunch, I suppose."

"I see." Dr. Hendrickson opens the door. "Well, should anything dire occur, you can always say we spoke of it."

It takes her a moment to realize he's making a joke. Irritation bubbles up and she takes a deep breath to quell her anger. "You should also know he exaggerates his symptoms. He fancies himself sick with everything and takes all sorts of patent medicines and tonics."

The doctor stares at her an interminably long time before he puts on his hat. "Very well, Mrs. Sullivan. I shall make a note of it."

She closes the door and heads for the stairs. A board creaks. A skirt is just disappearing around the corner in the direction of the kitchen. She's almost certain it belongs to the nanny.

"Anne?" There is no response.

The moment slides away, and the hunger is there in its place, a need she must satisfy. She climbs the stairs as quickly as her skirts allow and sails into the water closet. In the cabinet by the sink, behind William's numerous patents and pills, is a small knife. She draws it out, admires the wink of the blade in the sun seeping through the frosted window. Her hands tremble with the promise of it.

She places her boot on the ledge of the bathtub and hikes up her skirts. Across her thigh and shin rest scabs in various states of healing. She finds a spot just above her right knee that's unmarked. The skin there is as precious and pearlescent as a shell.

This is proof, she thinks, that she has feeling. That she's not a monster.

She presses the blade to her skin.

Chapter 4

St. George's Hall

Liverpool, England

Day 1 of Trial

The prison van judders along, advancing down streets choked with bodies. Conveyances are pulled over. Passengers and drivers gawp like carp as Constance passes in the Black Maria. Upper-story windows are thick with faces alive with curiosity, suspicion, scorn. Spectators watch from rooftops, clutching chimney stacks to keep their footing. What can they hope to see but the van, or, at best, a glimpse of a woman behind a veil?

A thud, and then a head of cabbage rolls away from the vehicle, bumping over cobblestones until it comes to rest before a sewer grate. The crowd jeers. Another thud and then another. The red whir of a tomato, the sickening crack of an egg. Her stomach drops and she shrinks from the window.

She's clothed head to toe in mourning, things her mother snatched from Torrence House before she was banished. If nothing else, she will attend court dressed respectably as a widow. Yet, cloaked in the hue of death, she feels as if it's she who's been buried.

The van veers left and parades down the 500-foot length of St. George's Hall. At St. John's Lane, it enters the Hall's gloomy portico. The driver jumps down, and she exits the vehicle with a female attendant and the prison governor. The door ahead leads to a long corridor. Soon they're descending underground to a series of holding cells. She is placed inside the nearest one with no instruction and takes a seat on the bench. The door screeches and bangs closed.

A lone candle lights her cell, flickering inside a mesh box. Fresh air seeps through a small grate in the wall. It isn't enough to dispel the odor of damp stone and body odor left behind by previous prisoners.

In the cool dimness, she feels as thin and brittle as glass. She crosses her arms to feel the comfort of her body, to remind herself that she will not shatter. She can't believe it. She is on trial for the murder of her husband. Of William. How is it she continues to breathe when everything is upside down? It's as if the world has cracked, the sky opened and rained fire.

Shadows gather at the edges of her vision. They are despair, hopelessness, fear. She needs release, craves it. There is no knife here, no garden shears or razor. But she's learned other ways to find relief within a prison cell: bites, scratches, gouges—anything that brings pain. Physical torment demands her attention and scatters the darkness. She removes a black glove, slides a finger along the scars at her wrist, picks at the scabbed-over cuticle of her thumb. Blood blooms, bright and welcoming, at the base of her nail. It tastes like an old penny and reminds her she is alive.

She is led through a series of corridors to a winding stone stairway, then ascends into a pool of light shining through a skylight. The main level announces itself with soaring ceilings, marble columns, tiled floors. The courtroom doors sweep open.

The room is thick with the heat of too many bodies. Voices cut. Heads turn. Every pair of eyes is a scorch, a sear. She advances into the room as if in slow motion, head up, heartbeat thrashing in her ears. She won't look down. She won't look defeated. That's what they want, the satisfaction of seeing her cower. She's halfway to the dock when the whispers begin.

"Adulteress."

"Poison."

"Murderess."

They've fastened these words to her as surely as they've pinned them to her dress. How dare they judge her actions when they know not her reasons?

She passes rows of press agents with notebooks and members of the bar in gray horsehair periwigs. At the court's center is the dock. It's little more than a narrow stage, raised to afford every occupant in the room a view. As she steps inside, she hears hissing to the left. It stops almost as soon as it begins. Her eyes cut to the source. In the upper gallery, women in feathered hats ransack her with their eyes, hand fans fluttering. In the front row her mother sits in rigid black, a smoky veil covering her face. She's struck with the odd impression that it is a mirror image, her own self staring back. She grasps the rail and prays her legs do not give out from under her.

On a raised bench before her sits Justice Stevenson, red robe blazing like a wound. He's a large lump of a man with furred sideburns and a bulbous nose. He scowls down at her, one hand coming up to scratch beneath his full-bottomed wig, replete with its rows of curls. Below him, to the left, is the witness box where the details of her life will be poured like vinegar from a bottle. Sir Charles, garbed in a black robe and wig, sits at a table centered below the bench, surrounded by papers and piles of books. He gives her an encouraging nod. Beside him, at another table, is Mr. Goodacre, representing Queen's Council.

To the right are two rows of men dressed almost identically, all with mustaches, most with beards—the twelve who will decide if she will swing from the end of a rope. They regard her solemnly, assessing her with eager eyes. She feels as if she's been skinned and looks away. Towering over all is a magnificent domed skylight through which the sun shimmers, blazing the wigs to a white-hot glow.

"Very well," Justice Stevenson intones. "The accused is now present. Let the clerk of arraigns read the charge."

The court rises. A small man with long sideburns calls, "Constance Sullivan, you are charged with having, on the 11th of May 1889, feloniously, willfully, and of your malice afore-thought, killed and murdered one William Sullivan by the administration to him of arsenic. How do you plead? Guilty or not guilty?"

A raspy intake of breath. "Not guilty." Said with force, as Sir Charles instructed. *You mustn't appear meek, Mrs. Sullivan. A submissive defendant looks guilty.*

With a rustle of silk, the room settles into their seats. In chairs flanking the dock are the female matron and the prison governor.

The judge clears his throat. "Mr. Goodacre."

The barrister springs to his feet and bobs his head in defer-ence, black robe swaying. "Your Lordship." He walks to the jurors, hands behind his back. "Gentlemen of the jury, it is my duty to lay before you evidence in support of the indictment you have just heard read. It would be idle of me to suppose

29

that you are not acquainted with some of the facts of this case, either from hearing of it or reading of it in the press. But I know perfectly well, now you are a jury sworn, you will have no difficulty dismissing from your mind all that you have heard."

A burn ignites in her chest. As if the lies printed in the papers can be erased from memory as easily as chalk from a board.

"I will call as witness William Sullivan's brother," Goodacre continues, "who will speak of him as an able, robust man. You will hear testimony from servants who considered their master strong and healthy, going regularly to the office before his untimely death. I will call a doctor and nurses who attended Mr. Sullivan, and saw his health decline sharply..."

Her head hurts. Her throat aches for water. There's no chair in the dock, only the cold brass rail to clutch. What if her strength gives out? She sucks in a breath and jabs the thumb of her right hand into the fleshy area between her left thumb and pointer finger. A burst of pain and she is lucid again.

"...your attention, in the order in which they transpired, to circumstances beginning in March of this year..."

She steals a glance at the gallery. Behind her mother, ladies stare down at her, opera glasses winking. She doesn't want them to know she's watching, how they pluck at her nerves. She has the sudden urge to cry out, release the venom sitting thick in her throat, but she won't give them the satisfaction.

Instead, she concentrates on Goodacre. He is portly, with a rotund chest and ridiculously thin legs. Younger than Sir Charles by a handful of years. A layer of sweat glistens on his forehead, which he periodically dabs with a handkerchief pulled from his robe. The clock behind the bench crawls to noon, half twelve, one. She's wondering how long Goodacre will drone on when the room is suddenly silent. All eyes are pinned on her. She has the sense that Goodacre is nearing the end and has paused for effect.

"Gentlemen, who did it?" he asks. The jury stares at her, as if expecting her to answer. "Who poisoned William Sullivan? There is powerful evidence that shows it was his wife." Goodacre elongates his arm, his chubby pointer finger an arrow to her chest. Another hiss from the gallery. "If Constance Sullivan was the person who administered arsenic to the poor man, then, gentlemen, Constance Sullivan is guilty of the cruel offense of willful murder."

Goodacre's eyes shine like jet beads. "How attentive to her husband was the accused in the two weeks you treated Mr. Sullivan?"

She's forgotten how big Dr. Hendrickson is. Even seated, the doctor looks a giant: broad shoulders, long arms. Even his voice is large, his tone deep and booming.

The doctor purses his lips, considers. "Very much, I think. She was almost always at his side when I examined him. In the beginning, that is."

"Ah," Mr. Goodacre says meaningfully. "Please continue with the summary of your visits."

Hendrickson shifts in the witness box and licks broad lips. "The first day, as I said, I gave him diluted prussic acid for the dyspepsia, prescribed a dietary, and told him to remain in bed. I rather expected him to be fully sound the next day, but I found him no better. I prescribed papain for his stomach pain, and iridine as he had a touch of diarrhea. I didn't see him the next day, as I told him unless someone from the house came round, I wouldn't call."

"You expected him to recover?"

"Completely. I did stop in the day after, as the house was on my way home from my other rounds. As I assumed, he seemed quite well. I prescribed Du Barry's Revalenta as a restorative to be prepared with his lunch."

"Who was preparing his meals, Dr. Hendrickson?"

"The cook, I expect."

"Not Mrs. Sullivan?"

Hendrickson rubs his chin. "Perhaps. She did feed him bedside, so she might have done. I didn't see Sullivan May 2nd. The next day, May 3rd, I called in the morning. He seemed quite well. But around midnight, Mrs. Sullivan sent for me. The deceased was suffering from what he described as a gnawing pain from his hips to his knees. I administered a suppository of morphia for the pain.

"The following day, a Saturday as I recall, I saw him early. The pain had passed away, but he was vomiting. He was unable to retain anything in his stomach. I advised him to take nothing, but to abate his thirst by washing out his mouth with water, or by sucking ice or a damp cloth. I gave him some ipecacuanha wine to allay the vomiting. The following day, a Sunday it was—"

"That was May 5th. Go on. He was getting worse?"

"Not exactly. I changed his medicine because it didn't make the improvement I expected. I gave him prussic acid again for the pain. He seemed in good enough spirits and spoke with me for some time. The next day I saw him early, about 8:30. He'd taken some Valentine's Meat Juice earlier that morning and it made him throw up."

There is a rustle from the gallery, whispers. Her face goes hot. *That blasted Valentine's.*

"We shall return to the meat juice," Mr. Goodacre announces, with a flick of his eyes to the upper seats. "Continue, Doctor."

"I examined two samples of his vomit but found no irritant."

"*Visually* examined you mean. You did not perform the Marsh test."

"Indeed not. I didn't believe at the time the man had been poisoned." Dr. Hendrickson's eyes settle on her then dart away. "I told him to stop taking the meat juice and gave him some Fowler's solution. I told Mrs. Sullivan he should be given Baine's beef tea and Neave's food for nourishment. Nothing else."

"His dyspepsia was persisting? The deceased was still suffering the effects of an irritant poison?"

"Yes, such as foul meat or dairy. I didn't believe then it was anything of the nefarious kind."

"By which you mean arsenic?"

"Yes. The next morning, he was much improved. He said, 'Hendrickson, I'm quite a different man today' or words to that effect. Later that day, I came round again. I administered a jaborandi tincture for his diarrhea and didn't return until the following day, May 8th. I remember Mrs. Sullivan looked very tired. Her husband wasn't sleeping well. I believe she was only resting when he was. I mentioned she might want to consider a nurse."

"It was your idea, the nurse?"

"Yes, I offered to have one sent from the Nurses Institute. I told the accused I would see to the telegram, and I did. I learned later that no nurse came from my request. Ingrid Berkshire, a friend of the Sullivans, saw to it later that day."

Whispers in the gallery. She can imagine what they're saying. *Couldn't be bothered to get a nurse for her own husband. What kind of monster is she?*

Goodacre approaches his witness. "That day, May 8th, turned out to be a significant one, did it not?"

"Yes. That evening Edward Sullivan, brother of the

deceased, came to see me at home. I'd never met him before. I told him my suspicions—that the deceased was suffering the effects of having ingested an irritant poison at the horse race. Bad wine, or something of that sort. He said he was astonished to see his brother so poorly. 'Reduced,' was the word he used, I think. He mentioned first the fly papers Mrs. Sullivan had been soaking a week before in the bedroom."

"Fly papers. Did he say anything more specific about them?"

"No. He then told me about a letter of Mrs. Sullivan's one of the servants had found. It was of a compromising nature, he said."

"I'm afraid you're going to have to be more specific than that, Dr. Hendrickson."

The doctor shifts in his chair, pulls at his collar. "I never saw the letter, but from what Sullivan told me, it was a love letter. It had been written that day, May 8th, and had language that indicated Mrs. Sullivan knew her husband would die. He went as far as to say Mrs. Sullivan might be scheming for just that result. He then circled back to the fly papers."

"Saying?"

"Nothing more."

"But you knew what he meant?"

"Yes. He was referring to the case a few years ago in Liverpool. The two sisters who soaked fly papers to extract arsenic, then used it to fatally poison members of the family. They were later hanged."

The ladies in the gallery stir like chickens in a henhouse. Her chest constricts. A veiled suggestion from Edward was all it took to turn her into a murderer. Hendrickson was a fool.

Justice Stevenson stands and pounds his fist on the bench. "Enough! The people in the gallery will refrain from speaking, or I will have you sent out. Do you understand?" Silence. "You may proceed, Mr. Goodacre."

"Is this the day, Dr. Hendrickson—May 8th—when you began to suspect William Sullivan was being deliberately poisoned?"

"Yes."

"Did you have a private conversation with Mrs. Sullivan the first time you attended her husband?"

"I did. She told me her husband often exaggerated his symptoms."

There is not a sound in the courtroom. The air feels heavy, loaded. A vision rears up: William in bed, wasted away to nothing, bones jutting from hollow cheeks. She blocks it out, swallows down the sharp reality of it.

"Meaning?" Mr. Goodacre prods.

"I think she was cautioning me not to take her husband's complaints too seriously."

By the time, two hours later, it's Sir Charles' turn to question the witness, Constance is worn out. She finds it difficult to concentrate. She longs to be somewhere, anywhere else.

And yet it's only just begun.

"Let's return to the conversation you had with Mrs. Sullivan after you'd examined her husband the first time," Sir Charles begins. "You said your recollection was that she cautioned you not to take her husband's complaints too seriously. But there was something more to it, was there not? She told you he often felt himself coming down with something when in fact he had no sickness at all. And *this* was what she was trying to make you understand, yes? He self-medicated with all manner of pills, patent medicines, and tinctures?"

Dr. Hendrickson lowers his gaze and says to the floor, "That's what she relayed to me, yes."

"During that conversation, did Mrs. Sullivan speak to you about her husband's habit of taking a white powder?"

He's got you now.

"Yes. She had strong suspicions he was taking arsenic or strychnine regularly. She said he didn't like her questioning him about it."

"Did you bring it up with him?"

"The very next day. He denied taking powder of any kind. Nevertheless, I told him the effects of strychnine, nux vomica, arsenic, and the like could be harmful, if not fatal."

"Have you ever heard of arsenic as an ingredient in so-called 'sexual nerve tonics?'"

Tittering through the courtroom. Justice Stevenson scowls and the noise quiets.

"Yes, but I'm not of the belief that arsenic has any powers of that kind."

"Could that be a reason the deceased might have taken arsenic powder?"

"He told me he didn't take arsenic powder."

"But if he did, might that be a reason?"

"I cannot say."

"Let me rephrase. Are you aware of men who take arsenic for the purpose of improving their sexual virility?"

"I am. But as I said—"

"We shall leave it at that," Sir Charles says. "In your testimony to Mr. Goodacre, you listed off a formidable list of medicines. You advised a strict dietary. How long did William Sullivan go without food?"

The question surprises Hendrickson. His eyes widen, graze the room. "I should say beginning May 3rd to May 6th, due to his nausea and vomiting. He ate—or I should say he was able to eat—only sparingly after that. He was also given brandy by his brother—"

"We shall get to that in a moment. Based on your instructions, Sullivan went four days, at least, on an empty stomach. Might some of the medicines you prescribed have been the reason for his vomiting?"

"With the morphia suppository I would say, yes. Perhaps the prussic acid, but I can't say for sure."

"Very well. Now then, regarding the brandy. You became aware Edward Sullivan gave William a brandy on May 10th when you had given strict instructions that the patient was not to have anything, isn't that right?"

"Yes. I didn't know about the brandy then. I learned of it later."

"And the result, doctor?"

"He vomited shortly thereafter."

Sir Charles lets the words settle over the jury, then says, "On May 6th, you gave the patient Fowler's solution. Can you tell us what that contains?"

Hendrickson's eyes narrow, as if he's suspected the question. "Fowler's is an arsenious acid solution. It—"

"Arsenious as in arsenic?"

"Yes. Fowler's solution contains one percent potassium arsenite, an extremely low level. In the deceased's case, I used it as a remedy for his digestive disorder."

The gallery shuffles. Sir Charles walks away from the witness box. With his back to Dr. Hendrickson, he says, "If you suspected an irritant poison from the outset, why didn't you examine all fecal matter and vomit to find the cause? Mrs. Sullivan had warned you the first day of the deceased's powder habits."

"I did examine them."

"Not until May 6th, in fact. You'd been attending him a week by then."

Hendrickson pauses, looks at Goodacre. Sir Charles notices the exchange and quirks a brow. "Doctor?"

"I did examine the feces again, along with the urine, May 9th."

Sir Charles raises his brows. "Ah." His eyes slide to Mr. Goodacre who looks like a child caught with his hand in a cookie jar.

He knew of this, Constance thinks. *Goodacre knew and he's kept it from the jury.*

"I boiled a tablespoon of the feces in hydrochloric acid. I was testing for metal—antimony, arsenic, or mercury."

"Arsenic is a form of metal?"

"Yes."

"And its presence would reveal itself if it were there?"

"Yes."

"And your result?"

"I did not find metal. The test was negative."

Sir Charles, still with his back to Hendrickson, opens his snuff box and takes a pull. "Why then did you arrive at May 8th as the day you began to suspect that William Sullivan was being poisoned? I don't mean with any irritant, but *feloniously* poisoned."

"My conversation with Edward."

Sir Charles shuts his snuff box, spins, and comes to the witness box in three brisk strides. "In other words, you were prepared to believe a foreign agent was at fault, such as bad fish or wine, until Edward Sullivan, a man who is no doctor, put ideas in your head. On the sole basis of a letter."

"After Edward Sullivan's visit, the deceased's symptoms began to take on a new light."

Just as Edward planned.

"Did they? If you believed the deceased was being poisoned by his wife, you must have, the very evening Edward came to you, returned to Torrence House. But you didn't, did you?"

"No."

"Why not?"

"I believed Edward had it all in hand."

"Did you inform the nurses of what Edward had shared with you, that Sullivan's wife might be poisoning him?"

"As I said, I believed he had it in hand."

A gasp from the gallery. Whispers from the press agents behind her.

"Oh," Sir Charles says, bristling. "Does Edward Sullivan have a medical degree of which I am not aware?"

Goodacre lumbers to his feet. "My Lord, Sir Charles is badgering the witness."

"I withdraw the question, my Lord," Sir Charles says. He turns to his witness again. "Now, you testified that Nurse Hawker gave you a bottle of Valentine's Meat Juice the morning of May 10th."

"Yes. She told me she'd seen the accused put it on the table in the landing where some of the patient's items were kept. When the accused left the landing, the nurse brought it into the bedroom where she could keep an eye on it."

"She took it from her person when she handed it to you?"

"No, it was on a table in the bedroom."

"It wasn't locked up?"

"No."

"It was accessible to anyone coming or going from the room?"

The doctor's brows furrow. "I suppose."

"Very good. I should like to ask you to repeat for the jury what you told my learned associate Mr. Goodacre this afternoon regarding the postmortem. Remind us, if you will, of your conclusion."

Hendrickson looks less substantial now, as if the weight of Sir Charles' questions have rubbed him down. "After having made the postmortem with Dr. Caldwell, recollecting the symptoms William Sullivan died of, I felt that death was due to an irritant poison, most probably arsenic."

"*Most probably*." Sir Charles heaves a sigh and pinches the bridge of his nose. "Dr. Hendrickson, have you ever conducted a postmortem examination of any person believed to have died of arsenic poisoning?"

"No."

"Can you absolutely swear—with one hundred percent certainty—that the irritant poison that caused William Sullivan's death was arsenic?"

"I believe strongly that it was, sir."

"I did not ask if you believed strongly. I shall put it to you again. Are you one hundred percent certain that the irritant poison that killed William Sullivan was arsenic?"

A pause. The question hangs, suspended in the moment. "No, I am not."

Jostling and whispers from the gallery. Constance closes her eyes to blot everything out but finds herself lurched back to the beginning. Where it all began three years before.

Chapter 5

Torrence House

April 18, 1886

A cramp spasms down Constance's leg. She adjusts her position in the Chippendale chair and sucks in a ragged gasp. Nothing alleviates the tightness around her belly, her aching back. Lately, sleep comes in brief snatches leaving her more exhausted each day. Two months to go before delivering this child. It can't come soon enough.

She rises from the chair unsteadily, belly-first, using her hands to lever herself off the seat cushion. Her brocade slippers whisper against the Turkish carpet as she crosses the room to the fireplace. The ormolu clock on the mantle proclaims the hour in a series of unnerving ticks.

Three o'clock in the morning. *Where is William?*

Of late, he doesn't announce his comings or goings, nor tell her his plans. Her days have narrowed to two predicaments that loop continuously in her brain: her discomfort and William's moods. The former is less serious; it will pass with birth. The latter is a different matter, one that scratches at her in the darkness when she can't sleep.

Where is he?

She bites her nail and stares into the fire. Alan, the new man Ingrid found to act as butler and valet to William, has turned the lamps low in the drawing room. Its furnishings—carved mahogany furniture upholstered in gold and light blue satin, lace curtains and velvet draperies, mantles imported from Carrara, Italy—are the best money can buy.

Her head aches. She needs sleep, but she won't go upstairs. Not yet. She sent Molly, her personal maid, to bed hours ago.

Her eyes wander to the framed coat of arms on the far wall half cloaked in shadow. William ordered it before they married. Though the Sullivan family are hardly nobles possessing land and title, he felt their union propitious enough to have the emblem commissioned by the College of Arms in London. She walks to the illustration, runs her finger along the gilt frame. At the top is a sparrow holding a sprig of hawthorn. Below, foliage winds around a crest topped by a scrolling 'S.' At the bottom is a legend.

Tempus omnia revelat. Time reveals all.

In the weighted, hushed air, it feels like a prophecy from the house.

Nonsense. It's *William* who's been doing the revealing. He'd stopped making love to her when the swell in her belly became apparent with their first child—William Jr, whom they called Billy from the start. She was relieved. She hadn't wanted to harm the baby, nor had she felt the least amorous once her body started to change. But after their son was born, William returned to her. He was more himself—kind, affable, charming William.

But she's come to know another side of him. William is

given to a morose and often gloomy disposition and, at times, an extremely hot temper.

Lately, his dark side has seized him. He has no interest in her condition, nor her company. While he delights in little Billy, he says little to her. He's at his office during the day, at friends' homes or the Palatine Club in the evenings. It would be easier to bear if William were not so distant when he *is* home—behind his newspaper or shut away in his office on the odd evening he isn't out.

There's no shortage of social engagements. Numerous invitations to suppers and balls arrive every week. These she answers with the same response: she is currently confined, but William will attend. He declines very few.

More often than not, William arrives home inebriated and smelling of sweet perfume.

She must face it; he's probably frequenting brothels. Is it not a well-known fact that men go elsewhere when their wives can't satisfy their urges?

Still, she thought William above it. Or at least averse enough to disease to avoid the pleasures of prostitutes. His fear of illness, of contracting any malady, however slight, is extreme. No, it's more than that. *It's beyond reason.* The pills and tonics have only increased in the five years of their marriage, as have the doctors who treat him. And yet, perhaps, in matters of the bedroom, his carnal desires win out over his abhorrence of contagion.

There is a word for William's condition: hypochondria. Dr. Hopper told her as much when she expressed her concern about William's patent medicines, his prescriptions from other doctors, his habit of dosing himself. "An unwarranted fear of contamination," the doctor told her. "Nothing to be concerned of in and of itself, as his illnesses are largely exaggerated, if not completely imagined. Not to worry, my dear." A chuckle and a pat on her hand and that was all they spoke of it.

The tumblers click and turn in the front hall and her thoughts go flying. The front door opens. She hears William's boots on the flags and then he's striding into the room. He tosses his coat on the back of a chair, walks to the mantle, and brings his hands before the hearth. He hasn't seen her in the shadows. His profile flickers in the firelight, his gaze on the coals. The scent of cigar smoke wafts to her.

Where has he been?

The rustle of her skirts brings his attention up short. William turns, scowling into the darkness until she advances into the gaslight.

"What the devil," he snaps. He returns his attention to the fire. "I suppose you told Alan to go to bed."

"There was no need for him to stay up merely to take your coat. I can manage the rest."

William blows air from his lungs. "That's what the man is for, Connie."

"Where have you been?" The words are out before she can check them. It's precisely the question she should've avoided: her suspicion laid bare.

"The Palatine."

"So late?" She steps closer. Then it comes to her. The scent of tobacco and bergamot, laced with something floral.

William moves to the sideboard and pours himself a brandy, tossing it back before setting the glass down and wiping his lips on his sleeve. "Why not? We're paid up until the end of the month."

"I wasn't thinking of the cost. You can drink here, at home. With me." She hates herself for giving words to her neediness. It makes her feel pathetic, the nagging wife. How has she become this, how have *they* become this, in the space of five years?

"I don't suppose you wrote to your mother today?"

"I'll not ask Mama for more money, William," she says, her tone sharp. "She's advanced funds on too many occasions. We must make do."

William pours another brandy. His cravat is askew, his eyes red. How much has he had to drink, and with whom? Last Sunday he disappeared for hours. There was no social engagement on his calendar.

He takes a seat in a chair before the fire, stretches out his legs. He holds up his glass and peers through it into the flames. "Make do," he repeats.

She sits down in the chair next to him, her body tense, coiled. She'd only wanted him home but now that he is, it isn't enough. She'd thought their marriage would be a meeting of minds. If she couldn't have marital equality in the matter of decisions—what woman did?—she could at least expect a certain measure of devotion. Now she feels discarded, a woman with no control and less power. "Must you go out again tomorrow, William? I'll ask Mrs. Hunt to prepare a special dinner. It's been so long since we spent time together, just the two of us."

He doesn't immediately respond. When he does, it's as if she hasn't spoken. "Do you know what I remember about the *Baltic?* Our little interlude on the sea?"

The *Baltic.* The vessel they boarded in Norfolk, Virginia, as strangers and, ten days later, disembarked in Liverpool as betrothed. "He is twenty-three years your senior," her mother had cautioned. But she was young and in love and cared not a whit. William Sullivan was handsome, the life of the party, and most important, he made her feel like a woman. She was seventeen.

William's mouth twists. "The impression, that is to say, being *given* the impression, that your mother had capital and assets in the way of property. Rather significant holdings, I believe you said."

The baby kicks and she flinches. "Yes."

He chuckles, low. "Then it is as I supposed. I didn't imagine it."

"Of course not." She doesn't like his tone. It's as if his only reason for marrying her were her assets. The ugliness of it is a stab to the throat.

"Then why is it, wife, we are hampered in the way of funds? Pray, tell me."

He's drunk. Little good will come of this discussion. She comes to her feet as best she can, thinking that not so long ago, he'd have leapt to assist her.

If only the baby would come. He will want me. He will love me again.

"Sit down," William says. The brandy glass dangles from his fingers. A muscle twitches in his jaw.

She has always adored his sandy hair, his heavy-lidded gray eyes, yet she wants nothing more than to strike him now. But she settles herself, one hand resting on her belly. "As for Mama's money, it's hers to use as she pleases. Surely you know that I receive a small allotment only. Whatever is left over at the time of her death will naturally come to me, but as she is young and in good health, I hardly think her money is something you should consider your own. As for my inheritance from my father, it wasn't large. A fact you are also aware of."

"And yet I wonder why it is your mother doles it out as she does, in rather paltry installments. It's yours, after all."

"She's managed her own funds for years. We thought it best she helped me manage mine."

"Yours."

"Ours, then."

"She isn't the one who should be holding the purse strings."

Could he actually think her mother is keeping them from her own money after she'd spent a fortune on Torrence House? "I promise you, Mama has no desire to keep me—us—from money that is ours." They never should have bought Torrence, but William insisted. "I think it prudent we keep to a budget. Mama has been more than understanding about our costs to set up house."

She'd preferred the expenditures—beyond the ones required for them to move in (a sound roof, working chimneys, repaired lines for the gaslight), spread over time so their finances wouldn't be depleted so quickly. She enjoys the trappings of a comfortable life as much as William, but her funds are limited and William's income as fickle as the cotton prices it depends upon.

But William had wanted all the repairs and embellishments done immediately, regardless of cost. Over the course of a year, stonemasons, glaziers, woodworkers, plasterers, painters, had plied their trade. And yet Torrence House remains a grim, drafty, three-story pile. The shadows, the oppressive air, the windows through which no sun shines have somehow remained unaltered.

As if the house is fixed in a permanent state of melancholy.

She massages her temples. No, it's nonsense. She's over-tired. The house is old, that's all. It isn't animate, for heaven's sake. It had been long abandoned, and she'd merely seen it at its worst and attached despair to it. *Torrence House*, she tells herself furiously, *does not have moods. It does not think.*

"If it's your own inheritance you wish to protect, dear wife, then perhaps she'd be amenable to a loan."

"A loan? Whatever for?"

"I must establish myself as a reputable broker, one who can afford a fine home, servants, the best that Liverpool has to offer."

He goes to the sideboard again, lifts the jeweled knob of the brandy decanter. "My own earnings will vary year to year based on the market, but your income will elevate us where we need to be."

"I don't underst—"

The decanter crashes down on the sideboard. William's eyes, hard as flint, bore into hers. "I need what was promised me, Connie. I don't take kindly to asking for what is mine."

From the inside of his waistcoat, he withdraws a small packet. He holds it over his brandy glass, tapping once. *That vile trickster of a powder.* It invigorates him, makes him feel alive, he says. But it's the powder that's alive, draining from him his vitality. She recognizes the signs: his ghostly pallor, his nervous tics, his explosive temper.

"I've furnished this home with the finest of things, William. We have all the servants we need. What is it you lack? Tell me."

"Our account is overdrawn until your mother's next apportionment." Her body goes still. "I have accounts to settle, Connie. Expenses. I want a valet who isn't a goddamn butler."

"I'm going to bed." She rises, takes a step towards the stairs, and turns. "Perhaps if it's your reputation you're so concerned about, you should avoid brothels. You stink of another woman."

In one quick sweep, William hurls his glass across the room. It crashes into the wall beside her. In the ensuing silence, the flickering shadows, she feels the house pulse. Watching.

She turns and lifts her skirts, her heartbeat as jagged as the broken crystal she steps around. Slowly, head held high, she climbs the stairs.

Chapter 6

Torrence House and Old Hall Street

July 8, 1888

Constance sits at her escritoire. She's written not a word and her tea has gone cold. She taps one foot up and down, up and down, on the floor, a nervous tic that sends tiny bolts of current through her. She's perfected her plan. All is in order. She must calm herself. She doesn't know how today will end, but she knows how it began: with a line—William's. *I'll just go down to the Palatine and see what the old chaps are doing.*

It's the same every Sunday and it is a lie.

She no longer recognizes her husband. Someone else has slipped beneath his skin. His expressions, his habits, his nature are not his own. Or perhaps William has always been obstinate, cantankerous, quick to temper. Perhaps it isn't that he's changed, but that his real self, the hidden one, has been laid bare these past few years. It's like the story on everyone's lips in tearooms and ballrooms alike, the shilling shocker that delights even as it astonishes. *The Strange Case of Dr. Jekyll and Mr. Hyde.*

It's hard to remember the way they fit so perfectly together: William's way of filling up a doorway when he entered a room and only having eyes for her, his gracious manners that saw to her comfort first. Their London wedding and the glittering parties, holidays, and social engagements that followed are now so lost to her she wonders if they were ever real.

Something is off. Something has tipped the balance.

They've fought over finances, squabbled over how best to use their money to fund Torrence House with its glowering rooms, its persistent drafts, its pair of peacocks that roam the grounds like azure gods. William barely speaks to her and arrives home late. He makes excuses—late meetings, an ale at the cricket club with friends—yet when she questions him, he's evasive. Sometimes he doesn't recall where he told her he was going, so his lies are easily caught, like fish in a net.

After the birth of Janie, Constance waited for the old William to return. Oh, how she waited. She'd coaxed, cajoled, begged. *Come to me, William. I'm not with child now. We can be close again.*

But things only worsened.

Over the course of two years, William's communication has become not words, but grunts of displeasure, hostile stares, suppers at the long dining table where barely a word is exchanged between them. In society, it's different of course. They must keep up appearances. At parties, at the theater, they are a united front. Smiles, clasped hands, shared laughter. "My, my," friends remark. "The Sullivans are quite the handsome couple. So suited."

She can't stand it. Their marriage has rotted like overripe fruit, and she will know the reason why.

She waits for the fall of William's step on the stairs. When it comes, her heartbeat quickens. He descends, the floorboards sighing as his soles hit the wood. She tracks his movements through the drawing room, his hushed steps on the Turkish rugs, and then the door opens in the front hall and bangs closed. She dashes to the window in the drawing room. Conrad, the stable-man, bobs his head to William, opens the carriage door. He waits for his master to climb in, then scampers up to the driver's seat. A slap of the reins, and they're off.

She smooths her skirts, waits for the carriage to turn out of the drive. When it disappears from view, she grabs her reticule and hat, pulls open the door, and sprints down the drive.

She imagines the servants peeping from windows, the scorch of their stares on her back as she makes her way to the street. She wonders if they know where it is her husband goes on Sundays, if she's the only one in the house who's unaware of William's destination. She hasn't been able to bring herself to ask Conrad, to reveal to a servant that her husband doesn't inform her of his activities.

The carriage is turning the corner when Constance reaches the street. She watches the cab parked a little way down leave the curb. It pulls to a stop in front of her and she jumps in quickly. Every minute counts.

They head north toward the city. The day is hot as Hades, the heat the kind that melts flowers and withers horses. Moisture is already beading on her forehead and the back of her neck. Though the windows are open, there is no breeze. It's difficult to breathe. Why didn't she bring a fan? She withdraws a handkerchief from her reticule and drags it across her neck, down her décolletage, pats her upper lip.

The horse trots up Sefton Street, the cab snaking along the River Mersey where bucolic Garston, with its broad trees and voluptuous parks, soon gives way to a string of piers to the west. They pass the docks with their clutches of ships and swarms of workers rolling barrels, hefting ropes, hoisting pulleys. The stench of seawater and fish is so strong she can taste it. This is the lifeblood of Liverpool, where coal and cotton arrive to fuel and clothe the city and fill its coffers. She has always loved the city proper—Williamson Square, Court Theatre, the Lyceum, but the wharves are a reminder of what Liverpool really is: a city made fat by trade.

The cab nears the Custom House and her pulse is in her throat. William's carriage doesn't turn. He isn't headed in the direction of the Palatine Club. It's just as she supposed.

Tempus omnia revelat. Time reveals all.

On they advance. The bells of St. Nicholas peal as they round the corner onto Chapel Street. They're close to William's office now. Why would he go there and not tell her? But the cab takes a sudden left onto Old Hall Street. She doesn't know it. It seems to be a mixture of shops and residences. The cab's pace slackens and crawls for another several blocks. Pedestrians saunter down the street in their Sunday best, shopping at market stalls, peering at window displays. Gradually, the shops give way to common residences whose doors open directly onto the street.

Her driver pulls to the curb, jumps down, and opens the door. "He's gone through there, ma'am." He points to a narrow alley too slim to admit a conveyance.

"And the carriage?"

"Parked about forty feet ahead. Driver's gone into the Cock and Owl, just there."

Of course. Conrad knows William will be occupied for the day.

"Very well." She pushes through the door, waving him out of her way. "Wait here."

The alley is shaded, a temporary relief from the sweltering heat. Still, her face is slick with sweat. Her armpits weep. The way opens into a cobbled courtyard of humble terraced homes of brown brick. No gardens. A dog licks from a shallow puddle at the base of a water pump in the middle of the courtyard, its skin stretched taut over thin ribs.

William is standing at a door across the courtyard. She steps back and peers around the corner. He tries the door, then fumbles in his pocket.

He has a key.

A creak of hinges and the door opens. A tall woman with red hair twisted into a knot smiles at him, hands on hips. He's about to step through when a boy of eleven or twelve appears. William tousles his mop of white-blond hair and the boy's arms go around him, eyes closed, a smile on his face as he holds William tight. The three disappear inside the house.

The boy's single utterance rings in her ears. "Papa."

A terrible confusion presses down on her and she slides down the wall of the alley, bricks scratching through her gown. Weeds sprout from the cobbles. The dog slinks to her and sniffs. "Go away!" she hisses. It moves off, tail tucked between spindly legs.

Thoughts come, unwanted.

William has a key to a woman's home.

He's a frequent visitor.

He has another son.

She rubs tears away with the heels of her palms, angry at her show of weakness. Now is not the time. She must go home. William can't find her here.

But her body is too weak to move. She is boneless, her limbs dead. Her vision blurs. The opposite wall of the alley shimmers, fills with stars.

"Deary?" Her heart flutters. She's been seen. "Are you all right? Dreadfully hot, dreadfully."

An elderly woman shambles toward her.

"I...have lost my way," she stammers, trying to push up. "I..."

The woman advances and puts a hand under her arm. For

an old woman, she has surprising strength. "You need some water, that's all. Come with me, deary. I live just there." She points to a nearby door, identical to the one William disappeared behind.

She allows the woman to lead her to her home. When the door has closed behind them, the woman guides her to a small sitting room with a window that looks out onto the courtyard. She helps her into a chair before the window. From the look of the seat opposite—faded and worn, armrests scored—the woman spends a good deal of time in it surveying the courtyard.

The woman returns with a tall glass of water and she gulps it down. The coolness in her mouth, down her throat, is a balm. She closes her eyes for an instant, feeling better. Until she remembers. Papa. *Papa.*

"Are you from around here, deary?" The woman is neatly dressed in a gown patterned with yellow daffodils, faded but otherwise well cared for, though the fashion is from seasons past. Her gray hair is piled neatly on the top of her head in a bun the size of a plum. Hazel eyes, kind and curious. "Goodness me, please forgive my manners. I'm Mrs. Kirby. Jemima Kirby."

The sitting room is decorated sparsely: a sagging couch, walnut tables in need of polish, knitted doilies everywhere.

"And your name, deary?" Mrs. Kirby prompts. She takes a seat opposite.

"Caroline Holbrook." The name comes easily to her lips. Her mother's, before she married her father.

"Well, Caroline, you aren't from around here, are you?" Mrs. Kirby's eyes sweep over her pink satin gown, her hat trimmed with cherries and rose-colored tulle.

"No. South of the city. Aigburth."

"Aigburth! Such a long way. What brought you here?"

Think. *Think.*

"I...found something. This..." she looks down at her lap, "reticule."

"I see." But Mrs. Kirby's forehead is creased as if she doesn't see.

"I found it at...St. John's Market. On the pavement. There's an address stitched inside and initials. The address is..." She glances out the window, marks the number on the door across the courtyard through which William had walked. "Number 18, Old Hall Street."

"Ah." Mrs. Kirby's face wrinkles into a smile. "You're being a Good Samaritan today, and in such weather."

"I didn't realize how hot it was."

Mrs. Kirby smacks her hands against her thighs. "I have just the thing. For special occasions." She scampers to a sideboard and brings a bottle and two small cups to the table between them. "I would say, Miss Holbrook, this is a very special occasion. Wouldn't you?"

Constance presses her lips together and wonders if the half bottle of cheap gin, sunlight glancing off it from the window, is really only brought out for special occasions, or if Mrs. Kirby is a tippler who's found in her an easy excuse.

The gin is a sharp bullet in her mouth. She swallows it down, throat ablaze, eyes watering.

"Now then, you've come to the right place." Mrs. Kirby gestures a wizened hand toward the window. "Number 18 is just there. I daresay Sandra will be very happy to have her reticule returned." Mrs. Kirby drains her glass and then closes her eyes in pleasure, the cup held to her chest.

"Sandra?" The name on her tongue is as sour as vinegar.

"Yes, the woman at number 18." Mrs. Kirby opens her eyes, runs them around Constance's face. "I believe you've a little sunstroke, deary. The gin will do you good. Restore you before you go back out in the heat again." She pours another for her, fills her own.

"I can't really read the initials she stitched inside the reticule," Constance says, her mind forming the lies easily. "I see how the first could be an 'S' now. But the other initial, do you happen to know Sandra's last name? There was some money in the bag, you see. I want to make sure it's going back to the right person." For a moment, she wonders what she will do if Jemima Kirby asks to see the stitching inside her reticule.

"Oh, I imagine Sandra was fit to be tied if she'd lost money. So many mouths to feed. Would you like a biscuit, deary?"

"She has more than—she has children?" She takes her glass from the table, glad now for the bolster of the gin. She's light-headed. The room has a watery look, the walls and furniture bowed in.

"Oh, yes." Mrs. Kirby squints into the courtyard. "Five, though they're not so little anymore. I believe the eldest, let's see —Jimmy is his name, I think. He's past twenty."

The words prick like darts. She is only twenty-five. *They can't all be William's.*

"The youngest, little Joe, I believe he's five or six now. Grown like a weed, he has."

She downs the contents of her glass. She's prepared for the burn this time. She closes her eyes, feels the gin's savage descent. *They aren't his. Not all of them, surely.* It would mean William had been with this woman—Sandra—years before she and William ever met. Decades. He's not that duplicitous. He doesn't have it in him. But the poison of the thought begins to spread, infecting all her memories of him.

"You've just missed William."

She blinks. "You know him?"

Mrs. Kirby cocks her head. "Of course I do, don't I? He lives there, deary." Her eyes flick to the courtyard. "Though he travels quite a bit. Not much at home. Traveling salesman. Comes home when he can manage it."

Blood pounds in her ears. None of this is real. She will wake up in her bed at Torrence House and this will all be a dream. She fights the urge to put her hands around Jemima Kirby's neck and squeeze until the old woman takes back every word and tells her it's all a joke.

"Sullivan's the name," Mrs. Kirby says, putting her empty glass on the table and wiping her mouth with the back of her hand. "William and Sandra Sullivan."

Chapter 7

Torrence House

July 8, 1888

Hours later, in the tangled web of the orchard, her thoughts fly unchecked. Jagged needlings that catch the air like sparks. *Lies. Woman. Children. Betrayal. Wife. Sandra, Sandra, Sandra.*

She'd mourned William's pulling away, wanted to make things better, but there's no way to put this rabbit back into the hat. William has always existed apart from her, he's kept secrets. She can never go back to the way it was. She'll never trust him again.

And if Sandra is William's wife, what does that make her?

Her whole body quakes with something more than shock, more than anger. She has a hunger to wound that exists almost outside of her, primal in its need. *If William were here, I'd kill him.*

She stops pacing. The leaves rustle and the trees watch. Under the gnarled boughs, the orchard is quiet and cool. Just a stone's throw from the house, but a place to think away from the servants' prying eyes. She's never sought it out before; she and the children avoid it. The listing agent had told them it was called the Witch Orchard and she doesn't doubt the origin of the name. It isn't difficult to find faces worked into the ebony bark: the shrewd eyes, the beaked noses, the poke of teeth. The gardener they'd hired that first spring had marveled at the age of the trees. "More than ninety years old, I reckon. Miracle they're still fruiting." But she knows it's the house. Its corruption extends beyond its walls, spreads like a cancer. She plucks a small yellow apple from a limb. It's scrawny and misshapen. She turns it over. Its bashed-in innards have rotted. The smell of decay hits her, and she drops it with a cry.

Torrence House, she realizes with a shudder, has infected more than just the trees. It's filled her with its darkness. How else can she explain her sudden urge to hurt William? Then her thoughts flash to a red-haired woman on a porch stoop and a blond boy saying "Papa" and she seethes all over again.

She lifts her skirts and makes her way down the row, tripping once over an exposed root. The sun is a bright pulse when she steps from the trees. One of the peacocks screeches and is answered by the other. The hothouse glints like a beacon and she trudges through clipped grass up a small rise. Behind her, some distance away, the children gambol about near the pond as Anne tries to catch them, three flaxen heads spinning like tops.

Inside the glass enclosure, the smell of earth and vegetation hits her nostrils. Pots of tomatoes and eggplant line the rows. The musty odor of marigolds almost overwhelms her. The gardener has set tools to hooks by the door. Spades, hoes, tillers. Rakes, shovels, pitchforks. She almost misses the shears. They've slipped from their hook and fallen, one pointed blade stabbed into the dirt. She snatches them up and casts around. The hothouse is empty. The slope leading down to the pond reveals no gardener bowed in work.

He'll be taking his tea in the kitchen. She hasn't much time.

She fusses with her cuff. The buttons are unaccountably small. Sweat prickles her brow. A bee drones at her ear and she shoos it away, temper flaring. At last, the buttons obey. She rolls up her sleeve. The underside of her left wrist waits, white and perfect, save for the scars there thin as spider floss.

Blue paint has long flecked from the shears' handle, but the metal is free of rust. She sets a blade to her skin and presses, testing the elasticity of it. The trick is to be light of hand. To slit, not gash. Still, she hesitates. She should go to the orchard. No one will see her there. But the thought of striding back in the heat and being seen by the children doesn't sit well.

And she's desperate. When her thoughts skitter to dark places, it's the knife that quells them. The pool of her blood mollifies as nothing else can.

She glides the blade across her wrist. A red line blooms. A thrum of pain, but only just; it's eclipsed immediately by a feeling of relief. She closes her eyes, soaks in the calm that threads through her like warm honey. Not since she was a girl of sixteen in New York City, where she was raised under social strictures that forbade her to show emotion or portray herself in an unfavorable light, has she bled herself. How she'd hated those days of turmoil, when every girl in her set felt the weight of expectation, of perfect manners, of never saying or doing what she wanted for fear of censure. Then she learned that a blade could release what her tongue and refined manners could not.

Plop, plop go the droplets to the earth floor, and she wants to sing at the satisfaction of it.

She doesn't know how long she stands there awash in peace before a cry jags the air. At first, she thinks it's one of the peacocks. Then it comes again, shriller this time. Not a bird, but a child. She runs.

Her legs don't carry her fast enough. Her skirts bunch, the sun blinds, her ankle rolls, but down the hill she dashes. Where are the children? The tall grasses that ring the near side of the pond partially obscure the water. It's not until she reaches the edge where the grass is clipped that she spies Janie at the waterline. Her daughter's face is white. She is pointing to the water with a trembling hand and when her daughter turns to her, her eyes rain tears.

Billy's wooden sailboat flits and dips above the churning surface. She wades in, each step agonizingly sluggish as she works against the water. When it's waist high, she goes under. She sees her son then, an arm's length away, his body weightless, as if suspended in amber. She cries his name, water bubbles streaming from her mouth, and takes him by the waist. She brings him to the surface and lugs him to the shoreline where they collapse. She lays him on his back. His eyes are closed, his face bloodless. She turns his face to the side, opens his mouth.

"Billy? Billy. It's Mummy. Breathe." She pats his cheeks, smooths the hair from his brow. "Can you hear me?"

Nothing. He is lifeless, still as stone. His lips are white. Water droplets fleck his eyelashes, and she thinks, *I shall never see his eyes again.* She can't stand it. She shakes him. "Billy. Billy. *Please.*"

Her son convulses and water gushes from his mouth. His eyes flutter. "Mummy?"

"Yes, darling. I'm here."

"My boat—"

"Never mind your boat. Can you sit up?"

He rises slowly with her help. More water streams from his mouth but he looks at her and smiles. She comes undone and hugs him fiercely to her, rocks him. Her emotions twist. She can't form words. All she knows is appeasement, that her beloved Billy is safe.

"Mistress?"

Anne stands a few feet away, worrying her apron into pleats. A breeze buffets her dress to her body, the nanny's slender frame and spindly legs discernible beneath, thin as a stork's. She scrapes pale hair from her forehead, and when she speaks again, she can't seem to steady her voice. "I told him it was dangerous, mistress. We've an agreement. The children are never to go near the water without me."

Anne is as white as Billy, frightened, and Constance wants to strangle her. Janie makes a mewling sound and clutches at Constance, buries her face in her shoulder.

Billy coughs and spews more water. A moment later, she helps him to his feet. His shoes ooze water. His short pants cling to him like a second skin. Janie burrows her face into her thigh. When her daughter looks up at her, her lower lip trembles. A smashed daisy falls from her chubby fingers.

Her heart lurches at how much she looks like William. Those gray eyes, that bow of a mouth. "Your brother is fine, Janie. There, you see? Good as new. Go inside, both of you. Ask Mrs. Hunt for some biscuits. Nanny and I will be along soon."

"Biscuits!" Janie jumps and claps her hands. Billy races toward the house, determined to beat his sister to the kitchen.

In the ensuing silence, her temper blazes, stoked by Anne's misery. "Where were you?"

Anne winces like she's been punched. "Just there, in the garden. We were making daisy chains as a surprise for you. Billy was with us and then...he wasn't." A spray of brown freckles stands out against her pallid cheeks. Her eyes, big and blue, are wide with dread. "He, he wasn't to—"

"It doesn't matter what *agreement* you had, Anne. They're children."

The nanny is young, seventeen or eighteen perhaps. A mere child. She hasn't been with them long, just a few months. Their former nanny had been older, more experienced, but had left to marry. She wonders if Ingrid made a mistake hiring a girl so green and then she feels ashamed for thinking it. Isn't she, the mother, just as guilty—more so—for allowing it?

Anne bows her head and wrings quivering hands. She can't look her square in the eye. "On my honor, mistress, I didn't see —" Her eyes widen, focusing on something past Constance.

She turns. The shears lay winking in the sun, blades pointed at her in silent accusation. Her cheeks heat. She picks them up and tosses them into the grass, mind working to invent a lie, but when she turns to Anne, the nanny is staring at her hand. Blood is traveling down Constance's fingers. A drop lands next to her shoe.

Before she can speak, Anne steps to her and grabs her wrist, turning it over. "You've hurt yourself," she breathes. Her attention flies from her wrist to the shears.

"An accident," Constance says, tugging her hand away and sliding her sleeve back into place. Her chest kicks. The nanny shouldn't be focused on her, but on the children. Billy had nearly drowned because of her negligence! She hears the slap before she realizes what she's done. Anne touches her cheek and takes a step back. Anger flares in the girl's eyes for a moment, then the anguish returns.

She's wondering if I'll sack her. The silence plays out and she realizes that watching Anne suffer will be immensely more satisfying than letting her go. At least for now. "See to the children. At once."

She stands at the pond a few minutes more, wrestling to order her thoughts. The sailboat glides across the water, indifferent to what has happened.

Constance sits with William in mutinous silence at the dining table, regarding his every movement under her lashes. He's barely said a word since he arrived home.

"Billy almost drowned today," she says, with the flatness of an undertaker.

William's hand freezes, the wineglass halfway to his lips. "What?"

She relishes his shock, the rapid retreat of his indifference. She won't speak of his betrayal yet; her thoughts are too unformed. But she can wound him by making him aware of how easily Billy could have been lost. She tells him in subdued tones of the pond: the cry, the water, his rescue. It's unlike her to be so serene in the recounting of it, considering how serious it might have been. She can only explain the blade across her wrist as the reason hysteria hasn't reduced her to ashes. "I've spoken with Anne—"

William, face pink, throws down his napkin and rises. "That foolish girl. I'll throttle—"

"Sit down," she says. How magnificent it is to watch him squirm. "I've handled it. Scolding her now won't change things." Her wrist, bound in gauze under her cuff, pulses once and she smiles inwardly.

"The devil it won't." He narrows his eyes. "She's too young. Too damned impetuous."

She raises her brows. What does he know of the girl? "Ingrid didn't think so when she hired her." Their family friend had hired all the servants when she first arrived in Liverpool, young and inexperienced. Later, when she was with child and they moved to Torrence House, Ingrid insisted on helping her fill out the rest of the staff.

Something flashes behind William's eyes, and she's reminded how little she knows of his inner thoughts. Who is this man she's been married to for seven years? What other secrets does he hide?

"It shan't happen again," she says. "I've told Anne they're to play only in the side yard or on the front lawn from now on." She twists the stem of her wineglass in her fingers, watching the light refract from the crystal. When she looks up, William's face is purple with rage. "What? Would you prefer I let her go?"

She should have done. It would've been easy. Nannies were two a penny. But somehow, watching the girl writhe under the cut of her words at the pond, and later, in the nursery, had been too gratifying. She wanted to prolong it; the girl's misery lessens her own. She feels a tremor come over her and thinks again of the corruption within her. Of the house's complicity in it.

William pounds his fist into his other hand and paces like a caged animal.

"Compose yourself, William. I've had words with her and that's the end of it. She was quite upset."

His eyes flare with suspicion. "What did she say?"

"That she was sorry, of course." The words seem to melt his anger and he looks like she could push him over with a feather. Billy's accident has truly frightened him. She's smug with the notion that his attention is on *this* family and not his other. "Should she put a foot wrong in future, she'll be gone. I shouldn't think being let go without a reference would go well for her."

"No. We must...I shall leave it to you, my dear."

To her surprise, he seats himself again, his dressing-down of Anne forgotten. There is a sheen of sweat on his forehead. A pang of pity hits her, quickly squelched. He doesn't deserve pity.

She feels the slow beating of her heart, wonders at the callous that must surely be forming around it.

That evening, Constance sits at her dressing table watching Molly work the brush through her hair. Despite her decision to confront William later, her veneer is starting to crack. Her face is unusually pale. Her heart trips. She can't seem to keep her hands still.

Sandra, she now realizes, was the reason William demanded they marry in London. Why he insisted on a small announcement only in the Liverpool papers. Had Sandra known of their impending nuptials, she might have come forward.

"Is everything all right, mistress?"

She starts and comes to herself, fingering the belt of her dressing gown to stop her hands from fluttering. "Yes. Yes, of course."

William enters the bedroom in his shirtsleeves, fumbling with the buttons of his waistcoat.

"That will be all, Molly," she says.

The young maid's eyes slide away, and she nods. No doubt the pond incident is being discussed in the kitchen. Molly has always been the suspicious sort, one who, she wagers, informs the servants of her master and mistress's every word. The problem with servants is, no matter how sincere they are, they're most loyal to their own kind.

"Goodnight then, mistress."

As Molly closes the door behind her, she is suddenly overcome with the realization that William will join her in bed. They will lie together. The image is a cool rankling and fury rises in her, biting and raw, and something inside her snaps. "Old Hall Street," she says.

William freezes, then tosses his waistcoat on the bed. She might've missed it if she hadn't been paying attention. "Number 18, Old Hall Street. You know it, don't you, William?"

His back is to her. "I don't know what you mean, Connie."

She turns in her chair. "Sandra. Sandra Sullivan. The home you share with her is on Old Hall Street. Where you've been sneaking off to on Sundays when you return from your fictional job as a traveling salesman."

The words skewer him just as she intended. He turns. Oh, his milk-pale face, the tremor in his hands as he tries to make sense of the buttons of his shirt. "I don't know what you've heard, but it's nonsense."

"Don't play me for a fool, William. Are the children all yours, or just a few of them?" She relishes the step he takes back, like he's been slapped. "What's the punishment for bigamy these days, I wonder."

He sits carefully on the bed, eyes brimming with something like dread. "It's rubbish. I swear it."

"If you continue to sit there and lie, I shall leave the house this instant. I shouldn't think your business would weather this, William. Don't think I won't speak of it. You'll be ruined. Your brokerage will be through by the time I'm done." The threat floats in the air between them and she waits.

"How have you come by this knowledge?"

"I followed you today."

The air goes out of him. He's caught. He can't deny anything now. "Very well. Sandra is my mistress. Has been for years."

The words are a dagger to her heart. She'd held out hope that somehow, *somehow* she was wrong. She closes her eyes and tries to swallow down the lump building in her throat.

"But we aren't married, Connie. I swear. Her name is Sandra Roberts, not Sullivan. I never had any designs to marry her. She takes my name for respectability's sake. Nothing more."

"If that's true—and I shall look into the matter myself—she

must leave the city within the week. If you truly aren't married, she has no power over you. I do."

William, eyes white as eggs, submits like a wounded animal. "I will see to it straightaway."

"I assume you're providing her financial support. You must withdraw it as well. All of it. I won't have your money, and certainly none of my own, spent on keeping your mistress."

"Very well, Connie. I give you my word." His face is haunted. For the second time that evening, she's unsettled him. Is she a fool to believe him so readily, to think a woman he's been with for years can be so easily banished? "And the children?"

"They'll leave too, naturally," William mutters.

"I meant, are they yours?"

He smooths his hair back, chances a look at her. "I don't know. What man ever does?"

A beat of silence. In the flicker of the gaslight, he looks as if he's been lashed with a whip. "You must sleep in the dressing room. I won't have you in my bed."

His shoulders sag. "If that's what you wish."

"What I wish is to be left alone. I must think. Decide what I'm to do."

His head snaps up. "What?"

"You can't honestly think I'll stand by you just because you've promised to send your mistress away."

"I've promised to do that precisely so you *will* stand by me." A muscle tics in his jaw and she gets a flash of the old William.

"The only thing I've agreed to is to remain quiet about your whore. And that's only if she leaves Liverpool. That doesn't mean I can stand the sight of you. Heavens, do you think it's as simple as that?"

He stands slowly, then withdraws a small bottle from the pocket of his waistcoat. He twists it open, places the dropper on

68

his tongue, dispels a drop, and replaces the bottle. It's a single fluid motion, one she's seen him do a hundred times, regular as breathing. "You're not going to leave me, Connie." His eyes flicker with menace. His humility has only been a show, something cast off as easily as his waistcoat.

She comes to her feet as he takes a step toward her. "You are in no position to dictate what I do, William."

"I'm your husband. I dictate everything you do."

She laughs. "Oh? What's to keep me from telling everyone about your other family? Do you think your clients would do business with such a man?"

"Perhaps not," William says with a cool shrug. "But they will certainly not respect the wife of one. Have you thought of what your liberal tongue will do to *your* reputation? No woman would have you in her drawing room. Invitations to suppers and balls?" He laughs. "Your social life would dwindle to nothing. Ah, I see you understand the point."

She stares at him, her body trembling. "You assume I'd stay in Liverpool? You forget. This is your home, not mine. In America, no one will know the shoddy details. I shall be a divorced woman, yes. But I'll be a free one."

William's lips curl in a sneer and he snatches her wrist. Her wound throbs and she winces in pain. "You aren't going anywhere, Constance. Not now. Not ever."

"You cannot forbid me from leaving you!" She struggles to free herself, but his grip only tightens.

"Listen to me," William says, pulling her to him. "If you leave me, utter a word about Sandra, there's little I can do. But I will never let you have the children, do you hear? You'll cease being their mother the instant you cross the threshold. Are you prepared to live without them?"

"You can't do that. I have a legal right—"

"Damn what's legal. I'll hide them from you if I must."

She pushes him off, stumbling back when he lets her go. She is speechless, awed by his cruelty. William straightens himself and approaches the door. "In return for your loyalty to me—keeping silent and remaining here as my lawful wife—I will send Sandra and the children away."

She doesn't speak. In any case, he doesn't require an answer. He's left her no choice. He lays a hand on the doorknob and turns. "I'm going to have a drink downstairs. May I bring you anything, dearest?" She can only shake her head, incredulous. "Very well. When I come up, I shall bed down in the dressing room, as you wish. For now, I shall be patient."

In the next instant, he's gone. She glances at her wrist. A bright-red spot weeps from her wound.

Chapter 8

Torrence House

November 10, 1888

Diamond teardrops sparkle from Constance's earlobes as she watches Molly work flowers into her hair. She fingers her necklace, also of diamonds, gifted to her this evening by William. "Please accept this as a token of my love, dearest," he said, bowing over her hand. She opened the box, withdrew the necklace, and said not a word. William, flustered by her silence, stomped downstairs to toss back a brandy and comfort his bruised pride. She pictures him now, pacing the drawing room before the guests arrive. Volatile, fidgety, dosing himself with that infernal white powder he calls his elixir of youth.

Four months may have passed since her confrontation with him over Sandra, but her anger hasn't abated a jot. She's settled into treating him with cool indifference, the most she can muster for a man who's lied to her since the day they met.

"The necklace is stunning, mistress," Molly says.

She wants to believe the young maid is sincere, but there's something of the fox about her—that little upturned nose, those small ears that peak from her cap. Her eyes have a way of sliding away at the wrong moment and she wonders if Molly knows the truth about William's other family. And there are the cameo brooch and tortoiseshell combs that've gone missing. Could they have been pilfered by the little vixen? But then, she's been so out of sorts, she might simply have mislaid them. She blinks and banishes the thoughts. She hasn't time for this.

In the mirror, she practices the smile she'll greet their guests with. Authentic, not forced. As if her joy can't be contained. The smile vanishes, quick as a candle snuffed. *Joy? There is no joy.* She concentrates on her reflection: her red-blond ringlets that look golden in the gaslight, her nearly flawless complexion, eyes of uncommon violet.

The gown is new and of gray silk, trimmed in deep-purple velvet and Brussels lace, gathered at the back and cascading over the bustle in a long train. The neckline is cut low, revealing the swell of her breasts. Fashioned by Madame Dupont in Bold Street for an outrageous sum. She's laced tight enough in her corset to burst.

Molly plucks the last artificial violet from the dressing table and holds it to Constance's temple, looking at her mistress in the mirror.

"I think not, Molly," she says. "A bit too much."

There Molly's eyes go, slipping off to the side, as if something waits in the corner of the room. She really must speak to her about her manners. But not tonight. Tonight, she needs all her wits about her. She may be withering inside, but she's young. Resilient. The women of their set look up to her, the men admire her. She won't let her failed marriage rot her from the inside out. She will wear beauty and happiness if she has to affix it to herself with pins and glue.

She sighs and flutters her fan. She prefers being a guest at dinner parties. It's easier to stray to a room William doesn't occupy. As hosts they are attached at the hip, automatons playing a role. Little do their guests know she ousted William from their bed in the summer. He still sleeps in the little dressing room off the bedroom with only a cot and his menagerie of pills, powders, and patent medicines for company.

The day after their fight over Sandra and for many days following, she visited church after church, looking for a record of marriage between William Sullivan and Sandra Roberts. She went back twenty-five years and found nothing. Nor were there any records of births or baptisms for a James or Joseph Sullivan, the children mentioned by Sandra's neighbor, Jemima Kirby.

Exactly a week later, she trounced up to Sandra's door, prepared to find her and her children still there. But William had been true to his word; Sandra and the rest of her family had vanished. An older couple lived there now. "Never heard of her, miss. You've the wrong address."

William has been good to her since she called him out. He's been at home, seemingly delighted with her company. No more shady evasiveness, no more late nights coming home stinking drunk. He's been cold to Anne since the accident at the pond, responding with frosty indignation whenever the nanny crossed his path, but she can't blame him. Though she's careful not to show it, she's pleased he showers her with gifts and dotes on Billy and Janie. He's only waiting for her to invite him back into her bed.

But William is good at pretending and even better at lies. She won't be so easily convinced.

She stands to scrutinize her gown in the cheval mirror. When she pulls on her gloves, her hands are trembling.

In the drawing room, guests hover around candles and lamps like moths to flame. Alan and Mary offer champagne on trays. Thirty invitations sent, not one declined. After dinner there will be dancing, and after that, another light meal. Guests will pile into their carriages at dawn dizzy with drink and sleep most of the following day.

Ingrid Berkshire enters the drawing room, her hair pulled severely back and betraying a few wisps of gray. Her somber features break into a smile as she reaches William. Heads nod in greeting. As a Liverpool native, there's scarcely anyone in the city—at least of the upper class—Ingrid doesn't know. She laughs at something William says, her sharp, angular features softening for a moment. He's always had a way of bringing out the best in her.

For an instant, she imagines racing to Ingrid and crying before the guests, *This man, this man you think you know? He has another family. A mistress and five children. He's a liar and a cheat.*

"You're fetching tonight." She starts. Edward cocks an inquisitive brow. "New gown?"

"Yes, thank you." She dislikes how close he is, how her skin prickles when her brother-in-law is near.

He takes a sip of champagne, his eyes searching over the rim of his crystal flute. "What's going on in that head of yours? Bored already?"

"Hardly, the party has only just begun." She smiles, though it feels thin at the edges.

"That artifice may fool most, but not me, Connie."

He's dressed in tails, his white waistcoat immaculate and well-starched. Seven years ago, when she and William married, the Sullivan brothers had never owned a suit of tails. They've come up in the world. Their cotton brokerage has done well, her income the icing on the cake. Still, there's something of the boy in Edward. While William assumed the role as a member of the upper class with ease, Edward still looks wet behind the ears.

"I don't know what you mean," she says. She takes a sip of champagne. Her head is beginning to pound.

"Did you get it, Connie? Did you read it?" Said softly, so no one will hear.

She can't look at him. She hates it when he ambushes her when he knows she can't easily walk away. "Of course I did." She smiles for the room.

"'Of course' you got my letter, or 'of course' you read it?" Edward, too, looks around the room. His profile is almost identical to William's. He's an inch shorter, but at thirteen years his brother's junior, his hair has not yet begun to thin as William's has.

"Not here, Edward," she whispers. "Not now."

"Then where, when?"

"I've told you," she says, low. "You must stop this...persistence. It's futile. For heaven's sake, I'm married to your brother."

"Not happily."

"Yes, happily—"

"You don't have to pretend with me. Surely you know that by now, after everything I've said."

In truth, Edward has said far less than he's written. She was shocked at first, that Edward would be foolish enough to send his own sister-in-law *billets-doux*—and not ten months after they married. How could he be sure she wouldn't go to William? But she realized, as did Edward, no doubt, that she would never speak the words that would fracture the brothers' relationship. Words that would not just sever ties but sabotage their business and divide the family.

If she's honest, she's as vain as any woman. She finds Edward's attentions cloying at times, yet it's gratifying to know —especially with the state of her marriage—she's still attractive, still a woman to be desired. Every one of Edward's letters is tucked inside her secret cache upstairs. She's kept them all. Lately, when thoughts of William's duplicity eat at her, she prizes them from their hiding place and pores over them, like a moneylender gloating over his accounts.

She'd assumed, at first, that Edward knew of Sandra. Her affair with William had gone on for decades, after all. But Edward would have used William's infidelity to convince her to stray herself—into his arms. For a brief instant, she considers confiding in Edward. But to what end? He'll only see William's betrayal as more motivation to win her.

"If only I'd met you first." Edward's eyes are red-rimmed. He's had too much champagne. "Everything would've been different. I leave soon for America. Laugh if you will, but I shall miss you."

"You'll be back come spring," she teases. Since their marriage, it's Edward who spends the cotton season in the American south. "Besides, William can't have you away too long." A grin plays about her lips as she looks up at him, willing him to smile lest the guests, or, God forbid, William take notice.

"I'd have swept you off your feet, you know."

A pang in her chest—regret? Longing? If she'd met Edward first and married him, would she be where she is now, living a lie? An image of Sandra naked and straddling William, fire-red hair falling around her shoulders, rears. Boisterous laughter snaps her back to the room, which feels suddenly airless and thick.

Ingrid has left William's circle and is speaking with her sister Martha and Christina Samuels. William pats his friend George on the back, eyes brimming with mirth. Another broker joins them, and the joke is retold. More barks of laughter. She must mingle, she must amuse. But the champagne tastes off, the room too loud. And Edward is standing too close.

"You aren't feeling well?"

"Pardon?"

"You're massaging your temple, Connie."

"It's nothing."

Across the room, Ingrid breaks from Martha and Christina and approaches them. "Hello, my dear. Edward." She inclines her head slightly. "You two look positively conspiratorial."

"May I get you ladies another champagne?" Edward says, casting a furtive wink Constance's way.

"That would be lovely, Edward," Ingrid says.

Her friend pins her with a look as soon as he's gone. "Is everything all right, Constance? You look odd."

"I've a slight headache, is all."

Ingrid is dressed in a simple mauve gown trimmed with gray. She's not what she would consider a handsome woman and no slave to fashion, but there is a strength in her, a confidence she has long wished to emulate. There is an art to knowing what food to serve at dinners, who to invite, and she doesn't think she could have mastered these things without Ingrid. She and William had grown up together, and Constance hadn't hesitated in naming her the godmother of their children.

"How fares the boy?" Ingrid's eyes access her. "He's not still misbehaving, is he?"

A flash of Billy; his plump cheeks, his infectious giggle. Earlier when she'd tucked him in, he'd held on to her as if he never wanted to let go. Ever since the pond he's been needy, demanding more of her time. "He's no worse."

"No better then."

How easily Ingrid reads her. After the dark day at the pond, she'd complied with Billy's requests to spend more time with her —taking walks with him on the grounds, allowing him to pick flowers with her in the garden, watching him run with his stick and hoop. It was his near drowning, of course. It was natural for him to want his mother. But her added attention had strained the relationship between him and Anne. "He's a good boy. It's just—"

"I agree with William," Ingrid says, her mouth pulled taut. "The boy needs a firm hand. He had a scare over the summer, but it's been months, my dear. Is he still throwing things about the nursery and speaking to Anne in strident tones?"

"He's coming along, I think." She cannot have this conversation now. It's beginning to feel like a scolding. She considers the older woman her truest friend, but now is not the time.

Ingrid lays a hand on her arm. "It's one thing to mother him, my dear. It's quite another to spoil him. You must stand firm."

Yesterday Billy had refused to sit quietly in a corner of the nursery after disobeying Anne. Constance had heard the ruckus and intervened, but Billy's behavior had only spiraled. *I hate Nanny! She lies! I shan't do a thing she says!* How he cried and flailed about. Janie had looked on wide-eyed, tears welling. Constance had lost her temper, telling him if he continued to misbehave, she wouldn't read to him or allow him to accompany her outside. It had done the trick, but something inside her had withered. Was he somehow feeling the coolness that had come between her and William?

"And now I've lost you," Ingrid says.

"Not at all," she replies with a thin smile. "It's a phase, I'm sure. You know how children can be." Ingrid's own children are grown. She'd divorced her husband before Constance came to Liverpool and she's breathed not a word about him.

"And how is Anne weathering this? I trust she's being stern with the boy."

"Anne's been a godsend, truly." It surprises her how well the nanny has managed with Billy. Not once has she asked her to intervene, even on Billy's worst days. It's as if the pond has changed her too. She is more sure-handed, more watchful. Only when she has come up to the nursery and witnessed Billy's behavior for herself had she known his fits persisted. Perhaps Anne bears so much guilt over letting Billy out of her sight that day, she can't bear to trouble her.

Ingrid blinks rapidly, tilts her head in that way that reminds her of a bird. "You're tired, I think. You aren't with child, are you?"

Bitterness blooms in her chest like a canker and she resists the urge to laugh. "No, nothing like that."

She's wondered for ages if the reason for Ingrid's divorce was infidelity. Now that her own marriage is in ruins, she's yearned to broach the subject but hasn't quite known how. She's held back from telling her about William's other family for fear of shattering Ingrid's good opinion of him. Once, when Ingrid's sister Martha drank too much at one of the Sullivans' soirees, she confided in her that Ingrid had once been in love with William. Years ago, before Ingrid married. She hadn't known whether to believe her. Ingrid has only ever spoken of William like a brother. Her emotions swim. Ingrid has known William all her life...could she know about Sandra?

The guests are engaged in conversation. For now, she has Ingrid to herself. "You've known William for many years. I wonder...It's only that I wonder if there was a woman. Someone special he knew before me."

Ingrid pulls in her chin. "He's more than twenty years older than you, my dear. Naturally there were women. He was—is— an attractive man, after all. He had his dalliances, I suppose, as does any man. What are you getting at?"

"He hasn't been...himself."

Ingrid looks amused. "You think there must be someone else because he's not as besotted with you as he was in the beginning." The way she says *besotted*. Like it's a dirty word. "I can't recall anyone who had such a tie to William. If he has a woman now, you can hardly expect him to own up to it."

Constance looks away, afraid her expression will reveal too much. When her gaze swings back to Ingrid, her dark-ochre eyes shine.

"Love doesn't last forever, my dear. The most beautiful, the most charming, the most suitable woman in the world can't hold a man."

A tremor pulses through her. Her head throbs in earnest and she can no longer stomach the conversation. "Forgive me, I'll just go freshen up."

She exits the room, nodding and smiling as she goes, feeling the weight of Ingrid's eyes on her. She ascends the main staircase and enters the water closet down the hall. The little brown bottle is waiting in the cupboard near the sink. She unscrews the cap, pours a bit onto a teaspoon, and tastes the bitterness of the liquid. She replaces the bottle and closes her eyes, hands grasping the sink. She can hear laughter downstairs, smell the sweet scent of pipe smoke. When she opens her eyes, she's relieved to see her hair is tidy, her eyes bright.

It won't be long before she feels the laudanum. It will numb the throb at her temples. Blunt the sharp edge of her marriage.

In the shadows of the landing, she lifts her skirts. The house waits. The hair on the back of her neck prickles, and she begins to descend. A cool rush of air. She stumbles on a step and somehow finds her footing. She feels as if... She looks behind her. It's almost as if someone—or something—pushed her. *This infernal house. I must ask William about having more lights installed here.*

A guest is being helped out of his coat in the front hall as she reaches the bottom. "Thank you, Alan," she says. "I'll show the gentleman to the drawing room."

The man turns, grinning slightly. "You must be Constance Sullivan."

"And you must be Timothy Worth."

He raises dark brows. "Does my reputation precede me?"

She laughs. "Not at all. You were the only gentleman on the invitation list I hadn't met. William was adamant you come. Welcome to Torrence House, Mr. Worth."

"Call me Timothy," he says.

The gaslights spit and pitch in their sconces on the wall, throwing a warm glow on one of the most striking men she's ever seen. Timothy Worth is tall and broad-shouldered, dressed in black tails with a waistcoat of deep green. His mustache and beard are neatly trimmed. A wave of deep-chestnut hair falls from his forehead. She has the sudden urge to brush it back. He is Edward's age perhaps, which would make him about ten years older than herself. Another cotton broker, she'd wager. It's a wonder she hasn't met him sooner.

"Forgive my tardiness," Worth says. "I hope I'm not too late?"

"For dinner? Goodness, no. Everyone is this way. We're having drinks."

They enter the drawing room. She leads him directly to William.

"Ah, Worth, old chap!" William says, putting an arm around his shoulders. "There's a good fellow. Glad you could make it."

Across the room, Edward holds her glass of champagne and looks at her like a lost pup. Ingrid gives her a questioning glance. Instead of approaching them, she heads for a small cluster of women and joins their conversation.

The ballroom isn't large, but the high ceiling and gilded pillars give it a palatial feel. The quartet in the corner is on a break. Dancers gather at a long table where punch waits in fat, orange-garnished bowls.

"Enjoying yourself, my dear?" William inquires, hovering at her elbow. Earlier, they opened the dance with a waltz while the guests looked on, rapt in the presence of such a happy, glittering couple. Now, William's strength has waned. He pats his forehead with a handkerchief. Beads of sweat speckle the skin above his lip. She can tell by his ashen pallor that he's indulged in his powder. She saw him tap it from a packet into a wineglass following dinner. After its initial spark, it's left him withered as a plucked flower.

"Of course."

William was solicitous at dinner, regaling their guests about the improvements to the house. How everyone laughed when she quipped the peacocks were William's idea. To her right sat Mr. Worth, a detail she'd arranged that morning. It was customary for a male guest unknown to the hostess be seated next to her. How fortuitous the rule; she enjoyed her conversation with him immensely. Between the first and second courses, her eyes fell on Edward seated farther down the table. His eyes went from her to Worth, a question in them, and then he looked away.

For a second, she felt a pang of guilt before she realized how absurd it was. She wasn't bound to Edward, and her husband was certainly never bound to her. No one owned her. She watched Timothy Worth's lips move as he told her about his cotton brokerage and wondered what it would be like to feel them on her own.

"If you don't mind, my dear," William says, scattering her thoughts, "I'll go have a smoke with George. Won't be long."

William motions to his friend and the two are soon out the

door to the garden. The string quartet returns to their instruments. She is on her way to the punch when she hears the eloquent strain of a violin being tuned and suddenly Timothy Worth is beside her. Tall, handsome, waiting.

"May I have this dance?" His eyes are kind and virtuous, a startling green. They haven't yet danced together. Has he asked her because William left the ballroom? She squelches the thought. Not every man is dishonest in his intentions. She's been soured by William.

"I would be delighted," she says. This time her smile is genuine.

"I promise not to trample on your toes," he says. "Trust me?"

She does, somehow, in more ways than dancing. Her insides twist and she thinks of how trapped she feels, and how very much she'd like to be swept away.

They approach the center of the room as other couples do the same. The music begins. His hand at the small of her back is as delicious as a secret. She wants to squeeze his shoulder where her left hand rests to confirm he's real. They step to the violins, and she feels a fluttering deep within her, as if she is capable of anything.

She floats across the ballroom floor in a gray satin whirl with a dangerously attractive man, and for the first time since the summer, she feels weightless, as if she hasn't a care in the world.

Chapter 9

Bold Street

Liverpool, England

January 4, 1889

Constance leaves Woolright's. From her hands dangle bags of sugared sweets for the children and a pair of butter-yellow gloves for herself. A hansom cab driver and a man selling flowers from a stand nod their greetings and she sees herself as they must, a young woman in a matching burgundy coat and hat that cost more than they make in a string of months.

The air smells of ice and mud. The sky glowers, waits to drop snow. There's little noise despite the traffic; the most fashionable street in the city is laid with wooden planking, a courtesy bestowed on wealthy patrons who turn down it in their handsome equipages.

She's usually lighthearted leaving the dressmakers, but

Madame Dupont has soured her mood. "We will settle your bill from last season's gowns, *oui?*" she'd asked, and her face had burned, for another customer had loitered nearby. How close she'd come to her debt being discovered, tumbled from the lips of a woman who cannot know how a careless word could find its way to William.

A year ago, she'd fretted over William going through money as if it were plentiful as air. But since the discovery of Sandra Roberts, she's found comfort in surrounding herself with luxury: expensive gowns, furs of fox and sable, shoes from Paris. Anything to sweeten the bitter pill of betrayal. William will only spend her fortune, so why should he be the only one to enjoy it? It's all part of the deception, their cleverly crafted illusion.

She remembers the London creditor, Mr. Seward. A man of means if the cut of his suit was any indication. She found his firm advertised in the *Liverpool Courier* last summer and took the train to London and back in a day.

> Seward and Sons. Agreeable terms
> Lender to ladies
> Privacy guaranteed!

She liked the sound of his name, the relief of knowing she wouldn't be turned away if William wasn't with her. "My terms are fair," Mr. Seward told her. The sparkle in his eye as he looked at her emerald necklace winking from its bed of black velvet was a relief. "As collateral," she said, and Mr. Seward smiled. "Sixty percent interest, Mrs. Sullivan. Do you know what that means?" She assured him she did and left with more money than she'd ever had in her reticule before.

The black iron clock that juts over the sidewalk announces

the hour: almost three o'clock. Hunger paws at her. Conrad isn't due to pick her up for another hour. She heads in the direction of Clayton Square and crosses Hanover, the clop and clatter of horse traffic jarring after the silence of Bold Street.

Pedestrians choke the pavement. A tall woman in a deep-green coat with a flash of bright-red hair beneath her hat startles her. Constance almost bumps into a man walking next to her. She can't see the woman's face. But she knows, she *knows*, even if the voice inside her head says it can't be.

Sandra.

She runs. She won't let her get away. Her bags crash against her skirts, her shoes pinch her feet. She jostles past pedestrians who turn to stare.

"Watch it!" someone shouts.

When she's close enough, she clamps a hand around the woman's upper arm and hauls her around. The woman spins, alarm on her face.

The face is wrong; the cheeks too hollow, the eyes too wide.

Her heart knocks against her ribcage. "Forgive me, I-I thought you were someone else."

"Clearly," the woman says, the word a knife. "You should be more careful."

Face aflame, Constance crosses Church Street to a coffee shop. The sharp scent of coffee beans wraps itself around her when she enters. She selects a small table by the window and gives the waiter her order, as if she hasn't just mistaken a woman for her husband's mistress and ambushed her on the street.

The door opens as her waiter arrives with the pot and a dish of scones. She's thanking him and pouring when someone steps to the table.

"Constance?"

She looks up. Her eyes widen at the sight of him, standing tall in a bowler and black coat.

"Mr. Worth. How lovely to see you." Her heart feels as if it's been pierced by an arrow. What wizardry has brought him to her, this man who's been on her mind since the dinner party at Torrence House?

"May I join you? I saw you from the window and noticed you were alone."

She nods and Timothy takes a seat. She waves to the waiter, motions for another cup. When her attention returns to the table, he's studying her. She feels the burn of a blush and hates herself for the open book she is.

"Have we resorted to formal names? Last time we met you were content to call me Timothy."

She smiles, a tremor running through her. The waiter brings the extra cup and she pours, hoping Timothy doesn't notice the way her hand trembles holding the pot. "Last time we met you were worried about stepping on my toes."

"I made good on my promise. Not a single toe broken." A wolfish grin. "I was wondering if I might see you one day about town."

She laughs and feels the weight of Sandra leave her. "Is my love for shopping that obvious?"

"No, no," he says. He clutches his cup in one hand, the other lying flat on the table. The memory of his hands touching hers when they danced is blade sharp, yet it's been months since she's seen him. "Running into you was more wishful thinking on my part."

His eyes are earnest, and she notices again how green his irises are, how dark the lashes that frame them. "Well, your wish has been granted, I suppose."

She lifts the tiny cream pitcher, hovers it over his cup. He waves it away and takes a sip. She adds cream to her own cup and watches the whorls of white and brown blend, wondering what to talk about, if he will note her nervousness. "What brings you to Church Street, Timothy?" She likes the way his name sounds on her tongue, the pleasure of uttering it aloud when, for months, Timothy Worth has only existed in her head as a recollection, a dream.

"Some banking business, nothing more."

"That sounds frightfully dull."

"Except for the fortune of spotting you."

The intensity of his eyes belies the lightness of his words. She feels a pulse in her throat. "And I thought you'd come from the Palatine Club on your way back to the Exchange."

"What? One of those drunken sods who's had a fine meal and goes tripping back up Castle Street?" There's mirth in his eyes though he doesn't smile.

"I've seen it, you know." *My husband is one of them.*

Timothy rasps a hand over his beard, considers the contents of his cup before looking up. "It may surprise you to hear it, but I think members of the Palatine are snobs with nothing better to do than talk of their own success."

"I take it you're not a member."

"I detest the exclusivity of it. Did you know no shop owner can join? How abhorrent for a high-class man of Liverpool to be seated next to his tailor."

His statements are so contrary to William's way of thinking. She realizes, in that instant, what a parvenu her husband is. How conceited she's become. They are pretenders, she and William, and she hates herself and their marriage so much she wants to scream. Her body has become a canvas of hatch-marks to vent her rage. Cutting herself is the only thing that stems her misery, and the balm is too short-lived.

"You're quiet," Timothy says. "I've shocked you."

She sips her coffee, bides her time before she replies. "I think your opinions are wonderfully refreshing. I myself hate..."

And there it is, the word she's looking for. "Pretense." *And yet look what I've become. What William and I are.* "I think honesty..." What is honesty? She can't even define it anymore.

"Is what makes the man?"

He can't know how close to the mark he is. "It does make the man, yes. But it's more than that. It's about character. About doing what is noble and good rather than doing what's self-aggrandizing or easy."

She sees it in him then, his quiet dismay over the Palatine Club's snobbery, his contentment to be alone and unfettered by what others think. Timothy Worth is a man of loyalty and honor.

St. Peters tolls the hour. They drink simultaneously from their cups. She cherishes the moment yet is terrified. She's afraid to speak, afraid she'll break the delicate bubble into which they've stepped.

"Were you with family for Christmas?" she says at last. She was surprised, following the dinner party at Torrence House, not to see him at other social engagements. Her eyes roamed dance floors and drawing rooms, but she was disappointed each time. She hated herself for the desperation of it, a man she'd only met once.

"Yes," Timothy says. He rotates his cup with his fingers. "I was in Rochdale. There were rather a lot of relatives milling about. Quite hectic, really. It's ironic I returned to Liverpool to get some peace and quiet."

When was the last time she and William were home of an evening that wasn't a social one with guests? She can't recall. To brim with movement and activity, to fall into bed fatigued and emptied, was to avoid introspection of her marriage. To admitting the failure of it.

"Have you a big family, Constance?"

"No. My father died before I was born. My elder brother passed away in Paris some years ago from consumption. There's really only my mother, who spends much of the year in France, though her home is in New York. I'm rather a foreigner here."

"Nonsense." He tilts his head, assesses her. "I must admit, I was a bit surprised when I met you."

"Oh?"

"I was expecting an older woman."

"Closer to William's age."

"Yes. But also, if I may be honest, someone more like him. Someone more..." She can feel the moment hang, drawn by a thread. She's afraid to breathe, fearful he will paint William as he is, and fearful he will not. "Tenacious. Rather stiff-backed?" He raises his shoulders and looks sheepish. "But you're none of those things."

"My husband and I are very different people. Much more than I believed at the time of our marriage."

A moment of torturous silence. Her stomach rolls like the sea. *I've said too much.*

Then, into the silence between them, Timothy says, "Do you walk, Constance? For pleasure I mean. I find the Wavertree Botanic Gardens enjoyable this time of year, provided the wind isn't too fierce."

She goes very still. The shop recedes and she has the sensation that it's only she and Timothy. That no one else, in this drop of time, exists but the two of them.

"I take a turn there, now and again," Timothy explains. "The air is refreshing and though there are no flowers blooming of course, the beds are still quite something."

"It sounds lovely," she says. She isn't quite certain, still, what he's asking. *If* he's asking.

"Next week at this time, weather permitting?" His voice quivers, as if he's not quite sure of himself.

Not a man experienced with romance or flings. This, more than anything, gives her the courage to respond.

"Weather permitting." She pulls on her gloves, hands shaking. They stand and say their goodbyes.

In another minute, he is walking away in the other direction.

Chapter 10

Wavertree Botanic Gardens

Liverpool, England

January 11, 1889

The days pass slowly with a dreamlike quality. Her mornings begin with thoughts of Timothy. The feeling of floating just inches from the ground is like the days counting down to Christmas when she was a child—the anticipation, the excitement. She doted on the children all week and had patience with Molly when she found the sheets folded clumsily in the linen closet. She'd even been kinder to William, who seemed surprised by her warmness at breakfast each morning. The world feels somehow benevolent and golden, even if Torrence House is as oppressive as ever.

When the day of her meeting with Timothy dawns, she's elated to see the sun's rays peeking through a scrim of clouds. He will be at the garden today. The thought of him sends a shiver down her spine. She deliberates all morning whether to have Conrad drop her at the garden entrance. Might he say something to William? Then she remembers there's a low wall and hedges around the garden's perimeter. But more than this is the realization of what Timothy will think—if his intentions are virtuous—if he sees her emerging from a hired cab. That she has fashioned his innocuous invitation into something intimate and illicit.

She arrives at Edge Lane a little after three o'clock and tells Conrad to return in an hour. If the driver wonders why she's walking a garden in the dead of winter, he's too well trained to comment.

She walks through the wrought-iron gate. The curator's lodge is a block of handsome sandstone. Straight ahead is a path that skirts a small, circular bed of bushes. Just beyond, the path opens up, intersecting a larger perpendicular footpath. It's here she spies Timothy leaning against a tree. He comes to attention when he sees her, his face somber as they step toward each other.

"You look surprised to see me," she says.

Timothy's breath plumes like smoke. His cheeks are red from the cold, his eyes alert and assessing. Her pulse quickens. She has the impression he will say this is a mistake, that he made a rash decision, and they should part ways. Then, the crazed kaleidoscope of her thoughts turns, and she is struck with the opposite—that he will draw her to him, plant a tender kiss on her lips, and never let her go.

But Timothy only turns and steps along the path, head downcast, hands clasped behind him.

"Yes," he says at last. "I thought maybe you would decide not to come."

She wonders at his mood, the way he is tense yet reserved.

"This garden," he gestures with a sweep of his arm to the

expanse of lawn and trees, "is quite secluded this time of year. I hope not too much so for your liking."

Is he suggesting he chose this spot so they can be alone? "I think it's lovely," she says. "It's quite its own world."

They share a smile. "If you haven't gathered already, Constance, I'm not one for crowds. The occasional party is expected, I suppose. That's why I came to Torrence House that evening. In truth, I find public life rather tedious. I'm perfectly happy to spend an evening with a brandy and a good book."

She remembers when she first arrived in Liverpool, when attending parties was daunting because she didn't know anyone. When she'd felt too young, too unfamiliar with all the things that were expected of her in her new role as wife. She was content to be with William and nothing more. When the children arrived, the four of them walking the grounds or sitting round the fire in the evenings was all she wanted. But then William pulled away and she lost herself in banal conversations, supper parties, and fancy balls.

She feels a wave of shame. "I've quite forgotten how immensely enjoyable reading can be."

For so long, she's pursued roomfuls of people, chatter, being busy. The simplicity of just being sounds like a dream. All those people around dining tables, in theater foyers, in ballrooms. What has she in common with any of them? Why does it matter so much to be considered one of them?

Because there's nothing else.

They've arrived at the main entrance to the glasshouse with its enormous, multi-story dome of glass.

"It's closed for the season of course," Timothy says mildly. "Have you been inside?"

"Once, years ago. When I first came to Liverpool. William was anxious to show me the city. I was lonesome for America. He brought me here to see the ferns."

"And are you still lonesome for it, America?"

I am lonesome always she wants to say but does not. "Sometimes." She thinks of the frigid air in Torrence House, how the winter has seeped into her bones that no fire in the hearths could vanquish. The house has only fueled her solitude. Yesterday, Alan, the butler, had come to her. Molly had complained of a strange stain in her room. The three of them climbed the steep stairs to the servants' floor. She had seen the black mold spreading under the eaves like tar and thought *the house is sick. It's changed me. Perhaps it's changing all of us.*

They turn down the central path, Timothy matching his gait to her own. The wind has picked up, but the sun is warm. The scrape of their steps on the gravel is the only sound. She's struck again that the world has somehow shrunk to just the two of them.

"Tell me of your children, Constance."

She smiles, pleased he's asked. "William Jr. is almost seven. Janie is two and a half."

"Is that all you have to say? Come now, you can tell me more than that."

She laughs. "Are you certain? I can go on forever about them." She glances at him, sees his mouth go up in a tight smile.

"Billy—that's what we call little William—was born a month early. He was such a delicate little thing, but you wouldn't know it now. He enjoys chasing after the peacocks and frightening the servants with tales of pirates on the open sea."

"A born storyteller."

"Perhaps. In truth, he's more like me. Quite pensive at times. Shy, too." Or he used to be. To her dismay, he's still acting out, refusing to obey Anne. She cannot understand why he's taken such a vicious dislike to the girl. She doesn't want to think it's the house...

"And Janie?"

"Much more like her father. Stubborn, not afraid of anything. She follows Billy around like his shadow, trying to keep up with him. She'd be more at home in breeches than dresses."

"You must be very proud."

They've arrived at the center of the garden. Raised beds stretch in every direction. The precision of the plantings is remarkably exact. She stops for a moment to admire bushes arranged in serpentine lines.

"You're right," she murmurs. "It's extraordinary even in winter."

"The designs are meant to emulate the tiles in St. George's Hall."

When she came here with William so long ago, he was in a hurry. They walked the paths and toured the glasshouse quickly, and then went someplace she can't remember. William said little of the garden itself; he merely brought her here to show her Liverpool was as grand as New York City.

They begin walking again.

After some moments, Timothy turns. "How is William?" The question startles her. It brings her marriage front and center in a way she'd rather avoid. "I only ask because...well, quite frankly, he didn't look well the last few times I've seen him."

"Let me guess. He looked pale and drawn, rather fatigued, sweating profusely, that sort of thing?"

"Yes."

They've reached the end of a path. A small, shallow cement pool sits empty, its shape reminding her of an eye. A flare of courage rises in her. Timothy has been honest with her; the least she can do is return it in kind. "My husband takes a great many medicines and sees a lot of doctors, I'm afraid."

Timothy raises his brows. "He's ill?"

96

"Not in the traditional sense."

Timothy nods slowly. "William is known in some circles, at least among the traders at the Exchange, to be a habitual arsenic eater."

She's wondered for years if William's powder is arsenic. She considered more than once while in his dressing room—coming upon an unlabeled packet of white powder here, or a small vial of liquid there—bringing these things to a chemist to determine what they were. But if she did learn William was taking something dangerous, what then? If she confronted him, he would be incensed. He'd see going behind his back the problem, not the toll his potions were taking on his health.

"I should think it was the malaria," Timothy says mildly. She frowns and looks questioningly at him. His eyes widen a fraction. "He never told you he contracted malaria in America?"

She shakes her head, embarrassment flaring in her.

"Forgive me." Timothy looks away. "I've said too much."

"No, please." She places her hand on his upper arm and then pulls it away, abashed at her forthrightness yet unable to let the conversation go. "Tell me. Please." She can see Timothy is at war with himself, weighing the risk of telling her what William has not. "I promise what you tell me will remain between us."

He turns to her slowly, eyes sweeping her face. "It was in '77, I think he said. Shortly after he formed the brokerage in Virginia. He said he languished for some time."

She pictures William telling the story: his exaggerated descriptions, his feeling of impending death. "And what has malaria to do with his arsenic habit?"

"He was given quinine. The usual remedy, he said. It was ineffective. The doctors prescribed a concoction of arsenic and strychnine which eventually did the trick."

The pity in Timothy's eyes is too much. Anger bursts like a wound inside her. "My husband is always on the verge of contracting some fatal illness, some disease of which there is no cure. *That* is his true affliction. When did he tell you this?"

"Months ago, when we were having lunch—the lunch when he invited me to your dinner party at Torrence, as a matter of fact."

"Did he admit to being addicted?"

"Not exactly," Timothy says. "I rather think he finds it therapeutic. Forgive me, once again. I shouldn't have mentioned it."

"Please," she says, "think nothing of it. I've known for some time William takes something that is ruining his health. I've wondered if it was arsenic. Now I know. I think it's the reason he's deteriorated as he has. He doesn't see it."

"Yes, it's quite dangerous. I shouldn't like to see you...suffer from his decisions."

Oh, but I have. The wind kicks up. Clouds wrestle. She wants to tell him everything—William's moods, his mistress, his children by her, how she hates him. Then, a dawning: Timothy Worth has asked her here out of kindness, perhaps to tell her only this. The sun scurries behind a cloud and the day darkens. Just like that, her happiness is gone. She wants to injure Timothy, to make him hurt as she hurts.

"Is this why you've invited me here? To tell me of William's addiction, his love of arsenic?" Her words are biting, sharp as a blade. Another thought rears: is his intent to pry into her marriage? Spy for William?

"Not at all. I had such a delightful discussion with you last week, I wanted to prolong it."

She doesn't believe him. She can feel her heartbeat in her ears, the coursing of her blood. "I imagine," she says with an acidic smile, "there are many ladies who'd find it their good fortune to walk with you."

"And yet not a one of them interests me."

She doesn't reply. Instead, she concentrates on the path.

They've reached a line of trees. Black branches reach to the sky and create a sort of tunnel. Wind rustles overhead, the whistling sound mournful, the creak of bark like a door on rusty hinges.

She can feel him looking at her, reading her expression, her body language. She doesn't care. This was a mistake. *I never should have come.*

He lays a hand on her upper arm, turning her gently to him. "I've upset you. I'm sorry. That was not my intent." His face is blanched, his mouth downturned in a scowl. "The truth is, I find you excellent company. I'd much rather be here with you than any other lady in the city."

"Come now, you haven't met them all, have you?" She cocks a brow and starts to walk again.

"I have met her." Timothy blocks her path and clutches her with both hands, his fingers tight around her upper arms. He doesn't let her go.

Her sardonic smile dies. Their eyes catch like fire. Timothy doesn't look away. His revelation hangs suspended between them. She can see it sparkling. *I have met you, Constance.*

"As God is my witness, I—" He stops. His eyes graze her lips.

They're standing so close she can smell the scent of limes coming from him. She hasn't imagined it. Her attraction to him —from the first sight of him in the front hall at Torrence House —is mutual. She takes a deep breath, the air filling her lungs with something wondrous and full of possibility. A sense of destiny settles in her, a taste of freedom that's as sweet as sugar.

The wind continues its banter in the boughs, but when his lips claim her own, they know only each other.

Chapter 11

Flatman's Hotel

London, England

March 21–23, 1889

From the window of her hotel room, Constance looks down at Henrietta Street. Dandies stroll with well-dressed ladies on their arms. A plump woman in a red hat walks a poodle on a leash. Carriages clatter by, the sorrel coats of the horses glinting like pennies in the sun. The breeze carries the scent of roasted coffee beans from the market. She wants to gather the scene in her arms like a blanket and embrace it. *This is living,* she thinks. *This is what it means to be happy.* When the bells of St. Paul's peal the hour, she brings the window sash down with a clack.

She turns and assesses the room with a critical eye. Overall, the sitting room isn't large, but is comfortably appointed. She wrote the hotel weeks ago asking for a suite: a sitting room with a bedroom and water closet, a good view out the window. Everything must be perfect this weekend. Everything.

Covent Garden, with its restaurants and theaters, its festive air, is a good choice for this...what? This *assignation,* this *tryst.* A smile lights her lips. Never in a million years would she have believed that she, Constance Sullivan, would be in love again. She thought her days of bliss long gone after she and William settled into the reality of marriage—the arguments over money, his capricious moods, his devious affair. But if these last months have shown her anything, it's that just when life seemed its most dreary, its most tedious and miserable, wonder could emerge.

She bites her lip and steps to the bedroom, heat clambering up her cheeks at the sight of the bed. Under the green counterpane and crisp white sheets, she and Timothy will lie together. The thought of their union hovers just out of reach. She can't quite imagine it. It's too hard to believe she's found him. That he is hers. That she, his. Her life had changed that January day at the botanic gardens when he kissed her, but if she's honest, it's more than that. Meeting Timothy at Torrence House kindled something in her she believed long dead.

Now it all seems destined, as if they are players in a drama that was meant for them all along. They are perfect together. More ideal than she and William ever were.

How quickly the pleasure of her days has become steeped in the stolen hours with Timothy—their meetings at the gardens and, later, Newsham Park. Each encounter became more intimate as the weeks progressed, their kisses deeper, their goodbyes more wrenching. Their feelings for one another warmed in time with spring.

But they were careful. They never ventured to parks too near Aigburth for fear they would stumble upon a neighbor or even Anne walking the children as she sometimes did on fair days.

Sometimes in the quiet hours when she's alone, she wonders if it's all too much, if it's too fast. There aren't enough hours to drink it in, and she refuses to reflect on what's wrong with what she's doing. She's passed the point of caring. She feels now, in the days before Timothy, she was sleepwalking, her life a series of duties and social engagements at which she clapped on a smile to play a role.

A knock on the door scatters her thoughts. A shiver drops down her spine. She smooths her skirts and opens the door.

Timothy stands before her, one hand clutching a small valise. "Connie," he breathes.

She tucks a curl behind her ear and steps aside, allowing him to enter. After the door is closed, they stare at one another, embarrassed.

"You had a safe journey?" she asks.

"Yes." Timothy looks around the room. "I didn't realize—"

"I thought a suite would serve us nicely." Her voice is tremulous. Has she made a mistake? Does he regret his decision to come?

Timothy sets down his valise and approaches the window. She's unsure what to do. Should she join him? Sit on the couch? She has no knack for this. Where are the instructions for how to engage in an affair?

"Connie?" Timothy has turned from the window. "What is it?"

She sees herself as he must, standing and wringing her hands.

He steps to her, brows knitted in concern. He places his hands on her upper arms. She can feel the heat of him through the sleeves of her dress.

"Do you..." Timothy licks his lips and tries again. "Have you reconsidered?" He watches her.

"No. I was wondering the same about you."

Timothy smiles, his face transformed. He pulls her to him, pressing her gently into his arms. With her cheek on his chest, she breathes him in: sandalwood and lime. How has she lived without it? She can smell the outdoors on his coat, too: the spring air, the earth. His hands rub her back, leave a trail of heat. Then he's clutching her face with his palms, thumbs strumming the skin below her eyes. She feels warm, captured in the moment. Snared by his eyes.

She's surprised how effortlessly it happens. One minute, they are in the sitting room. The next, they're beside the bed. He unbuttons the back of her dress. Time ticks by in precious seconds as he fumbles, cursing softly with the last few buttons, and then it is done. She tugs her dress down, standing in a corset and a thin white chemise. Her back still to him, Timothy kisses her neck, and runs his hands over her corseted breasts. Then he's tugging at her laces while she unfastens her corset. When she's free of it at last, Timothy turns her to him. She unpins her hair, the reddish gold locks falling well past her breasts. His eyes move over the contours of her, one hand tugging down her chemise to expose her shoulder.

"You are beautiful, so beautiful," he says, and his voice is hoarse with desire.

His lips move to her neck. As his mouth traces the line along the top of her shoulder, she slides his frock coat from his shoulders. His waistcoat is next. When it, too, has dropped to the floor, she begins to undo the buttons of his shirt. When both his hands find her waist, she feels him tremble. He helps her remove her chemise. His fingers find her nipples. She could cry out with the pleasure of it, but he gently pushes her to the bed to remove her shoes and then her stockings, the shimmy of his fingers down her shins bringing on a shiver of her own. He presses her down on the bed while he removes the rest of his garments, his movements hurried and impatient. When at last he lies naked beside her, his hands move up and down the length of her: her back, her torso, her legs, her buttocks. He cups a breast, traces kisses down her chest to her nipple and she feels like she could die with the ecstasy of it.

Her body grows warm, her blood heated. Timothy's hands continue their exploration, her skin coming alive wherever they touch. She marvels at the roughness of his cheek against her own, caresses the muscled contour of his back. His waist is slim and taut and when she rests her palms in the soft depressions above his hips, he winces as if in pain.

"Connie."

A murmured groan that brings on an ache between her legs. And then there is the thrill of his body on top of hers, the weight of him, the size. His knees part her legs and her world shrinks to texture and the taste of salt from his skin.

When he enters her, the pleasure is almost unbearable. The need to be taken, filled with him, seems matched by his own desire to take and fill. There is no restraint, only an urgency to give him what she wants for herself. When their bodies still, she lies with her head resting on his chest. She can hear the hammer of his heart, feel the rise of his ribs, as he works his fingers through her hair. They are damp and satiated, drunk with pleasure.

Through the bedroom door, Timothy tips the hotel waiter. She can hear the clink of coins, the squeak of the trolley wheels when, a second later, he opens the bedroom door and pushes in the tea service. He's clad only in a loose burgundy robe.

"Now for some restorative tea. You do have a way of depleting me." He maneuvers the trolley so they can access the tea from the bed. He pours a cup. "Sugar, yes, with milk?" He hands it to her. "No need for a saucer. It will only end up among the sheets."

She laughs. How had she ever fretted over this weekend? She's never seen him so content. She's glad they agreed to meet in London. Here, spending hours only with each other, they can be themselves.

He perches on the edge of the bed and fluffs the pillows, propping them against the headboard. He pours tea for himself and settles.

"I don't believe I've ever had tea in bed," she says. The tea is hot and sweet, just how she likes it.

"How can you say that you've lived?" he scoffs.

He is merely teasing, but his words settle over her and her mind falters. *Has* she lived? In the beginning of her marriage perhaps, when William was affectionate, and his addiction hadn't consumed him. But even then, when he was kind and attentive, Sandra was in his life. It was Sandra's children that first made William a father, even if they never married.

"You're miles away," Timothy says. He sets his cup on the trolley and cups her cheek, turning her to face him. "A penny for your thoughts."

She hasn't told him of the difficulties in her marriage. She mentioned William's infidelity but hasn't gone as far as telling him that her husband had been unfaithful with the same woman for decades. It was something she needed time to explain, more time than they had on their walks. And time discussing William or explaining Sandra would only sour the rushed hours they have together.

"I was thinking," she says, her eyes welling with tears, "when I saw you at the coffee shop that day, it was like the sun came out after days of nothing but rain."

He smiles. "That is perhaps the best compliment anyone has ever given me. And now you must imagine *my* shock when I arrived at Torrence House all those months ago, expecting to spend a dull evening and meet William Sullivan's very fussy, very stubborn, very matronly wife. You came down the stairway like a vision. I thought you the most beautiful woman I'd ever seen."

She places her hand inside his robe and strokes his chest. "Careful, you'll make me conceited." She moves her hand to his abdomen, and then lower.

Timothy moans. "If you keep doing that, we shall never leave this room."

She giggles. "Are we leaving this room?"

He sobers, lowers himself onto his side, and traces a scar along her thigh with his finger, never taking his eyes from hers. "Do you want to talk about this?" He moves to a scab above her knee. "And this?"

She pushes him onto his back and straddles him. "No." Her hair falls forward, enclosing them in a private, hushed world and she wishes again she could hold on to this moment. She could stay here and make love again and again and be perfectly content.

This time, they are slower in their movements. There is no urgency, yet she is astonished anew by his power to please, to give pleasure. As the moments tick by, a momentum builds in her, a frightening thought that she cannot be without him, that her life was nothing until he came into it.

The dining room is aglow with dozens of candles. They'd planned to find a restaurant along the Strand, but the restaurant in the lobby looked so cozy, they decided not to leave the hotel. Around them, diners sit at small round tables, huddled into private alcoves or divided by screens. She sips champagne. It's exquisite, the right combination of sweetness and bite. The candle at their table casts light through their bubbling glasses, burnishing them gold.

"You never told me what name you assumed this weekend," Timothy says. His arm is stretched across the table, his hand clutching hers, his thumb stroking the top of her hand. He does it absently; he really has no idea how his touch undoes her.

She smiles. She forgot she sent him a note before she left Liverpool with the hotel and room number only. "Sullivan, Mrs. Sullivan."

Timothy's thumb stills. "Truly?"

"Why not? No one will find us here. Mr. and Mrs. Sullivan."

He set down his flute. "Do you mean to tell me we're registered as Mr. and Mrs. Sullivan?"

"William is aware I'm staying here to visit one of my mother's friends this week. There seemed no need for an alias."

Timothy lets go of her hand. "But the register will reflect a couple, Connie. That you stayed with a man."

"Yes, my husband, for all anyone knows."

They break eye contact when a waiter appears. She fumbles with the napkin on her lap. She resents the intrusion and wants the little man gone. When he's placed their entrées before them —mutton for Timothy, salmon for her—he disappears with a nod.

"Connie."

In the low light, she can't quite see his eyes, but she can feel his coolness. "Timothy, please don't be upset. William will never see the receipt. If he does, I shall tell him the hotel made a mistake, and that, naturally, I stayed by myself."

Timothy frowns. "Covent Garden is a familiar haunt among cotton brokers. Did you know?"

"No. William never mentioned it."

"Why register as a couple at all?" he cuts in, his voice strained.

She feels stung. "So that we could have two room keys, for one. For another, so that I wouldn't have to smuggle you in and out of the room like a...like a..." She trails off. Like a clandestine lover. *Which is exactly what he is.*

Timothy doesn't speak for some moments. She knows he's looking for holes, worrying over details she can't change now.

"I wish we'd discussed this before you made the reservation," he says finally. He hasn't touched his food.

"You think we shall be discovered." She picks at her salmon and feels the happiness that has buoyed her up since his arrival shrink like a deflated ball.

He cuts his mutton. "I think you could have been less rash."

"I see," she says. But she doesn't. She can't look at him. The fish smells off, as if the tainted words between them have seeped into the salmon and spoiled it.

Minutes pass and gradually, they talk of other things. But the exuberance inside her is gone, replaced by a feeling of melancholy she can't shake.

———

They stroll arm in arm in the Victoria Embankment Gardens along the Thames. She likes the serpentine curve of the footpath, the low simmer of the spring sun. So rapidly have the days passed, their farewell is upon them already. She awakened this morning with a sense of finality, of something fragile cracking open, like an egg.

"What time is the train?"

"Five o'clock," Timothy says, checking his fob. "We've a few hours yet. Pray don't look so glum."

She smiles, though her heart isn't in it. Though she aches to see Billy and Janie, she doesn't relish returning home to William. She has a few days yet in London and she'll put them to good use. "I'm glad I shall see you Friday, at the Grand National race. I don't know what I would do returning home and not knowing when I'd see you next."

She settles her shawl around her shoulders and tucks her arm more securely into his. To the south, the Thames sparkles through the trees. Further downstream, the tip of Cleopatra's Needle daggers into the sky. Timothy leads her to a bench, and she takes a seat. She arranges her skirts while Timothy seats himself, his hand seeking hers.

"I've thought a lot about my marriage," she begins. "About William and me. I don't see it improving. My mother was right, all those years ago. I was so young. I should have listened to her. I should have waited. In any case, what's done is done." His eyes, that beautiful shade of green, blaze in the sunlight. "My mother has a dear friend I'm going to see tomorrow first thing. She's been like an aunt to me. I'm going to approach her and tell her of the state of my marriage. Her nephew is an attorney. I hope to get his advice."

Timothy's brows crease. "Advice?"

"I wish to divorce William."

Timothy goes very still and doesn't speak for some moments. "Why did you say nothing of this until now?"

She shrugs. "I didn't decide until recently. And if I'm honest, it wasn't until I met you that I realized how miserable I've been, and how much better things would be if William and I were no longer together."

Timothy takes both her hands and holds them tightly, angling his body toward her. "Connie, you must listen to me. William will never allow a divorce."

Surprise registers in her, replaced quickly by resolve. She

must make him understand. "It won't be his choice, Timothy. It will be mine."

He places his hand on her cheek and says slowly, "I know your marriage has been difficult, but you must be reasonable."

She cups his hand in hers and brings it down to her lap. "I have given this a lot of thought, Timothy. It's the only way I shall be happy."

"Aren't you happy now?"

She stands and walks a few paces away. When she turns, skirts flaring, she pins him with her gaze. "Is this all we are, Timothy? All we are to be? I can't live day to day, knowing I shall be miserable until I see you again."

"It's worked well for us so far."

Anger rises in her, hot and biting. "Just because I'm here, just because we've enjoyed one another these past few days, doesn't mean I'm content for things to carry on as they are." Her meaning hits him, and he looks away, almost cowed. "I see now I don't have your support." He returns her gaze. Something flickers over him that reminds her for an instant of William. Her hand flies to her throat. "Apparently, I have miscalculated your affections."

He rises and runs a hand through his hair. His face is thunderous. Her temper is well matched. "It has nothing to do with my *affections*."

"Then what has it to do with?" Her hands are balled into fists. She wants to slap him.

An older gentleman appears on the footpath, tapping his cane. He tips his hat and smiles. It takes an eternity for him to disappear. The minutes beat out and she works to calm herself.

When he's out of earshot, Timothy says, "This has nothing to do with how we feel about one another, Connie. It's about *reason*. Do you think your plans for divorce—whether William allows it or not—won't be all over town? He'll be furious."

She raises her chin. "I don't care what people think."

He laughs bitterly. "Don't you? You've made yourself and the parties you throw quite the thing. Why? Because it matters to you, and it matters to William. What happens when you walk by on the street and people whisper? When your friends don't dare speak to you, let alone invite you into their homes?"

"It won't be that way."

"No, it will be worse. Your fall—and that's exactly what it will be—will ruin you. Don't be naive. Whatever bliss you think a divorce will bring will be nothing but a silly, distant dream."

How can he say such things? "Ingrid divorced some years ago. None of what you say happened to her. She will aid me, I know it."

"Ingrid Berkshire, that sour-faced woman? I've never met her husband, but I'd bet he doesn't have half the temper William does."

"Her husband allowed her to keep her daughters."

"And you think William will allow you to keep your children?"

"I shall convince him, as will Ingrid, I'm sure. He'll see the wisdom of keeping them with me."

"What I recall of Ingrid Berkshire is that she's a very close friend of the Sullivans. I shouldn't count on her allegiance, Connie."

"Like I assumed I could count on yours?" She folds her arms and turns away, her heart kicking in her chest.

After a time, Timothy says, "Do you plan to tell William of us?"

"That's your principal worry? That you'll be exposed?"

"He will come for me. He won't take it sitting down."

"He won't learn of us because I shan't tell him. In any case, if he does, I have little control over what he'll do. William will do as he likes."

Up ahead toward Waterloo Bridge, she can hear the clop of horses, the rattle of carriages. The breeze carries the scent of seawater and sewage from the Thames. All around them, the world is unchanged—moving, working, thriving—yet she feels as if her world is breaking apart. "You're afraid of him."

"Yes, but not for the reasons you think. We'll come to blows most assuredly. Then he'll go about sullying my name, and that sort of damage won't mend. I'll be finished in Liverpool. William is well-respected and has far more clout, more friends, than I. I've only recently established my brokerage; William and Edward have been at it for years. They know the customers, they have more social contacts. I don't think you realize how much my parents rely on my income. Any kind of scandal with my name associated with it would kill them. It would as good as put them in the grave."

"I will not expose you, Timothy. Surely you must know that."

"I understand, but that doesn't protect me—or you—from the ugliness that will result should he learn of us. Have you thought of what life will be like without your children?"

He doesn't know she's got an ace in the hole. William will do anything to keep her from exposing his other family. She should've seen it sooner. He'll let her have the children because he can't afford the scandal. "William will see that I'm the one to raise them. I'm their mother."

"You've just told me William does what he likes, the hell with what's good for others."

She falls silent and chews her lip. This discussion hasn't gone at all like she thought it would. Tears sting her eyes.

Timothy steps to her. She flinches and steps back. "Connie, please. Promise me you'll think this through."

She nods, once. Let him believe she agrees. "Please go, Timothy. I realize now we can't go on like this. It's madness to continue. You're right; if we're discovered, William will make it impossible for us both. And as you cannot—will not—stand by me at the cost of exposing yourself, there's nothing more to discuss."

She turns away, the slow retreat of Timothy's steps beating in time with her shattered heart. She'd trusted him, thought him noble. A man of character who would stand by her. What a fool she's been.

Chapter 12

Torrence House

March 29, 1889

"This will be all over town tomorrow," William says, his brandy glass empty. "Do you hear? *All over bloody town!*"

Constance feels caged. There's not enough space in the bedroom for the two of them. She yearns to move past him and down the stairs, fly out the door, and leave him for good. "What a bully you are, William. We shall accomplish nothing if you continue to shout like a common street seller."

"You berate *me*? You took bloody Worth's hand on the track. I saw you. Something is going on between the two of you. You may as well tell me now, Connie. I'll get it out of one of you soon enough."

Fear ices her heart. Would William get the truth from Timothy? "Kindly lower your voice," she hisses from the chair of her dressing table. "The servants will hear you."

"I don't give a pig's arse what the servants hear!"

"Don't you? This whole conversation is about appearances, is it not?" She recalls how wretched William looked earlier that afternoon at the Grand National Race—his ashen pallor, the dark circles under his eyes. The red carnation pinned to his frock coat had wilted. It seemed to her, sitting under the pavilion waiting for the race to start, a silent mockery of their marriage.

William rakes his fingers through his hair. She closes her eyes, willing him to go downstairs and make another drink so she can lock the bedroom door.

"Don't lie to me, Connie. What's going on between you and Worth?"

Her chest kicks with outrage thinking back to yesterday when she returned from London to find a stack of letters from her mother on William's desk, all opened. He's been reading her mail for weeks, suspicious her mother is holding out on the proceeds from the sale of her extensive land in America. How many times has she told him that it's a legal tangle her mother and her attorneys have been fighting for years, that there are no proceeds to share? "I'll be in my grave before the money is freed up, is that what you're telling me, Constance? I shall never see it, is that it?" She thought he was going to strike her. She wished now that he had; it would give her even more reason to leave him.

William paces like an animal. His shirt is crumpled, his skin mottled. How much has he had to drink? She arrived home from the race well before he did. He must have gone to a pub or the Palatine Club to soak his rage in alcohol after he saw her with Timothy. Or maybe he went to one of his chemists for a pick-me-up of arsenic or strychnine, whatever it is that's slowly poisoning him. Following the race, she took the omnibus with Reggie and Christina Samuels, who were confused when William didn't accompany them back. She offered no explanation, but she wondered if the couple witnessed her take Timothy's hand as William had.

What would he do if he knew of the drawer in her dressing table? The one that, once it was removed, had a small cubbyhole with a blue box into which she places her letters from Timothy, letters from Edward, his own brother? "There's nothing going on between me and Mr. Worth, nor anyone else."

William stops pacing and sneers. His eyes glitter like diamonds. His glass is empty. "You're a bloody liar. I know what I saw, and I know what it means. Do you think me a fool? I won't be a cuckold."

"Then for heaven's sake, stop acting like one. I don't know what you think you saw, but it wasn't me taking Mr. Worth's hand." She stands and smooths her skirts, headed for the dressing room. Let him think he was drunk and mistook her for someone else.

Suddenly, William rushes at her, pulling her around to face him. "You're not going anywhere. I want the truth, damn it, and I'll have it."

She thrashes in his arms, averting her face. "You smell ghastly. You're drunk."

His hands squeeze her upper arms. "Answer me! What's going on with you and Worth?"

"Leave me alone!" She fights to wrest herself free, but his fingers only tighten. "You're hurting me!"

He shakes her, spittle on his lip. "You think this hurts? It's nothing compared to what I could do."

She wrenches one arm free and slaps him hard across the face. He staggers back, shocked by her boldness. He glowers and sets on her again, pulling her by the front of her dress, twisting the fabric so tight around her neck, her feet leave the floor.

She tries to push away. She can't breathe. Her vision clouds.

In the next instant, there's a sickening crunch and then the world dips, rings.

William releases her, wobbles backward. Shakes his smarting fist.

Her hands are at her eye. Stinging pain, the biting pulse of it. She's horrified to see, drawing a hand away, it's streaked with blood. Her skin throbs around her eye, the walls pitch. She feels sick.

"Molly!" William thunders at the top of his lungs. He flings open the bedroom door. "Molly! Have a cab brought round for Mrs. Sullivan at once!" He rounds on her. "Get out of this house."

He staggers out the door and takes the stairs. In the mirror, she is a monstrosity. Her dress is ruined: buttons are gone, lace is missing in patches. Tears stain her cheeks. Her hair has tumbled from its combs. Her eye is quickly swelling.

She never should have done it. Hours before, she lifted her opera glasses, swept the racetrack, and there was Timothy. It was like finding a diamond in the sand. Spectators were rising from their seats, collecting their things. She, William, and the Samuels shuffled into the aisle and made their way down. She tracked Timothy like prey. He was part of the melee in front of the stand, making his way slowly toward the gates. When at last they reached the bottom of the steps, they entered the throng moving right. But Timothy turned left. Constance dropped back. Just when she was going to walk the other way, William turned. He extended his arm, meaning to pull her up to him. He looked a question at her, baffled.

For an instant, she saw the hurt in his eyes, his vulnerability laid bare. She knew then he was sorry, that he would apologize later for reading her mother's letters. He was hopeful they would mend their rift. He *wanted* to.

She turned, uncertain, and took a step in the opposite direction. She glanced back at William. They were stones in a creek with water rushing past them, neither wishing to yield.

"Walk away from me," William said, "and you'll be sorry for it."

Not a shout, but loud enough. Passersby shot him a look. Had William been kinder, would she have gone to him? Would things have been different? Perhaps. But his words were like poisoned darts piercing her skin and she'd walked away into the crowd.

It was mad, of course. She had defied her husband in public. She didn't even know if Timothy was still here. She wove through the people, hoping for a glimpse of him, trusting he'd be glad to see her after their bitter parting in London. But the crowd was dispersing. Timothy had vanished. She'd provoked William for nothing. She stepped to the fence that bordered the track and rested her hands on it, reduced to tears.

"Connie."

Timothy stood beside her. His frock coat was linen fawn, his waistcoat a slightly darker shade that matched his topper. The flower in his coat was a perfect white rose.

She grabbed his hand and resisted the urge to bring it to her lips. The crowd thinned around them. They were exposed, easily seen. She didn't care. They walked a short way, his hand clutched in her own.

"I'm sorry for the way we parted," she said. Timothy didn't smile. "I, I cannot bear..." The words died in her throat. She wanted to be with him alone again, feel his skin against hers, but she couldn't make herself plain to him. Not here.

"Go home to William, Connie."

His words were a wound in her chest. She wouldn't let him see her cry, so she'd spun and walked away.

Downstairs, William screams like a madman: "Philandering wife! Bloody cuckold!" Has she time to pack? She runs out to the landing, opens the linen closet, spies her trunk at the bottom. No, too heavy. She'll never get it down the steps. She pulls a small satchel from the shelf and flies to the dressing room where she throws undergarments, a few dresses, a pair of shoes, into its yawning mouth. Downstairs, William screams again. The servants will have had an earful by the time the night is over.

She's poised at the stairwell when she thinks of the children. Can she leave them? Dare she? To pull them from their beds in the state William is in...No. He would terrify them. She'll return for them later.

She clatters down the steps and lands at the bottom unsteadily. The skin around her eye is tight and tender. The gaslights are on in the drawing room. The clink of glass. William is getting another brandy. She stumbles to the front hall, sets down her satchel, withdraws her fur cape from the closet, and quickly puts it on. There's no sign of Molly; she couldn't have sent for a cab in so little time. Her pulse hammers in her throat. She'll walk to Ingrid's. It's not so far. She can manage it. She grabs the handle of the front door, wrenching it open to the night. A waning moon, a few stars.

William stumbles into the hall, his breathing labored and erratic. She turns to him. *It will serve him right to drop dead*, she thinks. She's surprised by how relieved she feels at the thought.

"Take that off at once. You're not to leave with it."

The fur was a present from him before she left for London. "Do you mean to banish me from this house without a coat?" she says. He doesn't respond, only looks at her narrowly, his body swaying.

A footfall from the servants' stairs and the sound of the green baize door opening brings their attention to the corridor where a wavering light approaches. It's Mrs. Hunt, the cook. She carries a lone candle and is in her nightdress, her hair tucked beneath a cap. In the flicker of the candle, she is old and frightened.

"Leave us, Mrs. Hunt," William snaps. "You don't know anything about this."

The cook takes a step closer. Her feet are bare. "Please don't send the mistress away tonight. Where can she go? Let her stay until morning."

In the beat of silence, she decides to go. Let Mrs. Hunt distract him while she takes her leave.

"By heavens, Constance, if you cross that threshold, you will never enter this house again."

His change of heart confounds her. He is truly drunk. Yet, if she disobeys him, there will likely be another scuffle. In the end, it's Mrs. Hunt that makes her decide. She won't have the woman witness the humiliation of a physical altercation with William. She closes the door and removes her wrap, handing it to the older woman.

The motion seems to undo William. He staggers back and collapses onto a settee in the hall, dabbing at his brow with a handkerchief. She brings up the lights. William has gone rigid, his arm flung over his eyes. She has neither the strength nor inclination to speak further with him. He appears as if he's collapsed dead and she doesn't care a whit.

With a nod and a quiet thank you to Mrs. Hunt, she takes herself and her satchel upstairs. She enters the bedroom and locks the door, sinking down on the bed and putting her feet up. Sleep doesn't come quickly, but when it does, it is deep and dreamless.

Chapter 13

Livingston Avenue, Liverpool

March 30, 1889

Constance lifts a cup to her lips. The tea is sweet and hot and burns all the way down. Fatigue rolls through her. Her eye has swelled almost completely shut.

Ingrid sits regally at her tea table, back ramrod straight, and drops another sugar cube into her own tea, the tinkle of the spoon against the china the ring of tiny bells. "Is this the first time William has accused you of consorting with another man?"

"Of course," she replies, stunned. Morning sun plays tricks through the window behind Ingrid. With her friend's features in shadow, it almost looks like she's smiling.

"Timothy Worth is quite a handsome man, Constance. And nearer your age. You got on well last winter when you met him at Torrence House."

Does Ingrid think to trick her into admitting her affair with Timothy or offer reasons to start one? "He was our guest. Naturally I got on well with him." She won't tell Ingrid the truth. She promised Timothy. She wants him—the idea of him, the wonder, the delight—all to herself.

"What is it you expect me to do, my dear? William has a hot temper. He reacted like any man would have done."

Her eye throbs. She pads the socket lightly with her fingertips. The seconds tick with the scuds of her heart. She needs sleep; she would take her leave if it weren't for the reason she's come. "Tell me about your divorce. You've said so very little."

There it is again: a ghost of a smile. Ingrid takes a sip of tea. "It was years ago. It's not important."

"It's important to me now."

"You shall not have an easy time of it, if that's the direction you mean to take."

The words might have come from Timothy's own mouth. "But you were successful."

"My husband was a pliable man. William is not." Ingrid's eyes rove over her. "Divorce is a monumental step for a misunderstanding. You'll have no privacy. The papers will be full of it. You'll be ruined."

"Look at me, Ingrid. Am I not ruined now?"

Her friend chuckles. "Your eye will heal. Are you prepared to have your life raked publicly through the coals? Oh, why are we even speaking of this? I don't know about the laws in America, but here you must prove William has been unfaithful to you. And it doesn't end there."

"I don't understand."

"For a man to seek divorce, he must prove only infidelity. For a woman, she must prove infidelity and a second offense."

"Such as?"

Ingrid shrugs thin shoulders. "Desertion or cruelty. Bigamy." She leans forward. "Is it true about Timothy Worth? Is that why you've come? Are you afraid William will leave you?"

Her skin prickles. "It's rather the other around."

Ingrid's mouth drops open. "I ask for your complete discretion in the matter—"

"Yes, yes." Ingrid waves an impatient hand. "What is it?"

"Last summer I discovered William was keeping another woman. They have a family together. She goes by the name of Sullivan."

Ingrid stands so quickly, tea sloshes from her teacup. Her napkin slips from her lap to the floor. "I don't believe you."

"I saw her with my own eyes." She tells her the details of the day she followed William as Ingrid paces the room. "Later that evening, I confronted him. He admitted it, Ingrid. Naturally, I demanded the woman leave town at once." She looks down into her teacup and wishes for something stronger, something to blot her outrage. "I know you have a fine opinion of him. So did I, once. But the truth is the truth."

Ingrid stops and crosses her arms. "He isn't married to this woman?"

"I found no record of their marriage, nor records of births or baptisms of any children by a William and Sandra Sullivan."

Ingrid walks to the window, her body in profile. "Did he make good on his promise? The woman left town?"

"As far as I know. The family vacated the residence."

Silence plays out between them. Ingrid bites her lip, thin fingers working the pearls at her neck. Constance has never seen her so agitated.

"You must help, Ingrid. I can't bear it. I can't bear him." Misery saws at her and her eyes fill. Tears of resentment and indignation. She hates that she's here, that she needs Ingrid's assistance.

Her friend swings her gaze back to the room, eyes narrowed. "What will you do, Constance, should you proceed with a divorce?"

Her mind ticks to Timothy and she feels a pang of longing

for what might have been. "I suppose I shall return to America and take the children with me." *If William tries to stop me, he'll be disgraced.*

A corner of Ingrid's mouth lifts and she joins her again at the table. "Yes. I shall help you if that is what you wish."

———

The next day, Constance looks up from her escritoire as Mary enters the morning room. The maid wrings her hands and looks uneasy. Their row after the Grand National Race two days before has rattled the servants. They walk the floors on eggshells, poised for another explosion.

"Yes, Mary?"

"Mrs. Berkshire is here to see you."

Impatience burns in her and her eye pulses with pain. She's in no mood to see anyone. She's just read a note from Timothy. He plans to flee the country, scared out of his wits because Reggie Samuels told him William would 'pump him full of lead' if he discovered his affair with Constance. Reggie must have seen them on the track, just as she feared. She hadn't pegged Timothy for a deserter, someone her mother would call a lily liver. Timothy has changed her life, and he's casting her aside like, like—

"Mistress?"

She blinks. "Very well. Show her in." She whisks Timothy's note under the blotter. For an instant, she places her elbows on her escritoire and massages her temples, being gentle around the puckered skin of her ruined eye. She owes Ingrid a great deal for promising to help her. The very least she can do is be civil, even if her friend is visiting at far too early an hour. Yesterday, when she'd sought Ingrid's help, something hadn't felt right. Perhaps there was something to what Timothy had said. In matters of allegiance, Ingrid might well be more in William's camp than her own. She needs to be careful.

She rises as Ingrid enters the room. Her friend rushes to her and takes her hands. The gesture is so unlike Ingrid, she is taken aback. She doesn't recall, in all the years she's known her, such open affection.

"My dear," Ingrid says, squeezing her fingertips, "it's so good to see you up and out of bed." There's an exuberance in her she hasn't seen before: her eyes are bright, her cheeks flushed. Her hair is different too. It's clumsily arranged, easy to see, for Ingrid is hatless. She must've left home in a flurry. Her friend's eyes dart around the room, as if William might be hiding behind the sofa or pressed into a corner. "Are the two of you speaking? He hasn't left you, has he?"

She gestures for Ingrid to take a seat as she positions herself at the other end of the sofa. "All is well."

Ingrid pulls in her chin. "You've rectified things?"

"Yes. When I returned from your house, William was waiting for me. He wanted to talk." By then, his outrage had fled, replaced by a morning fog laced with regret. He'd sat drained and miserable in the drawing room looking at her with sheep's eyes: sorry for everything, willing to do anything to regain her trust. "He was quite a changed man by the end of our discussion. He apologized for mistaking what he saw."

Guilt had eaten at her, but only for a moment. So what if she had lied? How can she regret Timothy when William has done worse, and over the course of decades? She'd sat and restated her innocence and all the while she'd thought, *If ours is a case of tit for tat, I have more reckoning to do, dear husband.*

"Where is he now?" The color in Ingrid's cheeks has thinned.

"In the study." She can't quite reach Ingrid with her hand, so she places it on the sofa between them. "I must thank you for being so helpful yesterday. I wasn't myself. Without you, I don't know what I'd have done."

"Do you still plan to divorce?" The clock on the mantle ticks the seconds by. A bird strikes the window, startling them both.

"No." In truth she doesn't know, but it's better for Ingrid to think them fully reconciled. As far as William is concerned, they are.

Ingrid doesn't speak for so long she wonders if she's heard her. She merely looks at her hand, palm up and waiting to be grasped. "Well, this is a sudden turn of events. I admit I didn't think things would be so...*amicable* when I came to call." She sniffs.

She can see it now; Ingrid is upset. She flew to Torrence House in a fever to help, only to find she wasn't needed.

"I'm as surprised as you things have gone so smoothly." She waits for Ingrid to smile.

"Your eye is worse," her friend replies, her words snapping like teeth. "You look a sight."

The insult cuts like a scythe, but she casts it aside. Ingrid is wounded; she must be kind. Still, she can't stay. She needs to be alone, to think about Timothy, to consider what's to become of them. "I may look ghastly, but I'll mend. In the meantime, I shan't leave the house until the bruising has faded."

She rises and walks to the window. A raven lies in the grass twitching, its wing broken, one baleful eye raised to the sky. *I am this bird*, she thinks. *Struck but still moving. Desperate to fly.* "William plans to remain at home as well." She turns from the window. "He thinks some time together, just the two of us, will do us good. In any case, I needn't take any more of your time. We're getting on splendidly." An exaggeration, but it's all Ingrid need know. She waits for her friend to grasp her meaning and take her leave.

Ingrid intertwines her fingers in her lap, her knuckles white. "That is precisely why I have decided to stay."

Panic claws at her. "Pardon?"

"I've already given Mary my bag and asked her to unpack my things upstairs."

A flash of Mary wringing her hands as she informed her that Ingrid had come to call. No wonder the maid had looked ill at ease. For an instant, she thinks Ingrid is joking, that her friend will laugh at her little jest. Instead, the older woman rises and walks to the mantle. She draws a finger along it and lifts it, inspecting her finger. "I will see to everything. The meals, the children, the servants. You know how capable I am at these things. It's times like this when a woman needs a friend the most."

Her hand flutters to her throat. "I don't understand."

"You're still distressed, are you not? When a mistress of the house is distracted, the servants become lax." She crosses to her and takes her hands once more. In the light from the window, she sees the fissures in Ingrid's face, the wrinkles that frame her mouth, the tiny crevices that mar her forehead. "You must rest, my dear. I shall see to William."

She lets go of Ingrid's hands and walks away. "I know you mean well, but—"

"But what?" Ingrid quirks a razor-sharp brow. "You don't think you need my help? I can assure you that you do. You forget, perhaps, that I have been through a painful marriage myself. I know of what I speak and what is at stake." Ingrid's tongue licks dry lips. "Now, ring for Mary and we will have her bring tea, yes? And goodness, this room needs a thorough dusting. I shall conduct an inspection of all the rooms and see what needs to be done."

Constance lies on the bed staring at the ceiling. The house watches and waits. The laudanum hasn't yet wrapped her in its soporific embrace. Ingrid is downstairs barking at the servants for minuscule infractions. Snatches of her orders—*shan't tolerate laziness...must be cleaned of a morning...newsprint to clean the windows*—float up the stairs like smoke.

William is shut in his study, closed as an oyster. He's been courteous, though quiet, all morning and his pallor has improved, which means he's left off taking his arsenic for now, though it won't last long. She allowed him to kiss her cheek before she dressed this morning. Then, thinking to please her, asked her to accompany him on a walk later in the day. She declined, saying, "And my eye, William? Do you think people won't put two and two together?" Her words had the desired effect. He blanched and quit the bedroom.

If her eye didn't look such a fright, she'd go up to the nursery to see the children, but yesterday Janie hid behind Billy at the sight of her. It killed her to see the fear on their faces. Anne looked horrified.

"Mummy fell on the stairs, my darlings. A silly accident."

She wishes Timothy were here, his arms around her, his soft voice telling her everything would be all right. She wants him to promise he won't leave England. Promise he won't leave her.

A yell brings her up sharp.

"Constance! Goddamn it! Constance!"

She stands so quickly the room pitches.

"*Constance!*"

Downstairs, William's study door is open.

"William, my dear," she hears Ingrid say, "do calm down. You'll wake the dead."

She treads down the dark stairwell, feels again as if some hidden menace creeps behind her. Then, suddenly, she's filled with the urge to pitch herself down the steps. *It would be so easy.* She sees herself in her mind's eye: her body going lax, the jarring tumble of limbs, her twisted body at the bottom, her neck broken. *It's the laudanum,* she thinks. *I must be careful.* When she arrives at the study, William sits at his desk, his face dark. Ingrid stands next to him.

The room is William's private lair. She is seldom in it. Furnished in rich, comfortable pieces upholstered in bold reds and golds, it's wholly a man's space. She came upon him once staring at the German cuckoo clock on the wall. She realized, as William brought his hand quickly from the small, recessed area below the miniature Alpine roof, it was where he kept the key to his desk. She said nothing and the moment passed.

"Tell me this is a mistake." William thrusts a sheet of paper at her.

Laid out on Seward and Sons fine stationery is a short note stating her loan payments are in arrears. The last line is a subtle warning: *If this continues, Mrs. Sullivan, I shall be forced to apply additional fees.* A spike of fear stabs at her. Mr. Seward has never sent correspondence to Torrence House. Their agreement was for him to send correspondence to her post-office box. Apparently, now that her payments are behind, Seward cares little if she's discovered by her husband.

Blast him.

"I asked you a question," William says.

"Now, now, William." Ingrid's voice is spun sugar. "This is all a mistake, I'm sure." Her hands are clasped in front of her, veins rivering under her skin. "Constance, tell William this note cannot be to you. You would never do such a thing."

The deceit in Ingrid's face. Those glistening eyes, that half-smile. Timothy was right. *How had I never seen it?*

"You've been opening my mail again," she says, putting the paper back on his desk. She should apologize, but the words are out before she can check them.

"Bloody good thing I am!" William pounds the desk with his fist. "How long has this been going on?"

She turns to Ingrid. "I must ask you to leave. This is a private conversation between my husband and me."

Ingrid lifts her brows and then recovers, nodding sagely. "As you wish, my dear."

When she's closed the door behind her, she waits to hear Ingrid's footfalls retreat down the hall. There is only silence.

"If we are to discuss this, William, we must do so quietly. We've a guest in this house."

"Rather early for a visitor, isn't it?"

"Ingrid came of her own accord. She wishes to stay and help run the house while you and I make peace. I assure you, it was her idea, not mine."

William makes a waving motion. "Do what you want. I don't care if she stays or not. What I *do* want is for you to explain this." He picks up the letter again and throws it at her. It lands on top of his inkwell and teeters there like a hesitant bird.

She takes a seat across from the desk, determined to remain calm. "Do you really think my attire—the dresses I wear, the formal gowns, the wraps—comes out of my monthly allowance? The little left over from what I pay the servants wouldn't buy a pair of new boots."

"How the devil should I know what these things cost? If you needed more money, you might have told me!"

"And from what source would that money have come? Do you have funds of which I am unaware?"

William points a shaking finger. "You went deliberately behind my back."

"I took a lesson from your own book."

The remark stuns him, as allusions to Sandra always do. But it only lasts a moment. "How the devil did you manage it?"

"I used my jewelry as collateral."

"What? And the interest? Don't tell me you didn't bother to ask."

"Sixty percent."

William curses under his breath. For a moment, she thinks he'll come around the desk and throttle her. Perhaps the ruin of her eye stops him. Or perhaps the fact that Ingrid is in the house gives him pause. He reaches for a glass and the bottle of brandy on the credenza behind him. He pours himself a drink, tilts his head back and empties it. More brandy splashes into the glass. The sweet, spicy smell fills the room and combines with the scent of tobacco. There was a time when she loved to come here because the smell of William's study was the smell of William himself. How she adored him then, his scent something that had a way of both calming and exciting her.

William withdraws a small packet from his breast pocket and taps a smidge of powder into his brandy. She watches him lift the glass to his lips.

"Do you really think that will help?" she says.

William wipes his mouth across his sleeve. "How many other debts have you?"

"None."

"Seward and Sons is the only one?"

"I just told you so, didn't I?"

"How much?"

"Something in the neighborhood of £1,200."

William drains his glass. His hands shake. She picks at an imaginary speck of lint from her cuff. "I cannot see the difference between you racking up debt and my doing so."

"There was a time when you remonstrated with me to stop spending."

"That time was long ago. Things are different now." She looks at him meaningfully. Sandra has changed everything. But her blow doesn't land as it usually does. Instead, her words are

131

flint, and William the fire. He stands, pupils dilated, face crimson.

"I have relationships with my creditors—my tailors, the Palatine Club, the wine and brandy merchants."

She folds her arms. "Are you asking me to have a relationship with Mr. Seward? And I thought you a jealous man." She has the sensation that she's playing a part badly. That, one day, she'll regret it and work through these memories like beads on a rosary.

In a flash, William comes to his feet and leans over the desk. His breath stinks of brandy. A lock of sandy hair falls over his brow. "Don't you dare be flippant with me." She wants the words to wash over her, leave her unscathed, but her cheeks redden. "I pay my creditors when I can and they know I'm good for it, and I don't pay exorbitantly high interest!"

His shouts bounce off the walls and back again. She shrinks. Her eye smarts. A creak of a floorboard outside the door. *Ingrid.*

"This," he takes up the letter again, "is a different case. I don't know this man. We must pay him off completely before his fees overtake the original loan entirely. It's what these damn loan offices do. They prey on women like you who have no way of paying them back!"

The ensuing silence is almost as loud as William's cries. She stands. Her body trembles. He's right. She never should have gone to London and secured the loan. It was a foolish venture from the start. She never had a plan to pay Seward back. She only thought to pledge more jewelry to get more money. She thought, early on, to appeal to her mother. But, in the end, she'd been too embarrassed.

Conceding her mistake, however, is a different matter. She can't bring herself to apologize. Her marriage has ruined her; she's no longer the compassionate, loving wife she once believed herself to be. She blinks back tears and gathers her skirts. "Very well."

She opens the study door quickly. Ingrid stands there, caught like a rat in a trap. "Why Ingrid, shouldn't you be shouting at the servants?"

Constance pushes past her and takes the stairs. Her eye aches as if William has struck her anew.

Chapter 14

St. George's Hall

Day 2 of Trial

Ingrid sits in the witness box clothed in full mourning. Only her veil is absent, the better for the jury, press, and spectators to mark her grief. She sobs quietly into a handkerchief edged in black lace. She's cast everyone in her spell; the gentlemen of the jury lean toward her like plants to the sun.

Mr. Goodacre, who no longer bothers to pocket his own handkerchief, mops his face before the witness box while the sun continues its punishing bake through the skylight. "So the accused came to you the morning after a vicious fight she'd had with her husband over Timothy Worth?"

"Yes. She wanted my help because she claimed William had a second family she'd recently learned about. I don't think there was another family. I think she made it up to get my sympathy so I would assist her in a divorce."

Constance looks to the jury to see if they're buying Ingrid's lies. To her horror, they're staring back, faces brimming with judgment.

134

"And the day after, when you arrived at the Sullivans'?"

Ingrid launches into the story of her arrival, coming eventually to William's discovery of her loan. His shock and the jewelry she pledged for collateral are spilled like entrails from a bucket. "I think she lived so well on her mother's money, she hadn't the slightest idea how to manage a budget. I wasn't welcome in the house after that. She was livid I'd learned the truth. Poor William. She owed the creditor £1,200."

The gallery stirs. Press agents behind her whisper. Justice Stevenson, his face as red as his robe, glares down at her from the bench. She is stunned anew by Ingrid's guile. In that instant, it is as painful and calculating as William's.

"When did you see the Sullivans next?"

"When I didn't hear from her in over a month, I decided to call again. She'd lied to poor William about the loan, what else might she be hiding? I had a feeling—intuition if you will—that we'd only seen the tip of the iceberg." She works the handkerchief in her hands. "It was May 8th. I shall never forget. When I called, I was told by Mary, the maid, that William was ill and wasn't to have any visitors. It was the first I'd heard of it, and William a man in the finest of health! I knew then that *shrew* was planning something. If only I'd intervened earlier." Ingrid covers her face with her hands.

You've missed your calling. What an excellent actress you are.

Goodacre leans an elbow on the witness box, prepared to assist should his witness faint. "What did you do, Mrs. Berkshire?"

"Mary sent me away, so I went around the back. I thought I'd enter the house from the garden. I saw the nanny at the back door—she must have seen me from the nursery window. She came out and we spoke. I asked about William. She told me he'd been sick nearly two weeks and had scarcely left his bed. I asked why no one had sent for me and she said Constance had forbidden it.

"Anne asked me to wait in the garden. There was something she wanted to show me. She went back inside and came out with Molly, who had a sack with her. That was when Molly told me about the fly papers Constance had been soaking in the bedroom. There they were, lying in the bottom of the sack. Well, you can imagine my horror when I realized she had been scheming all along to sicken William."

Ingrid pauses to collect herself, but not before darting a look to the jury to see their reaction. There is not a sound in the courtroom. "I marched straight into the house and up the stairs to William's room. I saw for myself how wasted and pale he looked."

"And the accused?"

"She came into the room behind me, hissing at me to stop bothering William so he could sleep. I asked him if he was all right—for I had the way of things by then—but I don't think he understood me. He looked confused, poor man."

"Did you speak with the accused?"

"Oh, yes." Ingrid hardens her mouth and looks at her. "We had words. She told me the doctor thought William would recover. She said he'd sent for a nurse, but no one came. A lie if I ever heard one. I hated to leave William, but I needed another set of eyes in that house. I went straightaway to the Institute and ordered a nurse be sent as soon as possible."

"And then?"

"I went to William's office to speak to his brother, Edward. I told him about the fly papers, and we took the next train to the house. As we were walking from the station, we saw Anne. She was very upset."

"What did she tell you?"

"She said Constance had given her a letter to mail. On the

way to the post office, Janie dropped it in the mud. When Anne picked it up, she noticed the flap had come open. She saw some curious words inside, words the poor girl couldn't ignore. She then drew out the letter and read it."

"Anne Yardley showed you this letter?"

"Yes, both Edward and I read it. It was to Timothy Worth. It was very clear the two were on intimate terms. Edward was furious. What a fool I was to believe Constance wasn't involved with Mr. Worth. William was right all along that he'd seen the two of them holding hands after the race. It was all so clear the accused, the accused..."

Ingrid slumps on the stand and uses her handkerchief to maximum effect.

"Yes, Mrs. Berkshire? Take your time. I know this is difficult. It was clear?"

"It was clear the accused knew William would die."

Benches creak in the gallery. Fury settles in her chest as whispers unfurl into the stifling air.

Goodacre whisks the letter from the evidence table and gives it to Ingrid. "Is this the letter Anne Yardley showed you that day, the one dated May 8th and signed by the accused?"

"Yes."

"Which phrase gave you the impression that Constance Sullivan knew her husband would die? Please read it."

"She underlined it," Ingrid says. "It reads, 'He is sick unto death.'"

"I wonder, Mrs. Berkshire," Sir Charles says, walking up to the witness box, "I wonder if you might clear something up for me."

Ingrid straightens, as if prepared for an assault. She may have been heartsick over William for years, but she is no fool;

Sir Charles will throw water on every lie she's spoken if she isn't careful. *I hope you drown in them.*

"Did William Sullivan dose himself?"

For a moment, Ingrid is a hunted animal. Her furtive eyes go to the jury, the gallery. *Tell them the truth. Don't you dare lie.*

"I'm afraid he did."

"For how long?"

"Many years, I expect. I don't know the specifics. He never discussed his habits with me, but I saw him take tinctures and powders from time to time."

"This was generally known among his friends and family?"

A pause. "Yes."

"Do you know what these tinctures and powders consisted of?"

"No."

"Might they have contained arsenic?"

"I don't know."

"But it is possible, yes?"

"I suppose."

"He never told you, in all the years you'd known him?"

"No. As I said, he never discussed his habits with me."

"Fair enough. Did the accused ever ask you what her husband was taking? Did she ever express worry over his health from taking these powders?"

"No."

Liar.

Sir Charles lets it go. "You have testified that the accused told you she wanted a divorce. If that's true, why go to such lengths—poisoning over a succession of days with servants and family about—to kill him?"

Ingrid looks affronted. "Isn't it obvious? She wanted to be with Timothy Worth at any cost."

"She could 'be with Timothy Worth' without going to the

trouble of poisoning her husband. Without committing a felony at all." Sir Charles walks to his table and thumbs through some papers. "There was much happening at the house in the days surrounding William Sullivan's death. His brother was staying at the house, the servants were about, nurses were watching over him, a doctor was coming and going. Tell me, what was the accused doing the day her husband passed?"

"She fell into a swoon earlier in the day."

"In fact, in the forenoon, Mrs. Sullivan collapsed and was carried from her husband's bedside by Edward Sullivan to one of the guest bedrooms. Do you recall this?"

"Yes."

"She remained there for several days before she was arrested and taken to Walton Jail. Was she present during the searches?"

"She was in the house, yes."

"That's not what I meant. I mean, did she oversee or observe any of the searches going on?"

"No."

"Was anyone checking on her? Seeing that she was fed?"

"I don't know."

"Well, in any case, it's safe to say, you—her closest friend for many years—were not. No, the morning following Mr. Sullivan's death, you and his brother were conducting a second search of the premises, correct?"

"Yes."

"Had the police arrived that morning to conduct a search?"

"They arrived later."

"Very much later. About eight thirty that evening. By which time, of course, all the 'evidence' had been collected by the servants, family, and a friend. By friend, of course, I mean you, Mrs. Berkshire. Remind us again what you found in your search."

"In the bedroom, I searched Constance's dressing table and found letters. Seven, to be exact, from Timothy Worth."

Ingrid's eyes land on her. Time ticks out in slow seconds. The look is loaded with what Ingrid knows and is keeping back: the letters of Edward's tucked in the same blue box with Timothy's. Ingrid must have been outraged to find them. But Edward's *billets-doux* will never come to light. Constance may go down, but Edward won't be going with her. Ingrid is protecting him, protecting the Sullivan family.

"And in the dressing room, Mrs. Berkshire?"

"There were half a dozen bottles or so and a pile of written prescriptions. They were inside two hat boxes that were on the floor. We—Edward, and I—gathered them up and put them in a box."

"Prescriptions, you say? For the deceased?"

"Yes. Half a dozen or so."

"Do you remember what they were for?"

"No."

"Very well. Let's turn to Tuesday, May 14th. That was a very tragic day for the accused. Though she still lay very ill, Mrs. Sullivan was informed by Superintendent Browne that she was in custody on suspicion of causing the death of her husband. How did she take this news, Mrs. Berkshire?"

"She was frightened. We all knew what she'd done."

"Mrs. Sullivan asked that a cablegram be sent to her solicitor in New York, did she not?"

"She said nothing of that to me. She wanted to send a telegram to her mother in Paris but hadn't the money, so I advised her to write to someone who could loan the money to her."

"And that person was?"

"Timothy Worth."

Sir Charles pauses and lets the response sift through the

courtroom. "You suggested to Mrs. Sullivan she should write to Mr. Worth?"

"I did not suggest him specifically. I said only she should reach out to someone she trusted."

Liar.

"Mrs. Sullivan didn't know the nanny had opened her letter to him, but you did, isn't that correct? *You* had read her letter."

"Yes."

"Yet you did not *suggest* Worth?"

"I said I did not."

Liar.

"Why didn't you, a longtime friend of the accused, lend her the money for the telegram? Surely there was no harm in her mother being informed of what was going on. There was certainly no one else in the house to assist her."

Ingrid sits forward. The jet beading at her neck winks in the light coming through the skylight. She's forgotten to cry into her handkerchief. Her cheeks are dry. "Because William was dead. That was reason enough."

"You told her something that day, didn't you, about the meat juice? You mentioned it at the inquest."

Ingrid frowns and sits back. "I don't know what you mean."

"Let me refresh your memory. I don't take much stock in the tale that Mrs. Sullivan added something to the Valentine's Meat Juice. It does intrigue me, however, that arsenic was later found in a bottle of it. What you said was this: arsenic had been found in the bottle of Valentine's Meat Juice."

A nod. "Yes, that's right."

"How did you know, Mrs. Berkshire?"

"Because I heard it. Someone said arsenic was found in the meat juice Constance handled."

"Someone. Who?"

"I don't remember. What difference does it make? Arsenic was found in that bottle."

"Mrs. Berkshire, you stated that you informed Mrs. Sullivan of the presence of arsenic in the bottle on May 14th. When did you first learn of the arsenic in the bottle?"

"Sometime around then. I can't exactly recall."

"Nurse Hawker gave the meat juice to Dr. Hendrickson on the 10th. However, it wasn't analyzed until later. May 23rd, in fact. You could not have heard arsenic was found in the bottle from the doctor—an analyst had yet to determine its contents. You had to have been informed by someone else in the house. Who was it?"

Silence. Not a chair creaks. No one breathes. The air is as tight as a coiled spring. Ingrid mumbles something Constance doesn't catch.

"You'll have to reply louder than that, Mrs. Berkshire. I ask you again, who told you arsenic was in that bottle?"

Ingrid's eyes prick at Sir Charles before she utters louder, "I don't recall. Perhaps I was mistaken—"

"Might it have been you, Mrs. Berkshire? Might you have known because you put it there?"

Goodacre is up like a shot to intervene but, seeing the outrage on Ingrid's face, decides to let it play out.

"If you're asking if I tampered with that bottle, I did not."

The gallery stirs.

Constance's heart hammers in her chest. Ingrid was too devoted to William to have killed him. But would she have gone as far as to poison the meat juice to frame her?

"Let's return to the letter Mrs. Sullivan wrote to Timothy Worth. There was a particular phrase, you said, that gave you the impression Mrs. Sullivan was scheming to do away with her husband. That's a damning accusation. Might 'he is sick unto death' mean that William Sullivan was simply very ill? The

Sullivans spent time in the American south while Mr. Sullivan was building his cotton business. The phrase could be nothing more than a southern colloquialism that has been vastly misunderstood."

"No," Ingrid says, lifting her chin. "It's nothing of the sort. Constance Sullivan knew William would die because she was poisoning him to death."

Chapter 15

Torrence House

May 8, 1889

Constance sits at her escritoire and looks out the window. An otherwise beautiful day were it not for the events occurring inside the house. A nurse arrived from the Institute a short while ago. Though it pains her Ingrid had a hand in bringing her here, it's done, and Nurse Hawker seems capable enough. Ingrid hasn't returned since she stormed into William's room. The nerve of the woman—to go around the back and enter through the garden door! Dr. Hendrickson insisted on no visitors. In any case, she's glad Ingrid is gone. The woman would only try her patience by hovering at William's bedside and making repeated statements of her malfeasance.

She takes up her fountain pen, its golden nib winking in the sunlight, and begins to write.

Dearest,
  I hadn't expected to hear from you so soon. William has taken ill and I've been nursing him day and night. <u>*He is sick*</u>

144

unto death. Now all depends on how long his strength will
hold out. I cannot answer your letter fully today, my darling,
but relieve your mind of all fear of discovery now and in the
future. William has been delirious since Sunday and I know
now that he is perfectly ignorant of everything, even of the
name of the street. He has not been making any inquiries
whatsoever. You need not therefore go abroad on that account,
dearest; but, in any case, please don't leave England until I
have seen you once again. If you wish to write to me about
anything do so now, as all letters pass through my hands at
present. Excuse this scrawl, my own darling, but I dare not
leave the room for long, and I do not know when I shall be able
to write to you again.

    In haste, yours ever,
    Connie

Thoughts of Timothy thrum like a wound as she folds the
paper, addresses the envelope, affixes the stamp. The raw ache
of missing him is constant, even as she sees to William's every
need. She can't stand the thought of Timothy leaving the
country for fear of what William might do. It's laughable he
could be a hindrance at all when he lies so still and unlike
himself upstairs.

She slips the letter into her pocket, climbs the stairs, and
heads for the bedroom. Halfway down the hall, gooseflesh stipples
her arms. There's a presence there in the shadows. She can
feel it.

"Mama."

Billy. "What are you doing here, my boy?" She pulls him
into the dull gaslight. His violet eyes are round with fear.
"Where's Nanny?"

"She said she'd put me in the Witch Orchard if I didn't
behave."

"Anne?" It doesn't sound like her, but perhaps the young nanny's patience is finally starting to fray. "Have you been good today? You must do what she says."

She bends down so she's at eye level and strokes his cheek. Perhaps he's frightened his father is ill. Nothing has been the same since William's been bedridden: the servants move more quietly on the stairs, the children are only to play above in the nursery or outside. She didn't believe Torrence House could be more oppressive, yet the tension in the house is palpable, the air thick and loaded. "I'm going to see Papa. Would you like to come?"

"They eat children," Billy says. "But I shan't be eaten because I'm not bad and I'm too fast. They'll never catch me."

"Who?"

"The witches who live in the orchard."

"Has Anne been telling you stories?"

Billy shakes his head. "No." His lip trembles. "No. You mustn't say."

"Say what?" She takes his hand, flummoxed. "Why are you here in the hall?"

He looks at the shadows as if something might jump out at him. "To fetch a glass of water."

She moves to the table where William's medicines litter the surface. She pours water from a pitcher into a glass and hands it to Billy. He drinks greedily.

"There. Now, up you go. Wait." She kneels again and takes his arm. "What's this?" A bruise marks the underside of his forearm, but he squirms from her touch and races up the nursery stairs.

"He vomited last night sometime around ten o'clock and again this morning about half past eight," Constance says.

William watches from the bed. He's more diminished than she's ever seen him.

Dr. Hendrickson frowns and places his palm on William's forehead. "What has he had to eat?"

"Nothing yet this morning. He hasn't been hungry since yesterday at dinner."

William has hardly breathed a word since waking at six o'clock, and all her entreaties for him to eat have been met with a shake of his head. Nurse Hawker hasn't had any luck either. She sent her down to the kitchen to bring up tea.

Dr. Hendrickson takes a seat on the bed. "How are you, Mr. Sullivan?"

"My mouth is dry," he replies, his voice barely above a whisper. "Is there no medicine you can give me to get me out of this blasted bed?"

"I'm afraid it isn't that simple. Have you been able to get up to relieve yourself?"

William closes his eyes, as if the answer will take more energy than he has.

"No," she replies. "The nurse and I have had to help him to the water closet each time."

"Why don't I take you down the hall, Mr. Sullivan, hmm?" Dr. Hendrickson says. "We'll give your wife a rest."

She pulls the blankets down while the doctor helps William swing his legs to the floor. It takes an age. When William is standing at last, Hendrickson, with one hand at William's back, the other holding his hand slung around his neck, assists his patient out of the room.

Minutes later, Dr. Hendrickson speaks with William behind the door of the water closet. She hears the words *eat* and *strength*. In the beginning, William was embarrassed to talk about his trips to the toilet, his diarrhea, his vomiting. It chills her that these discussions are now commonplace. Of late, William's docility frightens her as much as his illness. She may want her freedom, but she won't desert him now. She will nurse him as best she can.

She's fluffing the pillows when they return. From the other side of the bed, she helps the doctor get William comfortable. By the time the sheets are drawn up to his chin, his eyes are already closed. Hendrickson gestures for her to follow him out to the landing.

When she's pulled the door closed, the doctor sets down his bag, his expression grim. "I think he will recover, Mrs. Sullivan, but I can't emphasize more how much he needs to get as much rest as possible. Please tell me you've been turning away visitors as I asked."

Her thoughts flash to Ingrid who'd barged in without her consent. "His brother, Edward, recently returned from America and has been staying with us since William took ill. They're business partners—"

"He shouldn't be concerning himself with business. He shouldn't be concerning himself with anything but getting better."

She tamps down her anger at his tone, as if she hasn't been working herself to the bone to see to William's every need. "I'll see that no one disturbs him. Do you still think it's the dyspepsia that ails him?"

"Yes." Dr. Hendrickson twists one end of his mustache, his eyes distant. "But I can't say what the irritant poison was that caused it. We may never know."

In the near distance, the children chase the peacocks. The birds turn in circles and then one takes flight and lands on a low limb in one of the trees. Janie runs to its base, looks up, and claps her hands.

Anne's cheeks are pink from exertion. In the sunlight, her hair is as blond as the children's. The nanny's mouth pulls into a grin. How lucky they are to have her. Since Billy's accident, Anne seems to have a special regard for her. Almost like worship. As for William, he can barely stand the sight of her. He's been unable to forgive her for her lack of vigilance at the pond.

"How's Master Sullivan fairing, mistress? I hope he's no worse."

Oh, Anne. You wouldn't worry overmuch if you knew how much he scorns you.

"No, no worse thankfully. The doctor thinks he'll recover. He just needs rest."

"I must say, you're holding up well. Being at home all day tending to him must be taxing. I know how you like to go about."

Constance's heart skips a beat. For an instant she thinks Anne is alluding to her walks with Timothy in the park. But that's ridiculous; Anne wouldn't know. Is she referring to her marriage, that she's put a wide berth between herself and William since last summer? *Stop imagining things. You're making mountains out of molehills.*

She holds up the letter. "I've an errand for you. Please mail this straightaway. You may take the children with you to the post office. They'll enjoy the walk."

"Of course, Mrs. Sullivan. Consider it done."

Billy barrels towards them, crashing into Constance's legs. "Come play with us! Nanny doesn't like to."

"What a silly thing to say, Billy," Constance replies.

For a moment, something dark passes over Anne's features

and then Janie trundles up, smiling in a pink dress, the tips of her white shoes stained green from the grass.

"Mummy! I almost catched a peacock!"

She bends and places her arms around them both. If only she had time to go with them. She'd like to be free of the house for a while. She wants to think she's imagining it, but the house's gloominess seems to have deepened with William's affliction. "I've asked Nanny to mail a letter. She's going to take you on a little walk. Do you promise you'll mind her? It's a very grown-up thing to accompany Nanny to post a letter."

Billy's eyes flick to Anne and down. "We'll be good."

She straightens and holds the letter out to Anne, who puts it in her pocket and takes Billy and Janie's hands. She blows a kiss to the children and steps back into the house.

She spends the afternoon reading *Great Expectations* to William who dozes on and off. She doubts he comprehends much of it. Still, it gives her something to do besides fret over the prominence of his cheekbones, the bruise-colored hollows under his eyes.

Nurse Hawker, upon seeing her sitting with William, busies herself with refilling the water pitcher, tidying the room, making sure the various bottles on the tables in the bedroom and landing are in order.

Hours later when William is asleep, Constance closes the book and stretches. Sleep paws at her. If she doesn't rest now, she'll regret it. A flicker out of the corner of her eye brings her to the window. The children play with a ball on the front lawn. Anne stands by a rose bush, her back to the house. Edward and Ingrid are with her. They're in deep conversation.

Edward's face is drawn, his lips tight. His eyes flick to the master bedroom window. She ducks, then approaches the glass again, angling her body so they can't see her. Ingrid and Edward look agitated, their mouths working quickly. They turn to each other, then back to Anne.

A throat clears behind her. She jumps and turns from the window, her face hot. Nurse Hawker. She'd forgotten all about her. "I was just...William is resting. I'll have a lie-down in the dressing room. Please let me know when my husband wakes."

Hawker, a short, rotund woman who appears to have a penchant for taking command, nods, jowls wobbling like curtains. "Of course, Mrs. Sullivan. I have it quite under control. Don't you worry about a thing."

The dressing room is small and windowless, cramped by the wardrobes and the cot. She sits, her mind racing. She can't shake the feeling that something is amiss. Yet she can barely keep her eyes open. She's making herself comfortable on the cot when she hears feet on the stairs.

"Nurse," she hears Edward say sharply. "Thank God you've arrived."

She opens the dressing-room door. Fury lights Edward's face. His eyes rake her then return to the nurse.

"From now on," he tells Hawker, "you are the only one, save the doctor, in control of the patient."

"Edward, you're too loud," Constance hisses. "You'll wake him. Whatever are you talking about?"

Her brother-in-law doesn't look at her. "Nurse, nothing is to be given to the patient by anyone but you, do you understand?"

Nurse Hawker comes to her feet. "And you are, sir?"

William stirs on the bed, turns to his side, and settles. Edward lowers his voice. "Edward Sullivan, brother of the patient. You must promise me that you will see he has nothing unless it is from your hand, and *only* your hand."

Constance's heart kicks. The audacity of it. "Edward—"

"Even Mrs. Sullivan," Edward breathes, shooting her another look of venom. "You must obey my orders, do you understand? If you have any questions, I'll be staying at the house. You are to direct your inquiries to me. Not the servants, nor anyone else."

"Yes, sir," Nurse Hawker says, her throat working as she swallows. "He'll be in good hands with me."

Edward leaves the room as quickly as he entered it, and she's fast on his heels. She chases him down the stairs, saying as she goes, "I don't understand, Edward. Explain yourself."

In the drawing room, he heads straight for the sideboard and pours a brandy. How like William he is tossing it back. Yet Edward is very unlike William. He's never behaved this way, never spoken to her in such a loathsome tone. Edward has only ever been kind. It frightens her.

Ingrid is settled in one of the Chippendale chairs before the fire. Her eyes snap to her. Emotions flicker in their depths: judgment, anger, arrogance. They're all there, fighting for dominance.

"Would one of you tell me what's going on?"

Edward breaks into a bitter laugh. "We could ask the same of you." His eyes meet Ingrid's, an understanding between them.

"We have suspicions, Constance." In the darkened room with the flickering fire, Ingrid's eyes are almost reptilian.

The blood drains from Constance's face. *Timothy*, she thinks. *They know.* For a wild moment, she pictures herself fleeing the house and showing up on his doorstep to seek the comfort of his arms. *No, not now.* She belongs here. With William. She must see his illness through, come what may. "Suspicions? What do you mean?"

"Why the devil wasn't a nurse called before now?" Edward says, his words like daggers.

She relaxes. They don't know. They're only concerned for William. *As it should be.* "Dr. Hendrickson sent for a nurse earlier this morning, but no one came."

Ingrid makes a noise in her throat. "If it weren't for me fetching one at the Institute, there'd be no nurse here at all."

"Dr. Hendrickson and I have been taking things day by day," Constance says, looking between them. "You've seen it yourself, Edward. In any case, William has preferred from the beginning that I attend him."

He takes a step toward her, his face red. "Oh? He's said no such thing to me."

"I sent Mary for a doctor the very morning he became ill," she counters. "You arrived that day, remember? You saw me do it."

A muscle works in Edward's jaw. "What's wrong with him, Connie? Tell me."

"What?" She pulls in her chin. "You know as much as I do. William has ingested something that's causing his illness."

"You shouldn't be caring for him." Edward rakes a hand through his hair. He looks ill.

"Who has a better right than I to care for my husband?" The impertinence. How dare they interfere. She raises her chin. "Think what you will, but I've worked continually to make William as comfortable as possible. Ask Dr. Hendrickson, he'll tell you."

Edward pulls the bell cord. A moment later Alan appears, bowing slightly.

"I understand Dr. Hendrickson lives close by," Edward says. "Do you know his address?"

The butler raises his eyebrows. "Yes, sir. It's around the corner, sir."

"Very good. I'd like you to show me the way."

Alan looks to her, and she waves her hand in acquiescence.

When the two are gone, only the popping of the fire punctures the silence. She must speak to Edward when he returns. *He'll tell me what this is all about. They've misunderstood everything.*

She looks up. Ingrid's glare bores a hole through her. Well, she won't give her the satisfaction of lingering. She turns and leaves the room, makes her way back up the stairs. On the landing, whispers cut. She frowns into the shadows. Two aprons swim in the murk.

"I was just asking Anne if the children needed anything," Molly says, coming nearer. "I thought to fetch a snack for them before supper if Anne were agreeable."

It's a lie. They've been listening to the confrontation below. Constance's face goes hot. She's glad, for once, the hall is as gloomy as it is. It will hide her embarrassment. "The children don't need a snack," she says, her words full of bite. "Your chores won't get done with the two of you loitering about. Off with you."

She turns and storms into the bedroom. William is sleeping. Nurse Hawker turns to her, her lips pressed tight. In the dressing room, she collapses on the cot. Despite the roil of her stomach, the rapid beating of her heart, she falls into an exhausted slumber.

In the dark dressing room, the wardrobes stare like sentinels when she opens her eyes. *It's all a dream,* she thinks as she sits up. *A sad, horrible dream.* When she enters the bedroom, Nurse Hawker watches her. She has dreamed nothing: Edward's hateful words, his insistence she desist from caring for William are all there in the nurse's face. The clock on the mantle reads half past eight. She's slept nearly three hours.

"Has there been any change?" The fire has been lit. A single lamp glows from the table next to the bed. William sleeps peacefully, though his face looks ravaged in the shadows.

"No," the nurse says, "though Dr. Hendrickson came."

A flare of impatience. "You should have awakened me. What did he say?"

"He was relieved Mr. Sullivan was no worse and seemed to be sleeping well."

"He slept through his visit?"

"The doctor didn't want to disturb him."

"Were Edward and Ingrid present when Dr. Hendrickson came in?"

"Yes."

She wants to ask more, but she can't stand the way Hawker watches her. Her eyes are hooks, her mouth set as if she holds a secret.

Chapter 16

St. George's Hall

Day 2 of Trial

Anne Yardley's eyes are enormous as she watches Sir Charles come to his feet. She reminds Constance of a filly she'd once seen, newly born, skittish at the nearest sound. She had answered Goodacre's questions without a hitch, though each word seemed to come from a place deep inside her she wished to keep to herself. It's clear she no more wants to be here than she wants to see Constance swing from the end of a rope.

I should have let you go after Billy's accident. It would have spared you this.

"There's a great deal being made of the fly papers Molly Laverty showed you last April," Sir Charles says. "She claims you told her to keep them."

"No." Anne's gaze finds her in the dock. *I'm sorry,* her eyes say. *I'm sorry for all this.* "I told her to throw them away."

The barrister stands at his table, a hand resting on his notes. "When your mistress asked you to post the letter, you did not intend to open it, did you?"

"No."

"You had no reason to suspect your mistress of anything?"

"No. It's just that, like I told Mr. Goodacre..." Anne's eyes well with tears. "Janie dropped the letter in the mud and the address was unreadable. I thought to fetch another envelope and readdress it. But it came open when I picked it up. The seal wasn't stuck. I...saw the words, 'my darling.'"

Whispers ripple through the court. In the press area behind Constance, a pen scratches furiously across a page. Her eyes dart to the gallery. At least her mother isn't present. Constance had written to her and begged her to stop coming. She would only be shunned by the ladies seated there.

Her eyes snag on a man moving down the row. *Timothy*. She blinks, refocuses. He's edging his way toward the aisle. He's leaving. Shame pools in her. His words in London echo in her ears. "Your fall—and that's exactly what it will be—will ruin you." She wants to drop through the floor.

"And then," Sir Charles is saying, "you read the letter. What did you do next?"

"We walked back to the house to get a clean envelope. That's when I saw Mrs. Berkshire and Mr. Sullivan walking to the house from the train station. I was upset. I was afraid the mistress would be angry I'd let Janie ruin the envelope. Mrs. Berkshire saw that I was crying and asked me what was wrong. She asked to see the letter. I remembered then the row the Sullivans had about a man named Timothy Worth. The letter was addressed to him."

"Earlier that same afternoon, before you were asked to mail the letter, you and Miss Laverty also showed Ingrid Berkshire the fly papers, isn't that right?" Anne bows her head. "Answer the question, Miss Yardley."

"Molly thought Mrs. Berkshire would know what to do."

"Meaning?"

"Molly got it in her head the mistress was soaking the fly papers like the Black Widows of Liverpool did, the ones who were hanged a few years back for poisoning their families."

"And that, my dear girl, is what started this loathsome witch hunt."

"Your Lordship," Mr. Goodacre says, standing, "I really must insist Sir Charles abstain from declaring his opinions."

"Agreed." Justice Stevenson frowns at Sir Charles. "You know better."

"Indeed," Sir Charles says with a small bow. To the jury, he says, "Please disregard my last statement." He returns his gaze to Anne. "When Molly showed you the fly papers, did you suspect your mistress?"

"No, sir."

"Did you open your mistress's letter because you suspected her of something?"

"No, sir."

"Did you show that letter to Ingrid Berkshire and Edward Sullivan to bring suspicion on your mistress?"

"No, sir."

"In fact, you thought highly of your mistress, did you not?"

A lone tear travels down Anne's cheek. "I did. With all my heart."

"In fact, you did not then, nor do you think now your mistress capable of poisoning her husband."

Silence stretches. Sir Charles lifts his brows. Her heart thuds. Why isn't Anne answering? The barrister tries again. "Miss Yardley, you do not believe your mistress was capable of harming her husband, isn't that correct?"

"I cannot say that, sir."

Intakes of breath in the gallery. It's a mistake. Anne has misunderstood the question. Sir Charles swings his gaze to Constance, and she can't stand the shock in his eyes. He'd asked her about Anne's loyalty, and she'd told him the young nanny had only ever thought the best of her. "Anne will support me," she'd said. "She worshipped me."

Anne bites her lip. Her eyes scurry around the courtroom. She doesn't look at her. It's then that she understands. *She's going to betray me. Just like all the rest.*

"Miss Yardley?" Sir Charles' voice is barely above a whisper. He looks as though he's stepped in a quagmire from which he cannot escape. "I shall withdraw the question."

"You will not," Justice Stevenson intones. "The witness will answer the question."

Anne swallows. "It's just that...last summer, sir, I noticed the mistress had a cut across her wrist. I didn't think much about it at the time. But then Molly mentioned that the mistress had an awful lot of scabs on her body, and a great many scars."

"I really do not think this pertinent—" Sir Charles begins, but Justice Stevenson waves him off.

"Go on, young lady," the judge urges.

"I came to know the mistress would take a knife and cut herself—on her wrists, her arms, her legs. She was in the water closet once and the door wasn't quite closed all the way. I saw...I saw her take a knife from the cabinet and slice her leg. Not deep enough to require a doctor, but enough to draw blood."

The courtroom is a tomb. Faces turn to the dock. Constance grasps the rail before her to keep her hands from trembling.

"And what, pray tell," Sir Charles says, fingers pinching the bridge of his nose, "does this have to do with your good opinion of Mrs. Sullivan?"

"It's only that, if the mistress could hurt herself, what might she have been capable of doing to someone else, sir?"

Chapter 17

Torrence House

May 9, 1889

S he is aboard the *Baltic*. Timothy attracts her attention almost instantly after they pull away from the pier. It's as if they're meeting for the first time, yet she's always known him. She's arrested by his good looks, his fine manners. He is equally smitten and soon, it is he who strolls with her on deck in the afternoons, he who escorts her into the dining room each evening. After a clutch of days at sea, they disembark arm in arm, pledged to each other in love. But as Timothy brings her hand to his mouth for a kiss, she spies William at the end of the plank. She laughs. *You can't stop us now. We're to be married, William! There's nothing you can do.* William draws a pistol and fires once, twice, three times. Timothy's chest explodes. Her lover staggers and reaches for her as his body teeters back, but his hands clasp only air. He falls from the plank, a black snarl of water swallowing him whole.

Constance gasps and sits up, the filaments of the nightmare dissolving like thin clouds. She runs a hand along her forehead.

It's damp. Her whole body sweats. She's fallen asleep in the drawing room again. William doesn't like to awaken without her beside him. She takes the stairs. The door to the sickroom is open. She has the absurd notion that the light coming from within is hesitant to invade the gloomy darkness of the landing.

Anne stands at the side of the bed. In her hands are folded towels. The nurse's chair is empty. Constance has always thought Anne a comely girl—not overly pretty, but pleasing in a simple, country way, with a sprinkle of freckles and hair of pale gold. But there's something about the way she's looking at William sleeping that is neither attractive nor simple. For an instant, she thinks the girl aims to smother him with a towel and then the thought scampers off as quickly and inexplicably as it came.

"Anne?" The nanny swivels to her. She expects her to recover herself, but she remains in some sort of fugue. "What are you doing?"

The nanny's lips draw down, her irises vacant. It's as if a magician has waved his hand and magicked a different person. "He doesn't care for you," she says. "He doesn't care for any of us."

Constance is taken aback. "What? Where's the nurse?"

Anne shifts back to William as if she hasn't heard and Constance's thoughts swim and connect. Anne knows William wishes her gone. Since the summer, the girl has read every message William has sent her: his clipped, over-sharp words; his affronted body language. She has only pretended not to notice.

Poor girl. How she must hate him. She stays for me. Me and the children.

Down the hall, the water closet door opens with a creak of hinges and brings Anne from her trance. She blinks and looks at Constance. "Can I mail another letter for you, mistress?"

The old Anne. The moment is gone.

"No. You may put the towels on the dresser there."

Anne does as she asks, nods with diffidence, and slips from the room just as Hawker's replacement, Nurse Callery, enters.

"Did you ask Anne to deliver the towels?" Constance's tone is ice water. Whatever the nurses have been told, they haven't confided in her, and she's left with the impression they lie in wait to catch her out. But at what?

"I did, Mrs. Sullivan. She asked if I needed anything, and I said I'd just duck into the water closet for a second if she'd handle the towels."

Constance takes a seat and clutches William's hand. It isn't the hand of the man she once knew as spirited and vigorous. It's the cool appendage of a man diminished by pain. His eyes are closed, but earlier, before he'd succumbed to sleep, they'd stared unblinking at the ceiling. A log shifts in the fireplace. The shadows in the room are growing long. It's after seven o'clock. She runs a hand over his forehead and through his hair. Worry saws at her. William doesn't know she's here. His lucidity comes and goes, fickle as the wind. Dr. Hendrickson told her yesterday morning William would improve. That his 'grave error of diet' wouldn't persist. But it isn't true.

William is worse. William is dying.

Dr. Hendrickson has already made two visits today. William suffered from loose bowels much of the morning and afternoon, combined with rectal straining that exhausted him, shunting him into a state of confusion and incoherence until he had, at last, fallen asleep.

Voices in the front hall trickle up and footsteps pound the stairs. Nurse Callery sits in watch behind her, her eyes as suspicious and blaming as Hawker's.

Edward and Ingrid enter, followed by Dr. Hendrickson. She stands and her chest constricts. She hates that the bedroom is jammed, that they've invaded a place that was once private.

There is only suspicion and hate now, and a liberal dose of blame.

And soon there will be death.

"Mrs. Sullivan," Dr. Hendrickson says, inclining his head.

The gesture is deferential, but his eyes are not. He holds her gaze a bit too long—enough for her to see the suspicion in them—before considering his patient. So, Edward has infected him with his baseless accusations of her neglect of William.

"He hasn't stirred since the pain earlier," Nurse Callery offers, coming closer to the bed. "The suppository of opium did him good."

Edward's eyes pin her. "Constance, if you'll step outside."

She wants to lunge at him, curse him, but to argue in front of Ingrid, in front of the doctor and nurse, is too shameful for words, and she won't risk waking William. She steps back from the bed and leaves the room. The door is abruptly closed behind her.

Damn them. Damn them all.

She grinds her teeth, unintentionally clamping down on her tongue. She winces, the coppery taste of blood sticky in her mouth. She starts for the stairs, but reconsiders. The voices behind the door aren't too low to hear, not if she stands close enough.

"The rectal straining from the lower bowel is troubling." Dr. Hendrickson. "I made an effort to examine it, but it caused him such extreme pain, I was unable to continue. I examined the urine and feces this afternoon. There was no sign of an irritant. No hint of metal. No mineral deposits."

"Look again." Edward. "It's there. You've only to find it."

Someone makes a comment she doesn't catch and then the doorknob is turning.

She tiptoes as quietly as possible down the stairs.

163

May 10, 1889

Weak sun filters through the panes of the drawing-room window. It's the twilight hour when shadows and light collide, and the lamps haven't yet been lit. In the semi-darkness, it's easy for her to pretend the house is as it was weeks ago. Before sickness, before doctors, before Edward looked at her as he does now. But once the gaslights come up and the fires are lit, she will see the detritus of illness—the unopened mail, the bedpans, the vomit basins—and know that everything has changed, and nothing will be the same again.

And something else.

Last night she was on the landing, her eyes sweeping over the items on the table as they had so many times before. Making sure it was well-stocked, organized, that nothing was needed from the kitchen. She'd seen it then and her heart had skipped. There among the folded linens, the water pitchers, the towels, the bottles of camphor and lotion was the little turnip-shaped bottle. She crept closer, cursing the infernal darkness that perpetually hovered there. She lifted it off the table, turned the label to the gaslight just to make sure.

Yes. It was a bottle of Valentine's Meat Juice, and it shouldn't have been there. In that instant, she felt the house waiting, the shadows coalescing, gathering around her ankles. What did it mean?

She'd been so engrossed in making sure it was what she believed it to be—an interloper among the innocent items there —she hadn't noticed Nurse Hawker come to the door of the sickroom. There must have been a sound. A creaking floorboard? A rustle of clothing? It hardly matters now. Constance had looked up and seen the formidable figure of Hawker scowling at her from the doorframe.

And Constance had jumped.

She wanted to protest about the bottle. It didn't belong there. Dr. Hendrickson had vanquished the last bottle of Valentine's from the house after it made William sick. But poised there in the gloom, Constance knew that uttering a word would be futile. Complaining would only bring attention to her deposed position in the household because wasn't everything she said met with suspicion and scorn? She hadn't wanted to give Hawker the satisfaction.

And so she'd set the bottle back down and drifted downstairs without a word.

She wishes now that Nurse Callery had remained for the night, that Hawker hadn't relieved her last evening. Callery might have been kinder, more sympathetic perhaps. She might have *listened* to her about the wrongness of the bottle being there.

Now, the mood in the house has shifted from unease to expectation. Though Dr. Hendrickson hasn't stated it in so many words, they are waiting for the inevitable.

She recognized it in the doctor's face when he came this morning and saw that William was worse, grimacing and writhing from the pain in his bowels. He gave William phosphoric acid for his stomach upset, but it did nothing to comfort him. Not a single thing the doctor has given William since the onset of his illness has relieved him.

Ingrid and Edward roam the house in a different orbit than she. If they chance her on the stairs, in the front hall, on the landing, they move away and avoid her eyes. When this is over, she will vanquish them from Torrence House. She will leave England for good and return to her mother's home in New York City. She misses America. It's familiar. It is home. Billy and

Janie will never know their Uncle Edward, nor Ingrid Berkshire, their godmother, and she doesn't care a jot.

And Timothy. Her insides twist, and she flinches with regret, that she gave herself to another man as readily as she took a brush to her hair. Thoughts of them tangled in sheets, laughing together, collide. There's a small chance a letter is waiting for her in her secret post box, but if he was concerned for her after receiving her letter, after telling him how ill William has become, he would have arrived at her door in the guise of a fellow broker worried about William's illness.

He'd have come for her. He'd have found a way to see that she is well.

She's sifted and weighed their tryst in London, laid it all out in her mind's eye like clothes on a line, and gathered that Timothy never wanted anything more than a mistress. It pains her to admit it, yet she is strangely relieved to face the truth of it.

On the threshold of the sickroom, she motions for Nurse Hawker. When she's pulled the bedroom door closed after her, she says, "I would like to have a private conversation with my husband. Now, before..." She falters, her throat strangled with emotion. *Before it's too late.* "I'll leave the door open if you require it, but I ask you to give us some privacy, if you will."

Nurse Hawker considers her, the same hard tilt to her mouth when she'd spied her with the bottle on the landing. Only now her eyes gleam with satisfaction, as if Constance's jolt on the landing has fully convinced her she is guilty of whatever it is they suspect her of. "I'll move my chair just outside the room, but the door stays open."

With a nod from Contance, Hawker installs herself outside the door and looks on. Constance pushes the sour woman from her mind and arranges herself on the bed. "William." She takes his hand in hers. The network of veins on the top of his hand stands out against his flesh. His cheeks, once so hale and hearty, are caved in. "I must speak with you. There are things you should know."

William's eyes flutter open. They're clear enough to convince her he's lucid.

"I have been so angry at you for so long," she begins softly. "I've hated you, even. But I regret it. Ours was—is—a good marriage. We were good for each other, weren't we?"

His head nods ever so slightly. The motion seems to bring on pain and his eyes close. "You were my bright light, Connie. The best decision I ever made."

She feels the prick of tears. "I don't know if you wish to hear this, but I must clear my conscience." Another ripple of pain crosses William's face. "I have been unfaithful to you. I didn't set out to be, not exactly. I have kept it from you for months."

William's eyes swim open and find her in the room. "Oh, Connie. How could you do it?"

Tears rain down her face. "I can hardly believe it myself. I was furious at you over Sandra. I couldn't get past it. I hated her and I despised you. More than anything, I felt lonely. Unloved."

"You were never unloved."

William must be dying, for he would demand she name Timothy as her lover were he himself. Oh, to have that man back. She longs for his mercurial nature, his temper, his loud guffaws. The old William. She wants to smell his cigars in the house again, hear his step in the foyer announcing his arrival home. "I ask your forgiveness, William. For all of it—the lies, my anger. You cannot know how seeing you like this has broken me. I can't bear the thought of you, of you..."

"Hush, Connie." William removes his hand from hers and wipes her tears with his thumb. "All this silly talk will make you sick. I forgive you, of course. I was far from perfect myself. I wasn't good to you."

"You were."

"Not good enough." Another spasm of pain crosses his features. She wonders if he will die now, this very moment. Perhaps he's only been waiting for this.

"We were enough for each other," she says. "Billy and Janie will grow up knowing their papa was a good man." She is astonished at the realization. She's always known this. It was her blind jealousy and her pride that hid the truth.

She's filled with so much pain, she must quit the room. She won't let him hear her sob, how much she hates herself. But in the end, it doesn't matter. William is breathing deeply. He's asleep.

She runs past a glowering Hawker, down the corridor to the water closet. After closing the door, she leans over the sink. The sobs come, loud and wrenched from her in gasping heaves. The woman in the mirror has blue crescents under her eyes. Her dress is mussed. She holds out her shaking hands. Her wedding ring mocks her: who she is, her infidelity, her lies. She tries to remove it from her finger. It won't budge. She twists it until her knuckle swells, the skin red and pulsing around the band. Finally, she forces the ring free and flings it to the floor. Her hair is tumbling from its bun. She pulls at it, tugging at the ends until her scalp screams. She rakes her nails down her cheeks. This is who she is. This is what she's become. She is despicable. Pathetic.

But more than anything is the realization that William will die and there is nothing she can do to stop it. Nothing. She fumbles for the knife in the cabinet.

"I won't bother with this now." William's voice is an exasperated stage whisper. "Leave me alone, damn you!"

Constance listens outside the bedroom door. Apprehension

scratches at her insides with tender claws, pulling at her ribs. She's about to place her hand on the knob when she hears a response.

"You must tend to this now, William. You know how important it is." Edward's voice, edged with urgency. "You must see reason. There's no other way. You know as well as I it's the best course and the only one, given the circumstances."

"Christ, if I am to die, why must I be worried with this?" William again, his voice loud and grating. A pause. Papers rustle. "There, I have done it. Now leave me in peace!"

She turns the knob. It doesn't give. She beats on the door. "Edward, open this door at once." A low conversation, nothing she can catch. She pounds again. "Nurse, unlock this door!"

"Is everything all right, mistress?"

She spins and there in the semi-darkness is Anne. Shame singes Constance's cheeks. How pathetic she must look, locked out of rooms in her own home. Kept from her dying husband. "Tend to the children, Anne. Please."

Thoughts seem to flicker under Anne's lowered lashes, but she nods and makes her way back up the nursery stairs.

The door opens. Edward stands like a wall, his gray eyes sparking with malevolence. *Who are you?* she thinks. *What's become of kind, charming Edward?* He turns and reclaims his seat on the bed where William sits propped on pillows. There is no nurse in the room.

"Connie, my dear." William smiles weakly and stretches a hand to her. The smile turns to a grimace as a wave of pain lumbers through him.

"You should be resting." She glares at Edward. "You've upset him. How dare you."

Her eyes mark a stack of papers in Edward's lap turned face down, a bottle of brandy on the table at the window, a half-empty glass of amber liquid clutched in William's hand. A spike of fury flares in her and she reaches for the glass.

"He wanted a brandy," Edward says impassively. "Under the circumstances, I didn't see a reason to deny him one."

"We're to obey the doctor's orders. William is to have nothing. *Those* are the circumstances."

"Connie." It's more croak than word. William lifts his brows. "Please."

"I can't allow it, William. I'm sorry." Edward bristles. She's about to reprimand him again when Nurse Hawker darkens the door. "Nurse, I expected you at my husband's side."

"I told her she could have a cup of tea in the kitchen," Edward says.

"I wasn't gone more than ten minutes, Mrs. Sullivan," Hawker snaps.

"Enough time for Mr. Sullivan to upset my husband. Take this glass and the brandy bottle there," she says, gesturing. "It seems my brother-in-law is taking liberties with my husband's diet." She turns to Edward. "I won't tolerate this. No food or drink, even if William asks for it."

Edward lifts a brow. "Forgive me, Connie. I'd forgotten how good you are at denying William." His eyes travel down her body and back up.

It is a clear reference to their sleeping arrangements. Edward must've noticed the cot in the dressing room. Or perhaps William told Edward they haven't been living as man and wife. Her face burns. She resists the urge to slap him. William seems oblivious, his eyes half-mast.

"That's a nice stroke of madness," Edward says between clenched teeth. "Telling me what William should and shouldn't have."

Nurse Hawker grabs the glass from her. "I'll take it from here, sir." She rounds on Constance, her chin jutted. "Ain't a soul who can gammon me, no matter how sly it creeps in the shadows of the landing."

Constance quits the room with a flounce of petticoats, her heart leaping in her throat. Her mind skirts the edge of something, the bones of it showing through skin like the stays of a corset.

They, all of them, think she's poisoning William.

Chapter 18

St. George's Hall

Day 2 of Trial

Eugenia Hawker licks her lips. Her eyes, small and dark, are twin raisins in a doughy face. She's without her nurse's cap, her hat failing to hide ears as big as fists. Through Mr. Goodacre's examination, she'd told the jury about Edward's angry insistence she guard William, his taking control of the house, and her witnessing Constance on the landing with the bottle of Valentine's Meat Juice—later found to have arsenic in it. The jury took it all in their stride, as if it were perfectly natural for Constance to be judged a murderer based on the veiled suggestions of strangers.

The jurors tug at their collars and the ladies in the gallery work their fans as Sir Charles comes to his feet. Constance longs to lift her veil for air but doesn't dare rid herself of the only privacy she has.

Sir Charles approaches the witness box. "Though Ingrid Berkshire and Edward Sullivan appear to have been on edge about Mrs. Sullivan's plan to poison her husband, they shared none of their suspicions with you, the patient's nurse, once you arrived. That's very odd, wouldn't you say?"

Nurse Hawker purses thick lips and examines the barrister through narrowed eyes. "Mrs. Berkshire told me enough when she fetched me from the Institute. She said to watch over Mr. Sullivan very carefully and that's what I did."

"Did Mrs. Sullivan seem concerned with her husband's condition?"

A shrug. "I suppose."

"She seemed caring, did she not? She read to him, she sat and talked with him when he was awake."

"Yes."

"In fact, he wanted her at his side, did he not?"

"Yes."

Sir Charles walks before the bench, hands clasped behind him. "Your first day, May 8th, did Dr. Hendrickson tell you no one in the house was to give him anything except for you?"

"No."

"But in the days following, *after* Edward Sullivan's visit to him, Dr. Hendrickson acted differently, didn't he? He was suddenly very concerned about arsenic."

"He was more concerned, yes. Mr. Sullivan was vomiting and—"

"Edward Sullivan had planted theories in his head about fly papers and a letter."

Goodacre is on his feet. Sir Charles sighs and waves him down. "Never mind. My apologies, my Lord, Mr. Goodacre. I shall keep to questions. Now then, you didn't witness Dr. Hendrickson give any medication to the deceased the evening of May 8th, did you?"

"No."

"So according to Dr. Hendrickson, the deceased needed none. Now, let's tackle this extraordinary story of the

Valentine's Meat Juice. You testified that you saw Mrs. Sullivan put a bottle of Valentine's *on* the table outside the room. That landing is very dark. Are you sure you didn't see her merely pick it up and put it back down?"

"That's not what I saw. I saw her put it there."

The gallery rustles. Someone hoots. Constance looks to the jury. At least half the men stare back, taking her measure. She grips the rail. Blood pounds in her ears.

"Dr. Hendrickson testified that on May 6th he instructed the patient not to take any more Valentine's because it had made him sick," Sir Charles says. "The doctor removed that bottle from the house. Could not Mrs. Sullivan have noted another one had suspiciously appeared and was attempting to remove it?"

"Mrs. Sullivan had that bottle in her hands. When she saw me, she put it down on the table."

Constance curses herself for not speaking up. Or worse, for not removing it. But Nurse Hawker thought her a schemer. Had she argued about the Valentine's being there, the nurse would have cried foul.

"Have you an explanation, Nurse Hawker, how another bottle got there when the doctor removed the first one three days before?"

"It was Edward Sullivan," Hawker says. She looks from Sir Charles to Mr. Goodacre. "He told me there was a new bottle on the landing and I was to use it if necessary."

Edward. The bastard.

Whispers flit through the gallery. For the second time, Sir Charles is taken by surprise. "Edward Sullivan told you this? Why didn't you say so before?"

Nurse Hawker crosses thick arms. "Mr. Goodacre didn't ask."

174

The room turns to the seated barrister. Goodacre pales and moves a trembling hand over his brow.

Sir Charles walks to his table and searches impatiently through his notes. "And yet Dr. Hendrickson had prescribed the deceased was not to have any food or drink. You were aware of this?"

"Yes, but if the deceased woke up hungry, Mr. Sullivan said to give him the meat juice."

"Edward Sullivan instructed you to do that? To 'give him the meat juice?'"

"Yes, if the deceased needed it."

"Did you give him any?"

"No. By that time, the poor soul couldn't tolerate much of anything."

"After you saw Mrs. Sullivan handle the bottle, you took it from the landing into the bedroom where you could watch over it, correct?"

"Yes."

"Had the bottle been opened?"

"Yes. The white seal around the cap was broken. Mr. Sullivan said he'd put a fresh bottle there, but someone had opened it. I knew just who that was."

"Ah, then you witnessed Mrs. Sullivan add poison to the bottle?" Hawker's mouth hardens and her cheeks redden. "Ah, I see you did not. However, you say the bottle had been opened because the seal wasn't intact. Which means *you* could have unwittingly administered poison to the deceased." Sir Charles' eyes dance. "That was the goal of the culprit, I daresay. But to say that Mrs. Sullivan is unequivocally the poisoner is a step too far, given that you didn't witness her add anything to the bottle. You didn't even see her open it. No witness, so far, has testified to anything of the kind. However, it's quite clear—since you are absolutely certain that once you took it from the landing you guarded it exhaustively until you handed it to Dr. Hendrickson —that *someone had already* added arsenic to it. Half a grain of it, in fact. That someone could have been anyone in the house who had access to the landing. Which is to say everyone."

The gallery erupts. A few reporters dart from the courtroom. Justice Stevenson rises and the noise settles.

"I may not have seen her do it," Hawker says, her eyes skimming the jury, "but I know what she did. Mr. Sullivan put the bottle there, but *she* added poison to it. I saw her replace that bottle on the table and jump out of her skin when she saw me looking on. If it weren't for me spying her, poor William Sullivan might've had another dose."

Chapter 19

St. George's Hall

Day 3 of Trial

The morning is hazy, the low boil of the sun sharp as a needle. The air feels fetid and ready to burst. The Black Maria rolls through the portico of St. George's and pulls to a stop. A uniformed policeman, the prison matron, and the governor lead Constance through the building, up to where the courtroom sits in marble splendor.

As they near the cavernous hall that leads to the courtroom, she hears the echo of voices. They turn a corner and suddenly the way is jammed. Policemen stand with their backs to her, trying to subdue a mob. On seeing her, there's a roar. Bodies swell closer. The crowd raises angry fists, shouts obscenities. Someone throws a browned apple. It hits the floor and explodes.

"Murderer!"

"Give 'er the noose!"

She raises her hands to her ears to shut it off, shut it out.

"Stand back!" an officer cries. Another raises his billy club, prepared to use it.

The policeman with her beckons for their party to retreat, but her gaze snags on a face. She gasps. The room seems to narrow and elongate, the shrieks to muffle. For an instant, time seems to slow, and then she's jostled down a passage, pushed through another. A moment later, they enter the courtroom through a side door.

She barely registers any of it. She can't rid herself of that hair, that face. *Sandra.*

Entering the dock is like stepping onto a stage. It is an irony that she is so intensely visible, yet unseen. They think they know her, all of them, but they know nothing. She is more than what the witnesses say, more than what they think they know. She can't be defined simply by the words they utter, the lies they declare as truth. She is multifaceted, like a diamond. But they see only the parts of her that reveal the story they want to tell.

She grabs the bar in the dock and winces. Her nails are bitten down to the quick. In the darkness of her cell each night, the rip and pull of the tender flesh around her cuticles is a reprieve from the horror that she could hang. Like her veil, the gloves disguise what weeks in jail have done. Namely, carved her down to the baseness of an animal. She is all bared teeth and haunted eyes. A shadow of her former self.

Two local chemists are called by the Crown to testify to her purchase of fly papers, which Mr. Goodacre quickly links to her intent to leach of arsenic. Sir Charles counters admirably by getting both to admit arsenic from fly papers is often used by women as a cosmetic to rid the face of eruptions or lighten the skin. Both chemists profess it feasible that she purchased the fly papers for just this purpose. The barrister also gets them to admit William frequented their shops regularly for pick-me-ups, mostly in the form of liquor arsenicalis.

Small wins, but her heart remains heavy. Edward is due to

testify in the afternoon, and she worries he won't be so equally mastered.

"From time to time he took ordinary liver pills, nothing more."

All through the Crown's interrogation, Edward remained calm. His replies to the questions Goodacre put to him regarding the Valentine's Meat Juice he suggested to Nurse Hawker were perfectly composed. Goodacre must have fore-warned him about it. Edward's self-control is broken only by his disgust for her. It rolls off him in waves, smacking into her like fists.

But he's attempting to deceive the jury about William's life-style: his drug habits, his myriad of doctors, his hypochondria. When had Edward become so cunning? She always believed him a younger version of William, one with more heart, but without William's gregariousness, his maturity. Edward's Machiavellian nature must have always been there. How she underestimated him. Though he might well have framed her for William's death, she can't comprehend why he would murder his own brother. Not for the first time she wonders if William merely died by his own self-dosing. Perhaps there was no murder at all.

"In all the time you spent with your brother—including the years you ran your brokerage together—you never knew him to dose himself, even with patent medicines?" Sir Charles asks.

"No, I did not."

"Yet you helped collect over 100 samples of medicines—pills, liquids, powders, and the like, from the house in the days following your brother's death."

"We didn't know what belonged to whom." Edward glances at her, the bald scorn in his eyes another slap.

"Were you aware your brother took arsenic?"

"I wasn't aware because William did not take arsenic."

"The prescriptions you found in the dressing room didn't contain arsenic?"

"We didn't find prescriptions in the dressing room."

Sir Charles searches his notes. "Ingrid Berkshire told the court yesterday that you both found written prescriptions in the dressing room inside some hat boxes, along with several bottles."

"Well then," Edward says, brushing lint from his sleeve. "Superintendent Browne must have them."

It's a lie. There were no prescriptions among the evidence. *Which means Edward destroyed them, just as he did his letters.*

Sir Charles sighs and moves on. "You returned from America on April 25th, around the time your brother took ill. Was it customary for you to stay at Torrence House overnight?"

"Yes. William was impatient to hear how the season went in Norfolk. Every year upon my return, I stay a few days, sometimes a week, until I find suitable lodging in Aigburth for the remainder of the year until I return to America."

"Whose idea was it that William see a doctor?"

"His own."

"Did you believe at the outset of your brother's illness the accused was poisoning her husband?"

"No." Edward stares at her. "I believed at the time, as we all did, that my brother's wife was devoted to him in every way. When I learned she'd written a love letter to another man while my brother lay dying, I knew. The fly papers only confirmed it."

"In point of fact, Mr. Sullivan, on May 8th, the day you learned of the letter, Dr. Hendrickson still expected your brother to recover. He was not, technically, dying."

Edward's face is white with rage. "My brother perished three days later. To me, sir, he was dying."

Each word is the slash of a knife through her, every mention of the letter a wound cut deeper. She cannot look at him.

"Did your brother give you any indication his wife was poisoning him?"

"No. And before you ask, I'll tell you he wanted only Connie to nurse him. The poor fellow had no idea what she was doing. If it hadn't been for that bloody letter, none of us would have known."

"Yet from thenceforth, you never said a word of your suspicions to Mrs. Sullivan."

"I informed the nurse immediately after I learned of the letter that only she was to tend him. I made sure Connie gave him nothing from that point forward."

"Why didn't you inform Mrs. Sullivan she was suspected?"

"And give her a way to wiggle out of it? No. We didn't tell her because we knew what she was doing and wanted to catch her red-handed."

Liar. You were jealous another man stole my heart.

"Nurse Hawker testified you gave your brother a glass of brandy on May 10th."

"Yes. Connie came in and complained about it and saw that the nurse took it from him."

"Something a dutiful wife would do, Mr. Sullivan. Wasn't she simply following the doctor's orders?"

"By that time, William had lost a stone. Do you have any idea how badly he wanted it? I saw no reason to deny him a drink."

"He asked for it then. It wasn't your suggestion?"

Edward glares at Sir Charles, his eyes glittering with hate. "No, it wasn't my suggestion."

"Are you aware your brother vomited a half hour later?"

"If he did, it was because that woman was poisoning him." He jabs a finger at the dock. She feels everyone in the room turn and stare. She clutches the railing, her ruined fingers throbbing with pain.

"Let's turn to the bottle of meat juice you directed Nurse Hawker to use. Where was it when you mentioned it to her?"

"On the landing. As William had eaten so little in the last few days, I thought it might help sustain him. And no, I hadn't any license to do so. I was acting on common sense."

"Was it a new bottle? Had it been opened previously?"

"The seal wasn't broken. It was new."

"If you believed your sister-in-law had designs to kill your brother, what prevented her—or someone else for that matter—from adding poison to it on the landing and waiting for a nurse to give him some?"

"You're insinuating anyone could have added poison to the meat juice. Perhaps *I* did, isn't that what you're saying? But you see, Sir Charles, I prefer to consider the evidence. Connie handled that bottle, and it was later found to have half a grain of arsenic in it. She purchased arsenic before William got sick. And let's not forget her lover, Timothy Worth." Edward's eyes scrape to hers and her legs go numb. "He seems to have escaped this circus. Perhaps you'd best interrogate *him* with your blasted theories. I'll wager Connie and Worth wanted nothing more than to see William in his grave. Well, they got their way, but I'll be damned if I'm blamed for it."

Chapter 20

Torrence House

May 11, 1889

"I wish there was more we could do," Dr. Hendrickson says.

He is monstrous in the drawing room, a giant of a man who made promises that never manifested. How could he have got it so wrong? Now, in the garish dance of the gaslights that amplify their white faces, it seems a cruel trick.

Constance whole body quakes. One tug and she will fall to bits, like beads from a necklace. She doesn't recognize the woman she's become—on edge, full of self-loathing. William's imminent death doesn't fit into their carefully constructed life. He can't pass. It's too soon, too horrible. Who is she, who are the children, without him?

It's late—well after midnight. Another day has turned without them noticing, for what else is there to consider but William's end?

"Will he regain consciousness?" Edward asks, his voice cracking.

She can't look at him. She sees too much of herself in him:

his wrinkled clothing, his chaotic hair, his haunted eyes. As for Ingrid, her eyes blaze every time she looks at her.

"I think not," Dr. Hendrickson says.

The cook, Mrs. Hunt, brought in coffee a half hour ago. The silver urn sits untouched on its tray, as if it, too, waits for William to draw his last breath. She wants the burn of the black liquid down her throat to feel that she's alive but fears her hands aren't steady enough to pour.

Edward collapses on the sofa and drops his head into his hands. "How long?"

"I doubt he'll last the day," Hendrickson says. "For now, I've made him comfortable. He won't likely be lucid again. Though sometimes, in cases like this, patients rouse themselves."

"Then we're wasting time here," Ingrid says. "He may yet speak."

She means William will tell them what he apparently hasn't yet—that Constance has poisoned him. It's the only thing that explains their behavior. It's absurd, the stuff of a poorly plotted play.

Edward stands and comes at her. "You did this."

She stands her ground. "I did nothing. All you've done is deny me access to my husband in his last days. I shall never forgive you for it. Were he well enough to know what you're doing, he'd have you both thrown out."

Edward's lip curls and he raises his hand to strike her. Dr. Hendrickson lunges and grabs his arm. She waits for the doctor to say something in her defense, but there is only silence.

She raises her chin. "I'll wake the children. Unless, of course, you think they're a threat to William too?"

Edward mumbles a curse and looks away.

The light of her kerosene lamp plays tricks against the walls as she climbs the narrow stairs to the top floor. Never has she felt the house more alive.

The first door on the left, beside Anne's room, is the children's room. Their beds rest against opposite walls. On the left, Billy lies on his back, buried in blankets up to his chin. He looks so peaceful, unaffected by the tragedy playing out one flight below.

"Wake up, little one."

Billy's head rolls to one side and then the other. One eye opens. He instantly cowers from the light, a pudgy hand coming up to protect his face. "Nanny?"

She frowns. Is he frightened of Anne? "No, dearest, it's Mummy." She moves the light so he can see her better. "You must come downstairs to Papa's room."

Billy sits up and rubs his eyes. "What's wrong?"

She sets the lamp on the dresser and urges him into his robe and slippers. As she's reaching to pick up her daughter, she's jolted by a stir of air at the door.

Anne stands at the threshold. She's still dressed in her uniform.

"You scared me," Constance says. "I thought you'd be in bed." She picks up her daughter, inhaling her sweet scent. Janie murmurs and settles herself against her shoulder. "Help me with them on the stairs."

They make their way slowly down. She's careful to hold the light so they can find their footing.

In the bedroom, Nurse Hawker and Edward sit on chairs on either side of the bed. Billy runs to his father, who lies under a coverlet that's been immaculately turned down at his chest. His hair is newly brushed. She's suddenly filled with loathing. The nurse has tucked William so perfectly, he might already be lying in a coffin. For a second, she envisions demanding everyone leave the room so she can clear the medicines from every surface with the sweep of an arm, muss the sheets, and lie beside him. Pretend that William is only dozing, that these last weeks have been nothing but a bizarre dream.

The dressing-room door opens, and Ingrid emerges. Their eyes catch. *What the devil was she doing in there?* Something simmers below the surface, something Constance can't quite place and she longs to be inside Ingrid's mind, see everything from underneath her bones, her skin. Ferret out what it is she's keeping to herself.

Her thoughts are interrupted by the tug of Billy's voice. "Is he sleeping, Mummy?"

She comes to Billy's side and sets Janie down on the bed. "He is."

"Why is everyone watching him?" Billy's wide eyes take in his uncle and come to rest on the nurse.

"Papa is very sick, Billy. He will..." Her voice cracks. "He will be with the angels soon, so you and your sister must say goodbye."

Janie's hand reaches back for her. When it finds her skirts, her daughter leans against her.

"Must he go to the angels, Mummy?" Billy's eyes search hers and when he sees the tears in them, his own fill. "Can't he stay here with us?"

She shakes her head, too overcome with emotion to speak.

"Papa?" Janie says. She leans forward and pats William on the cheek with a pudgy hand. She then brings herself closer, leans in, and kisses his forehead, looking back for approbation.

Constance nods, blinking away tears. "Good girl. Billy, would you like to tell Papa goodbye?"

Her son is solemn for a moment, then he reaches out his hand and gingerly places it on top of his father's. To her surprise, William's eyes flutter open.

"Billy." Little more than a whisper. "My boy."

"Farewell, Papa," he says.

William's eyes float to Janie. "My dearest girl." He doesn't move.

He knows they're saying goodbye. He knows he's at the end.

His eyes rove the room, noting the nurse, Edward, Ingrid. "Anne."

They all turn in unison. The nanny stands in the doorway. William lifts his hand as if to bid her to him. She steps to the bed and looks troubled by her master's attention.

He wants to apologize for the way he treated her.

Anne looks down at him. "Sir," she says, bowing her head.

For a tense moment, no one moves. William stares at the girl but his gaze seems far away. When his hand drops again to the bed, the moment is over.

Constance takes the children from the room.

———

A loud shot shudders through her. She sits upright in bed, heart knocking in her chest. *Thunder, only thunder.*

The door, slightly ajar, moves on its hinges as if someone has just left the room. She's in the guest bedroom. The crowd around William made it impossible for her to get any rest in the dressing room, so she's been sleeping here.

A white flash illuminates the room for a split second, long enough for her to glimpse a cup of tea steaming on the table beside her. Thunder groans in the near distance. She takes the cup and brings it to her lips. Hot. Strong too. Mrs. Hunt forgot to add the milk. She can't blame her; the whole house is out of sorts. She takes another sip and sets it back on the table. She's been too long from William.

Outside the master bedroom, Edward and Dr. Hendrickson talk in low tones. She crosses into the sickroom. William hasn't moved. Were it not for the rise and fall of his chest, he might be a figure wrought from wax. Ingrid is seated in the chair closest to him sniffing into a handkerchief. Nurse Hawker sits in another chair on the other side of the bed.

Suddenly, Constance's stomach seizes, and she thinks she might be sick. She wants the world to stop. Each minute could be her husband's last and there are precious few of them left. She takes William's hand. It's heavy, the skin around his nails dry. There's a large mole in the shape of a heart where two veins meet. She teased him about it once, years ago. "I've heard of one wearing a heart on his sleeve, but never his hand." He'd laughed and kissed her, and they'd never spoke of it again.

Her vision blurs and her stomach rolls. The room begins to sway and suddenly Nurse Hawker is behind her.

"You should sit, Mrs. Sullivan. Take my chair."

"No." The floor undulates like the sea. "No. I'll sit here on the bed."

Seated, she feels better. The room stops pitching. The next instant, there's a lick of lightning at the window. The sun is up. Dark clouds scuttle across the sky. The trees billow like cloth. Rain pounds the roof. Another flash illuminates William's face: white, calm, unmoving. The air is charged with electricity.

It's here, the moment she's feared most. She's rehearsed how William will die, turned the details over in her mind like stones. During dark, sleepless nights, Death has hovered over her saying, *I will come. There is no avoiding me. There is no escape.*

But is it Death lingering in wait or the house itself? She no longer knows the difference.

A snarl of thunder brings her to her feet. She's sobbing now. *William, William.* Her head throbs. Her stomach lurches. She's going to be sick. She casts about the room, looking for something, someone to anchor her. Ingrid sits cold and judgmental. Edward leans against the doorjamb. The nurse speaks, but she can't hear what she's saying. The walls shuffle in, bleed. Someone tries to pin her arms and calm her.

She wants to leave this evil house. Leave it all. But she's trapped. There's no place for her now. There's nowhere to go.

The last thing she remembers before sinking to the floor is looking to the bed and seeing not William, but a skeleton lying upon the sheets. Bones and gristle, empty eye sockets, the wide grin of teeth.

Chapter 21

Torrence House

May 12, 1889

Constance awakens to a murky room. The smell of vomit fills her nostrils, sour as milk. She has a dim recollection of retching over the side of the bed. Her limbs feel weighted and bruised, as if they've been trampled upon. Beyond the door, men's voices rise and fall. Her mind floats back to her last memory: William lying still in bed, the death vigil playing out in precious minutes.

She comes to a sitting position. Is he dead? The sharp image of the skeleton lying where William should have been unfurls in her mind. Her heart thumps erratically. She must have fainted. Yes, someone carried her from the room and put her here. She lies fully dressed on the counterpane; the sheets aren't even turned down.

She swings her legs to the floor, a sob wrenching from her as it comes to her that William is dead and she's been sleeping. The knowledge of it, her selfishness, burns in her. She should have been stronger, shouldn't have succumbed to her own weakness.

Her stomach clenches as nausea rises in her throat. The smell in the room sickens her. Her skin prickles with sweat as she sinks back against the pillows. Thin wedges of light stream from the window slats to the door. The bell pull is there. She could fetch Molly. Easy enough, could she stand.

Her mouth is dry. What she would give for a glass of water. Her eyes flick to the table beside the bed. The tea is gone. She sifts through the chambers of her mind. She fell asleep after speaking with Molly. She brought her tea. Or was it one of the nurses? It tasted strong. Mrs. Hunt forgot to add the milk. And then she went to William. Ingrid and Edward were there, daggers for eyes. Had she suffered a fit? Said horrible things? She remembers the nurse. What was her name? She tried to restrain her.

She closes her eyes. She must think clearly if she's to get up from the bed. There are things to do now that William is gone. But is he? Is she a widow?

Widow. The word snags in her brain like a fly in a web.

The door bangs open. A silhouette stands in the doorway. She fights to sit up, wrestles to keep the bile from her throat. The shutters are flung wide. Sunlight pricks her eyes.

Edward comes to the bed, grimacing as he steps around the vomit. He's dressed in the same wrinkled clothes she'd seen him in last. His cravat is askew, his eyes red wounds. "Where is it?"

Her hand flutters to her throat. "What?"

"Don't play games with me." He smells of sweat and stale smoke.

"Is William dead? Please tell me, Edward."

There is a hesitancy, a particular expression—half contempt, half suspicion—that has prefaced conversations with Edward these last days. She sees it now.

"You know, Constance. You above all."

"Why do you say that?"

Edward laughs. "Oh, but you're good. Of course he's dead. He expired last evening, a good many hours after your theatric swoon."

William was still alive when she was with him. It's a tiny comfort. "Were you...was everyone there when he—"

"All but you."

Footsteps outside the room. The hall-closet door creaks open.

"What's happening?" she says. "Who's there?"

Edward leans down, nose wrinkling at the stench of her. "Tell me where the key is."

"The key?" She pulls in her chin. "The key to what?"

Edward's hands shoot to her upper arms, and he shakes her. The room blurs and dips. When he stops, she fights to keep focused on him. "You fool. The key to his desk."

She frowns. "William always kept it. I don't know." Her thoughts trip, try to make connections. Why the key? Why now? "His study. He keeps it in there."

"You'll have to do better than that."

She's certain the key is in William's study. She remembers the cuckoo clock, the peculiar way William twitched when she came into the study one day and saw him standing before it. His hand in the little space under the roof. Space enough for a key.

Ingrid's voice punches through the room. "Find it. Find all of it!"

She's in the master bedroom. Who else is there rifling through William's things? It's despicable. William so soon dead and they're clutching and clawing at the pieces of him like animals.

"Answer me, Constance." Edward's fingers dig into her arms. "Where's the key to William's desk?"

She wants to curse him, tell him to quit the room, but she hasn't the strength. She wants him gone before her stomach empties. "The cuckoo clock in the study."

Edward raises his brows. His eyes search hers, and then he turns on his heel and is gone.

The contents of William's desk were always his business, not hers. The only thing she's hidden away are Timothy's letters —and Edward's. Tucked away where no one will find them. Where no one will think to look. It's the only consolation as she leans over the side of the bed and retches.

Her secrets will remain her own.

"He said there's something that's happened near the hothouse, mistress." Molly's eyes cut sideways, shifty as a thief's. "He asked me to come fetch you straightaway."

"My husband is dead," Constance snaps from the guest bed. Her head aches. She needs a bath. "I cannot—"

"He said it were important." Molly's hands shake. Her face is as pale as her apron, and she shifts from one foot to the other. It's the shock of William's passing, the disorder in the house. But the girl should know better than to pester her at such a time. What could the gardener possibly—

"Mistress? He says it's urgent. He doesn't want the children seeing."

Whatever is she on about? "Very well." She sits up. The room tilts, but she waves Molly out.

On the landing, the stillness is broken only by the hiss of the inept gaslights. The air is thicker, colder. It's as if the house has absorbed William's death, taken him as its own.

The master bedroom door is closed. She wonders if William still lies there, a sheet covering him. Or if he's already been taken away. A wave of nausea rolls through her, and she steadies herself against the wall. She can't think of it now. She takes the stairs slowly, cursing the persistent darkness. At the bottom she hears low voices in the drawing room. Ingrid and Edward. Something else she must tend to later, throwing them out. Another roll of nausea. She staggers down the corridor toward the kitchen and exits the house through the back.

A chill in the air as she steps out, the scent of rain. The storm has wreaked havoc on the lawn: tree limbs lay like cast bones, their snatches of leaves fluttering like hands. She heads left and rounds the corner of the house. The pond's surface is smooth as a mirror. The dark presence of the orchard plucks at her nerves as she passes, its sickly-sweet scent permeating the air. Matthew, the gardener, leans on a shovel at the top of the rise. He pulls at his cap in deference as she approaches.

"Mistress." His face is lined from years of work outdoors. He smells of grass and milkweed. "I surely apologize for disturbing you. I know the master...God rest his soul."

She nods once, her patience spent. "What is it?"

"I didn't know what to do, mistress." He gestures behind him to a green tarp on the grass. "It's bad timing to be sure, and I do apologize, but I was afraid the little ones...I thought it best—"

"Yes, yes. Just show me, Matthew."

He bends and grips a corner of the tarp, then turns it over like the page of a giant book. At first, she doesn't know what she's looking at. A riot of jewel tones: sapphire blue, emerald green, golden tourmaline. And then she sees them: the royal blue eyespots at the top of the feathers. There are so many of them. It's the peacocks. They've been hacked to pieces. Heads, wings, tails, breasts severed into bits. Blood stains the grass. Flies buzz and the stink of death smacks into her. A bloodied axe rests among the ruins, its blade crimson.

"I don't know who woulda done such a thing, mistress,"

Matthew says. "But I didn't want the children coming upon them. I—"

She shuts her eyes and it's as if the ground shifts under her, as if she drifts on dark waves. She staggers back, turns, and retches in the grass.

Chapter 22

Torrence House

May 14, 1889

"Mistress. Mistress?"

Warm palms pat Constance's cheeks. A round face hovers over her.

"Hand me the smelling salts, Mary."

"Should I fetch the doctor, Mrs. Hunt?"

"Heavens, no," is the terse reply. "He's done enough for my liking."

Constance blinks and the face sharpens, the nut-brown eyes coming into focus. Mrs. Hunt's hair is pulled back, gray tendrils escaping from her bun. The cook waves something under her nose. The smell of ammonia singes her nostrils, and she brings up a hand and bats it away.

"That's right. There you are, love. Come back to us."

Mrs. Hunt's words stir something deep within her. A sob escapes, a quick mewl, before she can hold it back. She breathes, wills herself to act the woman of the house, not a bedlamite unraveling at the seams.

"Mary, go get a bucket to clean the floor. And bring a new dress for the mistress. It's high time someone took care of her." When the door snicks closed, Mrs. Hunt returns her attention to her. "Do you think you can sit up, mistress? I can bring you some beef tea if you're up to it."

She nods. Mrs. Hunt gathers the pillows and helps prop her up.

"I don't want the tea just now," Constance says, once she's settled. The pain in her head is a dull drum beating behind her eyes. Her voice is hoarse, not hers at all. She clears her throat and tries again. "I want to know...what day is it, Mrs. Hunt?"

The older woman places a glass of water in her hands. She gulps it down greedily, remembers how thirsty William had been, how he begged for water but Dr. Hendrickson saw he had none.

"It's Tuesday, mistress. The fourteenth." Mrs. Hunt pushes a curl from her brow. "Mrs. Berkshire told me you fainted a few days ago, the morning the master...you do know he passed? Please tell me she or that brother of his had the decency to tell you."

She nods, looks down at the counterpane fisted in her hands. "Edward told me. He came in demanding to know where the key to William's desk was." She would never, weeks before, have shared such a personal detail with a servant. But weeks before seem a lifetime ago and Mrs. Hunt is more family to her now than Edward ever was.

"Did he." Mrs. Hunt chews on this morsel like a piece of fat, a knowing coming into her eyes. "Well, if you don't mind me saying so, we've seen his true colors, haven't we?"

Mrs. Hunt refills the glass and hands it to her. She takes a sip, ruminating. What had William kept in his desk that was so important Edward stormed the house to find the key to it? Slowly, as her mind settles, the room reveals itself. The fire doesn't look like it's been lit since she's been sleeping here. The sheets are twisted. There's a spot of vomit on the counterpane and the room stinks of sour waste. Her gaze returns to Mrs. Hunt, and she feels laid open like a book, her pages telling a terrible truth.

"Why are you here? Where is Molly?"

A sigh escapes Mrs. Hunt. "I sent her to the grocers to make herself useful, and if I know that girl, she'll take her time doing it. I didn't realize you were in such a state, mistress. I thought she was taking care of you. She said you weren't hungry, so I assumed you were grieving. I had no idea..." She gestures to the disordered room. "That fool girl. I'll give her a tongue-lashing when she's back, I will."

"Tell me what's been happening." There's a pause, and the cook looks uncertain. "Please, Mrs. Hunt."

"Very well. You'll learn soon enough, and I'd rather you hear it from me than...the others." She lays a hand on her shoulder. "Dr. Hendrickson wouldn't sign a death certificate. He doesn't seem to know what caused the master's death." She's laying each word down like Constance might shatter if she's not careful. "They've cut him up, mistress, to find what they could. Right under this very roof."

Constance's heart races, an animal pitching itself against a cage of bones. "Cut him up. They gave William a postmortem?"

Mrs. Hunt nods. "There's more, I'm afraid. There are policemen in the house. They've been all over, poking around everywhere. The superintendent of police came and witnessed the postmortem. But that's not the worst of it. Mr. Sullivan and Mrs. Berkshire collected things about the house and gave them to the police."

"Things?"

"Evidence." Mrs. Hunt takes the glass from her, clasps both

her hands, and squeezes. "They've got it in their heads you poisoned the master."

Just as she supposed. Fear daggers in her chest and suddenly it's hard to breathe. *Poison.* She has the sudden urge to flee. Be gone from this horrid place that William will no longer fill. But she's pinned like an animal, one foot held fast in an iron cuff that will, she fears, forever hold her to this place.

"You must tell them it's nonsense," Mrs. Hunt says. "You must—"

The door swings open and a man in a black frock coat enters. Mrs. Hunt stands abruptly, holding her apron in her hands.

"Sir—"

"Mrs. Sullivan?" His eyes lock on Constance. "Wife of William Sullivan?"

"Yes."

"Sir," Mrs. Hunt repeats, "you must allow Mrs. Sullivan to dress properly. She will join you downstairs. It isn't respectable—"

"There's no time for that." He considers her, takes in the state of her clothes, her hair, the mess on the floor. "I understand you've been ill, but now that you are well—"

"She is not well, sir. She is still very weak. She hasn't had anything to eat, and—"

"Leave us, Mrs. Hunt," she says, not unkindly. "And please bring up the beef tea."

Mrs. Hunt nods and cold fear settles in her as the older woman leaves the room.

The man starts to step closer to the bed but thinks better of it, his lips curled against the stench of the vomit. "I'm Superintendent Browne. I'm going to make a statement to you. After which, you may reply. But I advise you to be careful what you say. Whatever you say may be given as evidence against you."

A movement in the doorway behind him. A uniformed police officer and Nurse Hawker stand at the threshold looking in. As if she is a circus freak to be ogled.

"Mrs. Sullivan," Browne resumes, "you are in custody on suspicion of causing the death of your husband three days ago."

Her face goes hot. She attempts to stand. With one hand on the mattress, she comes to her feet. She elongates her spine and lifts her chin. "I don't understand." The walls pitch. Her mouth waters. Bile surges in her stomach.

"Your husband's death was most unusual, Mrs. Sullivan. There are some who believe he died an unnatural death."

She works to keep herself still. She will not flinch. "I see. Am I a prisoner in my own home?"

"Until a formal charge is made, yes. In the meantime, a policeman will be placed outside the door."

The superintendent does not wait for more questions. With a curt nod, he exits the room. She falls back against the bed. The floor undulates. She can't remember the last time she's eaten. Yet the thought of food sickens her. Another movement at the door.

Ingrid enters the room. Her hair is scraped unattractively from her face, her eyes red and swollen. "You are up, I see."

Constance is surprised how quickly her fear spirals to anger. "Did you and the others find what you were looking for?" Ingrid's eyebrows rise; she appears surprised she knows this. "There are some in this house who are aligned with me, Ingrid. Not everyone is keeping secrets."

"Secrets? I think you would know more about those." Ingrid edges closer. "We bury William tomorrow. I planned everything. A shame you won't be there."

The words prick like darts. "I'm sure Superintendent Browne will make a concession in this case."

"He said he would not."

It takes everything she has to not give in to fear again, to panic. The anger is what she must hold on to. It buoys her up, keeps her above the waterline so she won't drown in sickness, in the hysteria that lurks below the surface. "If you came here to goad me, you may leave. In fact, I demand you vacate this house at once."

Ingrid cocks her head. "Don't you want to know what they found in the Valentine's Meat Juice?" A scene flickers in her head: Nurse Hawker finding her on the landing, her hand on the bottle she'd only meant to remove. Stupidly, she had jumped. As if caught out, as if she'd been doing something wrong. Stupidly, she'd remained silent. "Arsenic. That's what they found, Constance. *Arsenic.*"

Her heart shudders. "I don't...I didn't..."

Ingrid takes a step closer. "If I were you, my dear, I would protect myself. I would reach out to someone who can help. I am willing, given our closeness over the years, to help you this once. This *last* once. It is the least I can do if you will accept it."

Constance bites her lip. Ingrid waits, every muscle and sinew poised for her answer. Is she being sincere? There's no guile in her face, no artifice she can detect. Ingrid is a smart woman. She knows she's in trouble. If she distrusts her now, it's unlikely she'll get another chance. Her solicitors in New York must be notified. And her mother. She must send a telegram to France at once.

It's as if Ingrid has read her mind. "Your mother is awfully far away at present. Someone local may be of assistance. Someone close to you. Timothy Worth, perhaps?"

The silence stretches out, amplifies the hammering of her pulse. *They know of Timothy. They've found his letters.*

"Nurse," Ingrid calls, half-turning. "Fetch us some paper and a pen."

As much as she hates Ingrid at this moment, she needs her help. Timothy is her only choice. He'll come to her aid. He must. *It's only right to warn him he's caught up in this.*

Nurse Hawker waddles in and places the items in Ingrid's waiting hand. "I shall deliver your note at once," Ingrid says. "Time is of the essence."

Constance sits down on the bed and, using the side table, scribbles:

> *I am writing to you to give me assistance in my present fearful trouble. William is dead and they believe me culpable. I am in custody at Torrence House, without any of my family with me, and without aid to send even a telegram. The truth is known about us. Appearances may be against me, but before God, I swear I am innocent.*
>
> *Connie*

She folds the note, places it in the envelope, and seals it. She scratches down Timothy's address. "Thank you," she says, holding out the envelope to Ingrid.

In that drop of an instant, time seems to slow. Ingrid takes the paper and she notices what she somehow missed: Ingrid is dressed head to toe in black.

Just like that, the scales fall from her eyes. Ingrid isn't wearing lavender or gray edged with black one might wear to mourn an old friend. Her dress is unadorned. No embroidery, no flounces. Even her jewelry is black. Her veil has been pulled back from her face, but she has no doubt, once Ingrid leaves the house, she will lower it.

As a wife would. Ingrid considers herself the widow.

A brief flash of Ingrid's sister Martha telling her long ago that Ingrid was once in love with William.

Ingrid was never her friend; she was her enemy. How the older woman must hate her, how she must have hated her since the day she married William. No wonder she hired the servants. Ingrid wanted spies in the house, wanted to know the inner workings of their marriage. The reason for her being so supportive of her divorce now makes terrible sense.

Ingrid has only ever wanted William for herself and now it is too late. William is dead and she must pay.

The woman she once thought her friend turns and walks to the threshold. Without a hitch in her step, she hands the envelope to the policeman, saying to him though her eyes never leave hers, "I believe this may be of importance in the case."

Ingrid smiles, her lips pulled tight across gleaming gums.

Chapter 23

St. George's Hall

Day 5 of Trial

The prison van waits in the shadowy passageway of the portico. Constance clambers in, her limbs leaden from so much inactivity at court. The matron climbs up and seats herself opposite. They do not speak. Constance has grown used to the rides back to Walton Jail. In the quiet shadows of the wagon, she is no longer on display, a thing to be ogled or judged.

She's alarmed when, as the van begins to move, someone shouts, "Hold!"

The vehicle lurches. The door opens and Sir Charles steps in. The matron tucks herself into a corner and looks out the window. The barrister seats himself in front of her and they're off again.

"I've a message from your mother, Mrs. Sullivan." She feels a wrenching in her chest. "She misses you and asks you to be strong a bit longer. She believes you'll be acquitted."

Her eyes fill with tears, and she looks away. Her mother has said as much in her letters. Does she think her words falling from the barrister's lips will make them any truer?

"All *will* be well," Sir Charles says. He leans forward and puts his hand over her own. The gesture feels intensely personal. In the three months she's been at Walton, she's had almost no physical contact. She hadn't realized, until now, how precious it is, how much the lack of it made her an outcast, a thing to be scorned. "She has not been at court—"

"I know," she says. "I told her not to come. She'll only be hissed at."

Sir Charles leans back into the shadows of the seat cushion, his white cravat swimming in the murk. "I know there is much on your mind, Mrs. Sullivan." She can feel him assessing her, his need to soothe her nerves. "On the whole, I think things are working in our favor. Superintendent Browne's testimony of the police searches did not reflect well on the authorities. The jury must ask themselves, when it comes time to consider their ruling, why the searches were prioritized over contacting the police. Why the first things handed to Browne were your letter to Worth and those infernal fly papers. You were being set up."

"Yes," she says, her mind working. "The things found in William's hat boxes in the dressing room. He wouldn't have kept his medicine in them. It makes no sense."

"I'll wager that was Edward or Ingrid's doing," Sir Charles replies. "There's also the contradiction of the written prescriptions."

Though Ingrid had claimed seeing them, Edward had denied their existence. They weren't on the evidence list, which cemented her belief that Edward had destroyed them to make it look like William wasn't a drug fiend.

"As for the items found in your trunk in the hall closet, conveniently found by the nanny," Sir Charles continues, "the jury must see that the packet of cat poison, the morphia, and your handkerchief were placed there deliberately, just as the medicine bottles in the hat boxes were."

The cat poison, she remembers Browne stating defiantly from the witness box, contained sixty-five grams of arsenic. A tremendous amount. Justice Stevenson had glowered at her and, behind her veil, she'd glowered back. On cross-examination, Sir Charles had stressed to the superintendent that, at the time of her arrest, all he had were love letters, the fly papers, and a tale from a nurse about seeing her on the landing. None of which added up to murder. Browne had sniped, "Think what you will, but there was enough arsenic in that house to kill a regiment."

She'd clutched the rail as the courtroom buzzed, and the rest of the day had ticked by. One by one, doctors came forth on behalf of the Crown declaring William's cause of death, in their professional opinion, arsenic poisoning. His symptoms before he died—diarrhea, stomach cramping, rectal straining—were telltale signs. That little arsenic was found *in* him seemed of little importance. On cross-examination, Sir Charles had gone to battle, pointing to amounts too small to kill William—but with each new witness, inside her a terror crept: these men could hang her without any poison in William at all.

By the end of the day, the Crown had rested.

Sir Charles opened for the defense the following day. Dr. Caldwell, a pathologist for the Royal Infirmary, was the first witness. He testified at length regarding William's postmortem. His description of William's disinterment was even more gruesome. She felt a rush of horror at the hideousness that spilled from the witness box. "Coming to the head, I cut out the tongue, and, opening the skull, I removed one half of the brain." There was a roaring in her ears, and she'd come to herself when she felt pressure on her shoulder. It was the prison governor who led her to and from court each day. He bowed his head, pressed his lips together, and indicated a chair he'd placed behind her in the dock.

She took a seat but found she was unable to concentrate. Eventually, she released herself from the burden of listening, telling herself that none of this would have happened had she forgiven William for Sandra. If she hadn't wanted Timothy for her own.

Sir Charles clears his throat, shunting her back into the carriage. "Dr. Caldwell is a feather in our cap. For a man of his caliber to say it is impossible to differentiate the symptoms of dyspepsia from arsenic poisoning is significant."

She thinks back to the doctor's words. "There is no distinctive diagnostic symptom of arsenic poisoning. The diagnostic thing is finding the arsenic."

"The stomach and its contents, the intestines, the liver," Sir Charles ticks off with his fingers, "organs in which Caldwell expected to find arsenic were he poisoned, were virtually free of it."

In total, Caldwell had found less than 1/1000th of a grain in William's body. An amount so small, it couldn't be adequately measured by scientific instruments.

"This is why I have confidence you'll be acquitted, Mrs. Sullivan. Why I made it obvious in my line of questioning that—even though the superintendent *knew* your husband's postmortem results revealed insufficient amounts of arsenic to have caused death—he *still* arrested you. And following the body's disinterment two weeks later, which revealed even *less* amounts, you continued to remain behind bars."

"Because of the suspicions of those in the house," she says. "Their insistence of what I'd done."

"Yes." Sir Charles makes a waving motion with his hand. "Stuff and nonsense. In fact, Dr. Tyndale made it even more clear all this has been a waste of time. If the jury doesn't see it, I'll eat my hat."

Tyndale, a former analyst for the Home Office, was the last doctor called for the defense. After reading the reports of William's symptoms, he was certain he'd suffered from gastroenteritis, not from a deadly dose of arsenic. William, he said, would have had more vicious fits of vomiting and diarrhea if arsenic was the culprit. The doctor's belief was only strengthened by the results of the postmortem and the disinterment.

The finding of so little arsenic, Dr. Tyndale told the jury, was inconsistent with a deadly dose of it. *Yet someone added arsenic to the meat juice. Someone wanted William dead and me blamed for it.*

"Do you recall Tyndale's words to Goodacre, Mrs. Sullivan?"

Her mind spools back to the memory. The ill-humored barrister had picked at the corpulent Tyndale, gouging him with questions like stabs to the torso. "If the arsenic in William Sullivan's body didn't account for his death, why was it there?" Goodacre had pressed.

Dr. Tyndale had raised unruly brows. "For one, Dr. Hendrickson gave him, in the days leading up to his death, Fowler's solution. It's a one percent solution of arsenite potash—"

"Yes, yes. Besides the Fowler's."

Dr. Tyndale had remained silent for a moment. His dislike of being interrupted was evident in the scowl he threw Goodacre. "In my professional opinion, the small quantity of arsenic found in the body is consistent with what one would encounter in the corpse of a habitual arsenic eater. It would be only natural that some traces would be found in the corpse."

"Ah," Mr. Goodacre had countered, a gleam in his eye. "A habitual arsenic eater would have less severe vomiting and diarrhea, yes? The body would adjust to consistent doses over time?"

"Not in the case of a lethal dose, Mr. Goodacre. Give a man enough arsenic and he'll fall dead. But in this case, there was no lethal dose. Some other irritant, yes. But arsenic? Not a chance. I would bet my career on it."

"Dr. Tyndale was a superb witness," she says. "The jury seemed to believe him."

"Indeed. Goodacre's cross-examination was disastrous. And Mr. David's testimony was even more difficult for him to refute."

She thinks back to the chemical analyst, a man of short stature with ginger hair and a large, curling mustache. Blinking behind half-moon spectacles, he had regaled the jury with his knowledge of poisons. From the list Superintendent Browne supplied containing nearly one hundred and fifty items collected from Torrence House—pills, patent medicines, liquids, lotions—most had been found innocuous. Only a few revealed the presence of arsenic.

In his examinations, Mr. David found no evidence of soot or charcoal in the contents taken from William's body. Because the arsenic in the cat poison was colored in such a way, it couldn't be attributed to William's demise. It was removed from the list of possible sources of death.

"They didn't know, whoever it was in the house against me, that the cat poison would be eliminated," Constance breathes. Even now, it's difficult to wrap her mind around such wickedness.

"Yes," Sir Charles says, musing. "They placed it in your trunk to make it look like your stores of arsenic were vast. And as for the fly papers, well, Mr. David put those to rest as well."

Mr. David had found, when examining them under a microscope, the presence of colored fibers of cotton and woolen hairs.

Components, he said, of the papers themselves. His analyses of William's fluids and organs found no such elements. The fly papers, too, were struck from the list.

What remained on the analyst's list was white arsenic, in solution and solid form. He had been very specific about the difference. "Arsenic in solution is fully dissolved," he'd explained to the jury. "Solid arsenic is in clump or powder form. It is visible."

Neither Dr. Hendrickson nor Dr. Caldwell found visible arsenic in William's organs or tissues. And it wouldn't have broken down in William's body after death; it would have remained there to be discovered at the autopsy or, later, the exhumation. Evidence containing solid white arsenic was eliminated from the list.

This left one item in which arsenic was found, and in this case, it was arsenic in solution—the bottle of Valentine's Meat Juice she'd been accused of tampering with. It was curious. The solution had to have been brought in by someone and added to the bottle because there was no source bottle found in the house. Her head reels with possibilities. Had Edward planted it on the table outside the sick room with arsenic already in it or had someone added the arsenic later?

"We have, quite successfully, called into question the origin of the meat juice on the landing," Sir Charles says. "Everyone had access to it. Someone in that house was laying a trap for you, Mrs. Sullivan."

They turn a corner, the clip-clop of the horses striking in time with her heart. Evening sun slants through the window, casting the barrister in gold. Without his robe and wig, he looks younger. He is truly pleased with the progress of the case and this, more than anything, gives her hope.

"Tomorrow I shall call several gentlemen who knew your husband's medicinal habits. They'll testify he regularly and liberally dosed himself. I shall then conclude my defense. It's a good place to end. It will be firmly set in the jury's mind that William Sullivan was a chronic arsenic eater."

A memory swims before her: William tapping powder into a glass of wine. "I can't help but think," she says, her voice tremulous, "had these men come forward at the inquest..." Her throat closes and she cannot go on.

"Yes, they might've spared you the absurdity of this trial," Sir Charles says, his mouth twisting. "But it's not too late, Mrs. Sullivan. You shall go free yet."

Chapter 24

St. George's Hall

Final Day of Trial

Ill-tempered clouds scurry across the sky, their underbellies the purple-blue punch of a bruise. Constance can feel the storm building, a quickening in the air that carries the scent of rain as she travels south to St. George's in the Black Maria. Pedestrians line the streets once more to gawk. By the time the van enters the portico, thunder is groaning in the distance, white-hot lightning pulsing bright.

A short while later she enters the dock. Like chess pieces on a board, the jury takes their seats. The gallery is packed like tinned sardines. Reporters fill the front row, notepads poised.

Yesterday, a dozen friends and business associates of William's informed the jury of his chronic dosing, including strychnine and arsenic. Despite his attempts, Goodacre failed to bring doubt on their claims. The jury took it all in and looked appalled. Three had looked apologetically at her, as if to say, *A travesty. The man clearly killed himself.*

Now, all that remains are the barristers' closings and Justice

Stevenson's instructions to the jury before he dismisses them to deliberate.

Then we shall have an end to this abomination once and for all.

After a few swift inhalations from his snuff box, Sir Charles stands to address the jury. He begins with eloquent words. "The accused comes before you asking only that you grant a careful and intelligent consideration of the charge against her."

The barrister then begins his assault on the Crown's case, picking it apart seam by seam. He starts by concentrating on the Crown's failure to fix with certainty the cause of death. He reviews each doctor's analysis, taking his time to be thorough, emphasizing the contradictory opinions. "The question I have is this: can you say that you are satisfied as reasonable men beyond a reasonable doubt that this is a case of arsenic poisoning? If you are not, there is an end to this matter."

An hour passes. On he speaks, referring little to his notes. She finds her mind wandering, only to come to herself when she hears him say, "If the letter had not been read by Anne Yardley, the charge would never have been made. The lady would not sit in the dock on trial for her life."

He moves on to her unfaithfulness, saying with gravity, "Gentlemen, the lady fell. She forgot her duty to her husband."

Another hour passes. Fans flutter, the jurors shift in their seats. Sir Charles' points are flawless, his words polished to a sheen. The barrister takes his time with the sloppy way evidence was gathered, pointing out the members of the household who collected it, rather than waiting for the police to take the matter in hand.

"One hundred grains of arsenic were found in the house. The police never sought to prove any of it was acquired by the accused other than the fly papers. Mrs. Sullivan does not deny she purchased them, nor does she deny she soaked them. That she did so in plain sight of her maid is an indication not that she planned to use the arsenic therein to poison her husband, but that she used the arsenic as an ingredient in a homemade face wash for the skin.

"At first sight, it appears incriminating that Mrs. Sullivan handled the bottle of Valentine's Meat Juice on the landing. Why would she do so? I submit to you, gentlemen, that the nurse simply misunderstood what she saw. Mrs. Sullivan did not place the bottle on the landing; Edward Sullivan had already put it there. The accused *picked it up* knowing it didn't belong. When she saw that Nurse Hawker observed her, she was startled and merely returned it to the table. Why didn't she argue the bottle be removed? Why say nothing in her defense? Because Mrs. Sullivan's power had been usurped in the household, gentlemen. She knew that any explanation would fall on deaf ears.

"Furthermore, the contents of that bottle do not involve, in any way, the direct cause of William Sullivan's death. You mustn't forget that. The deceased had nothing from it. In fact, the Crown has failed to prove Mrs. Sullivan ever administered anything lethal to her husband. Not a single witness ever saw her doing so. William Sullivan never relayed to anyone he believed the accused was anything more than a loving wife he wanted near him in his time of need.

"You are not here to judge morals, gentlemen. I refer to the dark cloud that passed over the accused and rests upon her character as a wife. I entreat you not to allow your repugnance of her affair to lead you to the conclusion that because a wife has forgotten her duty to her husband, it follows that she would seek to end his life.

"And now I end as I began. If there is any doubt, any reasonable doubt, that arsenic killed William Sullivan, the second half of the charge—that the accused did willfully and feloniously administer it—does not matter. You must ask your-self, gentlemen, can you, with a satisfied conscience, say this woman is guilty? Without solid, irrevocable proof that arsenic was the agency of death, there is no case. You must therefore find Constance Sullivan innocent."

After a short recess, Goodacre stands, straightens his robe, and walks to the jury. As if on cue, the sky darkens. With his large belly protruding over legs thin as matchsticks, Goodacre begins by speaking of William as a model broker, brother, father, husband. So perfect is his character sculpted before the jury, she's surprised he mentions William's fit of rage that resulted in her black eye. But then that rage, Goodacre quickly points out, is what gave her motive to do away with him.

Goodacre describes Torrence House as a small paradise William set up for her, a utopia filled with loyal servants. As if Anne opening her letter wasn't a brazen invasion of privacy, as if Molly hadn't immediately attached a sinister intention to the fly papers. As for William's self-dosing, he disregards Ingrid's, along with other witnesses' testimony of it, saying, "What reasonable man would take medicine in quantities averse to his health?" Instead, he insists William only took prescriptions and the like on the advice of his doctors and only in the quantities prescribed.

An hour ticks by. Goodacre is composed but hasn't the flair and polish of Sir Charles. Do the jurors see it? She bites her lip and hazards a glance at the jury. She sees a frown on more than one, a sigh escape another. The energy in the room fizzles like a spent firework, the heat roasting them as the afternoon wanes.

Of the medical evidence, Goodacre attests to Dr. Hendrickson's assertion that arsenic was the cause of death.

"Who better to judge the patient's demise than the doctor who treated him?" he says. He then brings forth the testimonies of noted doctors who believed William was maliciously poisoned. "Sullivan's symptoms were precisely those of arsenic poisoning and who but the accused had motive and opportunity to see him in his grave?

"Constance Sullivan is a woman capable of duplicity. There is no question she's a fallen woman," Goodacre pokes. He launches into the 'London affair' with the zeal of a missionary denouncing infidelity. "But her affair was not enough. No, her deceits did not end there."

He shifts to William's illness and Dr. Hendrickson's initial call to the house. "It struck me as a strange conversation for the accused to have with the doctor," he says, rubbing his chin meditatively. "She wanted Dr. Hendrickson to know her husband was a man who took a mysterious powder. What was the doctor's response? 'Should anything dire occur, you can always say we spoke of it.' Was not Mrs. Sullivan laying the groundwork for her deception then?

"The night of the Sullivans' argument over Timothy Worth might have been the cornerstone of the accused's plan to silence her husband forever, gentlemen. It is always regrettable for a man to strike a woman, but the deceased had been cuckolded by his wife. He reacted in anger, and nearly threw her from their home. Was this enough to set Mrs. Sullivan on a straight path? No. While her husband lay dying some weeks later, she wrote to Worth. What words condemn her?"

He snatches up Constance's letter. "'I cannot answer your letter fully today, my darling, but relieve your mind of all fear of discovery now and in the future. William has been delirious since Sunday, and I know now that he is perfectly ignorant of everything.' Perhaps no statement lays guilt at her feet more than this one: '*He is sick unto death.*' I ask you, would you let such a woman go free?"

The glares from the gallery catch on her skin like fishhooks. She looks away only to meet the gaze of Justice Stevenson who looks for all the world as if he would like to strike her down.

The tension in the room builds as the sky glowers. A shadow moves over the skylight, darkening the paneled room to shades of brown and gray.

"Do not be distracted by Sir Charles' statement that the accused's tampering *did not involve in any way the direct cause of William Sullivan's death.* Gentlemen, such a statement is misleading. He would have you believe Mrs. Sullivan's presence— that is, her appearance on the landing with her hand on the bottle of Valentine's Meat Juice—has no import. It has every import. It places her in the vicinity of her husband's sickroom, tinkering with what the deceased might be given. Simply because Nurse Hawker put aside this bottle so that Mr. Sullivan would have none of it, does not mean there were not other times, many times perhaps, the accused went unobserved and did in fact poison her husband.

"Gentlemen, I put to you again the importance of coming to a verdict in this case that weighs all the facts—the state of the Sullivans' marriage, the witness testimony, the number of bottles and pills removed from Torrence House. In the words of Superintendent Browne, enough to kill a regiment. For a person to go about administering poison to a helpless man..." Goodacre lets the sentence hang. "It would take a certain mind. Did the accused have such a mind? Gentlemen of the jury, these are the questions you must consider."

A ripple of emotion along the gallery. A crack of thunder slices through the room. With a curt bow to the bench, Goodacre takes his seat.

Justice Stevenson turns to the jury. "Your role, gentlemen,

in the ruling of this case is an important one, one you must take seriously." He then launches into a long discussion about the charge: its meaning, its elements. "It is a necessary step, it is essential to the charge, that William Sullivan died of poison, specifically arsenic. This question you must consider at length, and it must be a foundation of a judgment unfavorable to the prisoner that he died of arsenic."

He then removes his spectacles, rubs his eyes with a thumb and forefinger, and laces his fingers together.

"It has been a long day, gentlemen. I will not belabor the points made by the counsel for the prosecution and that of the defense. However, I should like to remind you of the salient facts of this unfortunate case. An extramarital relationship took place between Mrs. Sullivan and another man. These facts have not been disputed. Shortly after, William Sullivan got sick. The accused, while tending to her husband in the sickroom, continued her liaison. We know this because of the letter she wrote to her lover while her husband lay ill.

"Now, I won't go as far as to say a murderous plot took shape in the accused's mind after the physical altercation with her husband, but we know the accused spoke to Ingrid Berkshire of divorce following the quarrel. What the accused may or may not have planned beyond that, what traitorous thoughts or acts may have been swimming in her head...well, I shall leave it to you to consider the evidence of this case—the numerous bottles containing arsenic removed from the house, for instance. What could it all have been for?"

A knot of fear pools in Constance's gut. Silence ticks heavy in the courtroom. In the snare of the judge's gaze, she is a bone picked clean. Fat raindrops pelt the windows. The wind stirs the bushes outside. She shuffles in her seat, her limbs itching to move, to be gone from this place.

"What did the accused mean by telling her lover that her

husband was 'sick unto death?' Did she forecast her husband's demise? It boggles the mind, does it not, that she might have predicted it? Perhaps she made a lucky guess. Or perhaps it wasn't a guess at all."

Out of the corner of her eye, she sees Sir Charles stiffen. Stevenson scratches at his wig and narrows his eyes as if he'd like to peer beneath her skin. Her face burns and panic spools through her.

"You must consider, gentlemen, the question of motive. When you examine that, you must remember the intrigue, that is, how the accused carried on with another man. It seems horrible to comparatively innocent people such as yourselves that a woman should plot the death of her husband in order that she might be left at liberty to follow her own degrading vices."

Each pronouncement is a stone tied to her, a weight around her neck pulling her down. Sir Charles begins to stand, then, apparently thinking better of it, remains seated.

The judge continues, speaking of William's worsening condition, his death, and the subsequent collection of evidence. He makes no mention of the searches made before the police arrived.

"Such a quantity of poisonous bottles and pills that came from the interior of that house! Gentlemen, I think there was undoubtedly a large amount of poison in which it might be said —I shall not go as far as to say purchased—Mrs. Sullivan had *access*."

Her head jerks to Sir Charles. The barrister's lips are white, his mouth set in a firm line.

"Regarding the arsenic, there is nothing to connect the deceased with it. Certainly, if Sullivan was in the habit of arsenic eating, he would not keep it in quantities which he could not possibly use."

It's a trick. He can't be making these statements. They're biased. Nonsensical. She wonders if she's dreaming, if she'll wake to find this a fantasy concocted from a hidden room in her mind. She places her fingers at her temples. Her head throbs. On Stevenson speaks, his words pulsing in and out of her mind as lightning flickers.

"...must consider not only medical questions, but you must rely on your own knowledge of human nature in determining the verdict..."

A crack of thunder and the rain begins in earnest, a vicious bucketing that pummels the windows and skylight. The court-room darkens, the dark polished wood sucking the room of light.

"...the very extraordinary thing of putting arsenic in the meat juice. Did she do it? Her silence when discovered by the nurse leads one to wonder, well, I can't find words moderate enough—"

Sir Charles is up like a shot. "My Lord—"

"Sit down, Sir Charles. I am addressing the jury."

The solicitor stands for a beat, his breathing labored, his fists clenched. His eyes flicker to the jury, as if weighing how damning it would be to contradict the judge. With a sigh, he sits.

She doesn't know how long Justice Stevenson goes on, only that when the storm has howled itself out, the silence startles her. All eyes are fixed on the dock. Sir Charles' face is unreadable. She swallows, her mouth dry.

"If the accused is guilty," Stevenson intones, "if these facts satisfy your minds, then gentlemen, we have indeed brought to light a terrible darkness—a murder founded on adultery, and carried out with a treacherous cunning rarely equaled in the annals of time."

She paces like an animal in her cell, her heartbeat slapping in her ears. She bites her nails, the tips of her fingers smarting. She stops and clutches her neck, starting when she realizes she's drawn her index finger across her throat where the noose will rest taut against her skin.

"Would you like to read a passage from the Bible, miss?" The matron slips a tiny Bible between the bars and lays it on the bench. It's battered, its cover scored and curling at the corners.

There's no time to answer. Footsteps approach. Sir Charles steps before the bars. "I attempted an audience with Justice Stevenson." His face is drawn, his pupils reduced to pinpoints. "The case must be thrown out. His closing to the jury was a mockery of justice. I cannot account for it. I've known Stevenson for years and never seen him so tendentious."

Fury spikes at the base of her stomach. She doesn't want to hear about the judge. She's heard enough from him. She wants to know what this means for her. "Attempted, you said. You attempted an audience."

"I'm sorry to say," Sir Charles says, his expression remorseful, "he refused to see me."

She closes her eyes. The room sways. She slumps down on the bench.

"Have a drink of water, miss," the matron says. She pours a cup from a pitcher and hands it through the bars. "It will make you feel better."

There isn't a thing on earth that will make her feel better. Not now.

"I'll try to see him again before the jury comes to a verdict," Sir Charles says. "I shall bring Mr. Goodacre with me. If the two of us can reason with him, he will perhaps see the wisdom of it."

He starts to go but a policeman appears before he's taken three steps. "Sir, the jury is ready. They have a verdict."

Thirty-eight minutes is all it takes for the jury to decide if she will leave the courtroom a free woman or return to Walton to hang. When she's led in, the jury is waiting. Not one meets her eye. She remains standing as Justice Stevenson pages through documents on his desk, raises his head, and regards the room over the top of his spectacles.

"Clerk of arraigns," he says, inclining his head.

The clerk rises. "Have you agreed upon your verdict, gentlemen?"

The foreman stands. "We have."

"And how do you find the prisoner, guilty or not guilty?"

"Guilty."

Cries from the gallery. She feels her legs soften, then begin to buckle. She claws the rail.

"Constance Sullivan," the clerk calls, "you have been found guilty of willful murder. Have you anything to say why the court should not pronounce sentence upon you?"

Roaring in her ears. "Everything has been against me. My Lord, I...I am not guilty of this crime." Her heart lunges in her chest. Hard, knocking thuds.

Justice Stevenson dons the black cap, placing it atop his wig. "Prisoner at the bar, I am no longer able to treat you innocent of the dreadful crime laid to your charge. The jury has convicted you, and the law leaves me no discretion."

No, it's you who convicted me. You merely instructed them to follow your orders.

"The court doth order you to be taken from hence to the place from whence you came, and from thence to the place of execution, and that you be hanged by the neck until you are dead. May the Lord have mercy upon your soul."

A dark bubble of horror opens up in her. The room is a

cacophony of voices. Reporters bolt for the doors. The gallery is a melee of moving bodies and gesticulating arms. She's shocked to see her mother there. A veil covers her face. Her body is bent, as if the weight of the verdict has withered her. A handkerchief is balled in her fist. When she screams, it is the bellow of a mother for her daughter, and it is the loudest thing in the room.

The scene tips, veers. The tunneling of her senses and then nothing.

Chapter 25

Walton Jail

August 22, 1889

She walks the prison yard, the gravel underfoot crunching like bones. The air is better here, a relief from the closed-in mustiness of her cell. The sun is already sharp as a lance. Over the wall, the vibrant greens of trees shimmer, reminding her that outside Walton, the world punches with color and life.

A sudden image: Billy and Janie running through the garden, hands held fast. With a convulsive hitch, she clears her mind. It's a trick she's learned, this sudden stowing of thoughts. Every happy memory of her life is the devil lurking to pounce.

Two matrons in caps stand together at the entrance of the enclosure alert to her every move. She doesn't eat, sleep, relieve herself, or take exercise without them looking on. They rarely speak to her and have taken on the guise of sentinels, watching her go through the motions of a reduced existence that's fast ticking away. They've been assigned to her to make sure she doesn't take her life before the gallows do.

There's no cheating the hangman's noose.

Though her limbs rebel, she forces herself to quicken her pace. She gets only a half hour each morning to walk the perimeter of the yard. Three months of confinement have left her body dormant. The exhaustion of inactivity is an irony she never could have imagined.

She casts her gaze to the desolate, low brick building that flanks the enclosure, fear pooling in her stomach. Her isolated cell, the private yard, and the building are links in a chain, as is her brown felt cape with its broad black arrow that proclaims her a condemned woman. She is set apart from the rest of Walton. She has yet to step inside the building, but she knows its interior will be the last thing she sees before her life is extinguished.

She shuts her eyes and presses her fingertips to her lids. She must blot it, like the children, from her mind. And yet. She's heard the whispers between the matrons. They're putting up the scaffold inside: cutting the cross beam, fashioning the platform, testing the trapdoor. She heard the hammering and sawing yesterday echoing across the yard and thought she'd go mad with the terror of it.

The scrape of gravel brings her attention to the gate. The prison governor, Captain Armstrong, is striding towards her with the chief matron.

"Mrs. Sullivan," he says, nodding.

His expression is shuttered as always. She suspects his years among convicts have hardened him. She's seen him only twice since the verdict: when she was first moved to the condemned cell to eke out her remaining days, and when he visited to tell her that her mother and Sir Charles are petitioning—*vehemently* was the word he used—to have her sentence reduced if not thrown out altogether.

In the morning sun, the governor's hair is lit yellow gold, his beard a few shades darker and laced with red. "I have come to tell you—" The governor twists his mouth and looks away.

The matron, a tall woman of perhaps fifty, knuckles a tear from her eye and studies her shoes.

They know. My day of execution has been set.

"Mrs. Sullivan," Armstrong says, "I want you to know that no commutation of your sentence has come down. It is my duty to tell you to prepare for death."

It surprises her how unaffected she is by his words. A few weeks ago, she would have whimpered and fainted. Walton has sunk its hooks into her. Its bleakness has found its way under her skin and seeped into her marrow. Nothing has the power to surprise her anymore.

There is a beat of silence and then they're gone.

While William rests in repose at Anfield Cemetery, she'll be buried a criminal, laid down cold and decaying, her neck broken, beneath unconsecrated earth.

That night, a loud knock startles her awake. The cell is ink black. The matrons shuffle in their chairs and whisper. Constance sits up in bed. A twist of a key in the lock, a moan of hinges, and then the door creaks open. Captain Armstrong holds a lantern aloft. Shadows pitch. A warder is behind him.

The matrons stand, smooth their hair, press their wrinkled skirts into submission. *He isn't expected. Even the matrons aren't informed when they'll come for me.*

She springs to her feet, the sudden motion bringing on vertigo.

The matrons rush to her, one on each side, and place their hands around her upper arms to settle her. She wonders if

226

they've done this before, witnessed a woman collapse before she's led to her death.

Captain Armstrong steps closer. "Pardon the intrusion, Mrs. Sullivan."

She wants to laugh. Such a time for manners, dangling on the precipice of death as she is. "There's no need to apologize." *I have succumbed to my fate, you see. The freedom I wanted will come in death.*

"All the same, it's nearly midnight. I wouldn't have come if it weren't important."

A strange choice of words. She has no time to consider them; there's a sound behind him. It's not a warder, but the chaplain, Mr. Morris. It's the sight of him that unhinges her. A man of the cloth here, in her last moments of life, come to hear her confession. She has knelt with him every day since the verdict to pray for the Home Secretary to grant a reprieve.

A wrenching sob escapes her. If it weren't for the matrons, she would fall to bits on the floor. Choke on her own misery.

The governor clears his throat and raises the lantern. His lips curl back in a smile. How can he grin at a time like this? She's never thought him a mocking man.

"It is well, Mrs. Sullivan. It is good news." The governor beams, the lantern swaying, pitching shadows against the walls. "I've only just learned by messenger come from the Home Office in London. Your sentence has been reduced. Your life is spared."

Part Two

You are abused and by some putter-on,
That will be damn'd for't; would I knew the villain.

—William Shakespeare, *A Winter's Tale*

Chapter 26

Woking Prison

Woking, England

August 1889–February 1891

Woking Prison enters her like venom. The great iron gates swing wide and Constance steps from the carriage through the yawning brick facade as though her skin is on fire. The yard smells of mud and masonry and assaults her eyes with its hard lines of wall and shadow. She wants to run, to disappear, but cannot. *This is home. This despicable pile of want is where I will die.*

In a windowless room she removes the uniform of Walton Jail to put on that of Woking. She is weighed, her height measured, her hair shorn to the scalp. The cell in which she is locked—a seven-by-four-foot space—is little more than a hole. She remains there for nine months and utters not a word, for speaking to anyone, even herself, is cause for loss of marks, and loss of marks means suspension of letters and visits, though these privileges are denied her, for now. Her single task is to sew a minimum of five shirts a week. She grows accustomed to stitching in poor light, the needlework her savior even as it ruins her eyes. She emerges from solitary confinement a shadow of herself, the insidious poison that is Woking coursing in her veins and thrumming hot.

Her probation period, lasting the next nine months, is little different. A slightly larger room, a floor of wood instead of slate, and a bigger window are a relief, but only just. She is not to speak, even though fellow convicts are near and easily seen. Her cell door is permitted open for an hour in the afternoons, but the bars remain closed. Insomnia plagues her and with it comes illness, brought on by the constant chill. In winter, the chilblains on her hands and feet fester and bleed. She suffers from pneumonia and influenza and lays for weeks in the infirmary, burning with fever, burning for her children. She wants to die.

A year and half later, the first two phases of her stay at Woking complete, she begins the third: hard labor.

March 18, 1894

The water in the sink has turned to gray sludge. Pieces of potato bob on the surface. Constance scrubs another plate of tin, dunks it in rinse water, places it in a stack she'll dry later. Behind her, seven other convicts are busy washing and drying, clearing the worktables, mopping the floor as voices near. Mr. Pennythorne, the director, advances into the room. Behind him, three visitors take in the kitchen: the still-steaming coppers, the fat stoves, the teetering piles of dirty tins. Their eyes linger, as they always do, on the convicts.

It's expected that prisoners stop their work and bow their heads when greeted by guests. She lowers her eyes and wishes them gone. When she's finished here, she'll have an hour of free time in her cell to talk quietly with her neighbors before she returns to the kitchen to begin supper preparations.

"Ah, Sullivan," Pennythorne says. He turns to a woman next to him in an exotic hat with long pink plumes. "As you can see by her uniform, she is a member of the Star Class." He gestures to the red emblem emblazoned on Constance's dress. "A first-time offender, as are all the women who work in the kitchens." His voice is full of pride, as if kitchen duty is light and pays.

He begins speaking to a man behind him in low tones and the pink-plumed woman sidles up to her. "How do you do?"

"Very well, ma'am," she replies. She studies the toes of her boots.

"Everything here is so nice and homelike!" the woman exclaims.

She lifts her eyes and tracks the woman's gaze. The windows that line one wall are filthy. On various work surfaces peels from three hundred potatoes have not yet been discarded. Gruel mars the floor in spots. The air is overwarm and stinks of animal fat. She wonders what the woman's kitchen is like, if she employs a bevy of servants who work unceasingly to keep it clean. Except for her hours asleep, she spends all but two hours a day here. Exhaustion has drained her of all vitality. She is an automaton.

"How long are you in for?" the woman asks.

"I don't know." She itches to turn away, resume her work.

"How long have you been here?"

"Five years." She feels a tightening in her chest. At her sides, her hands ball into fists. *Just go.*

"Oh, well," the woman says with a laugh and a wave of her

hand, "they must have passed quickly as busy as you are. Your remaining years will soon fly by."

Her pulse crashes in her ears as Pennythorne and his visitors exit the kitchen. She turns to the sink, skinned by the words, her heart like a raw wound bleeding.

Aylesbury Prison
Aylesbury, England

In 1895, Woking Prison closes and Constance is transferred to Aylesbury. It's kinder to the female inmates who reside within. For new prisoners, solitary confinement lasts four months instead of nine. The coarse brown bread is replaced with white, the watered-down cocoa with strong tea. She's allowed a small looking glass in her cell, a hot bath once a week. Within a few years, she's the only prisoner who served under the hardship of the old system at Woking; those who accompanied her to Aylesbury have been released into the world or are dead.

She's known for her exemplary behavior. It's she the wardens seek to calm a raving convict, she who gives hope to new arrivals who sink under the weight of prison life. With the passing of each year, her former life takes on the veneer of a long-forgotten dream and she wonders if she ever lived outside prison walls at all.

September 29, 1902

Constance sits in her cell on a log nailed perpendicularly to the floor, placed where the matrons can see her. It's the hour when prisoners are allowed to chat quietly through the bars. Whispers float through the air of the hall, but she is distracted.

She moves a finger over the tattered photographs of her children and pretends she can feel the warmth of their skin. Edward had written, once the children came of age, that Ingrid sent them to boarding schools in London, far superior, he claimed, than any Liverpool school could have offered them. She'd been shocked to hear it and angry she'd had no say in the decision. Do they languish at school missing their mother or has Ingrid poisoned them against her?

Edward had dutifully sent one picture of Billy and Janie every year the first four years, then stopped. She'd written him pleading he continue, and when that failed, she'd appealed to Ingrid. The thought burns in her that she'd had to beg for what should've been freely given to her as their mother, but her desperation had burned hotter. Ingrid, too, had failed to respond. The most recent pictures are seven years old.

Billy will be a strapping lad now. He favors her; his eyes and nose are her own. To think, her son is twenty years old. A man. And Janie, what a lovely girl she must be. Her daughter stares back at her with William's defiant mouth, his angular cheekbones. Does she still wear a bow in her hair as she does in the photograph or, at sixteen years, has she decided on another style?

Her heart fills with a familiar perplexity that eats at her: time behind bars has passed at a snail's pace but galloped to age

235

her children to near adults. By every important measure she is dead, but that they live has pulled her through the ache of solitude.

The swish of skirts brings her from her reverie. A matron stands at the bars.

"Sullivan." She thrusts a letter through the bars and Constance takes it, thanking her.

It's postmarked from Paris. She recognizes her mother's handwriting. She opens it to read,

Dearest,

I have most distressing news. I fear by the time you read this you may already know. If so, I apologize for not having reached you first, as revelations such as this are best conveyed by a gentle heart.

My dear, Sir Charles has died. He passed in his home last month after a sudden, unexpected illness. Surely, from what you conveyed to me, he did not know his demise would so soon be upon him when he visited you in March.

I beg you, do not lose hope in the petition to have your sentence reversed. All is not lost. I will do everything in my power to find a legal advocate who will address your case with the same fervor Sir Charles demonstrated these thirteen years.

I shall write to you in full later. I merely wanted to dash this off as soon as I learned the tragic news.

In sympathy,
    your loving Mama

She reads the letter again, and then a third time. Her hands shake. Sir Charles, dead. She can't believe it. Over the years, he'd written regularly to tell her of his progress on her case. He believed she ought never to have been convicted, would not have been if it weren't for Justice Stevenson's remarks to the jury. The former barrister's star had risen in the courts; he is —was—Lord Chief Justice of England, a man of great importance.

She recalls his first letter, received while she awaited the noose at Walton. She's read it so many times she can recite it by heart. *Within half an hour of the trial ending,* he'd written, *a petition against the verdict was signed by every junior barrister and every Queen's Council attending the Assize Courts that day.* Even the prosecutor, Mr. Goodacre, signed the petition. In the ensuing weeks, petitions for her release were signed by half a million American and English citizens and forwarded to the Home Office. They'd mattered not a whit; the Home Secretary, in his write-up explaining the basis for her reduced sentence, had cited only reasonable doubt as to cause of death. The judge's biased comments to the jury were never mentioned.

As for her release or retrial, there has been no development. Unlike America, in the case of capital crimes, there is no Court of Appeal in Britain to which the verdict could be referred. But Sir Charles had promised he wouldn't rest until he found a way to have her acquitted. He'd given his word.

When she isn't dreaming of her exoneration or the children, her mind works over the details of William's last days. The puzzle of who framed her and if William was truly murdered are questions that plague her more than the lack of human contact, the knowledge that she may never go free.

Beneath her skin, a fury has burned for all of it: forever hungry, never appeased.

She stands and paces, bites her thumbnail. Bitterness rises in her for the injustice of the trial, for Sir Charles' untimely death. She wants to rage, to rend her clothes, throw her tins and Bible against the bars, but a fit will only cost her marks.

She swallows down the scream in her throat, folds the letter, and places it on the shelf beside her bed.

———

The knife is long, its wooden handle worn with use. Constance has used it countless times to chop potatoes, slice carrots. She'd slid it up her sleeve after she finished the supper dishes. It astonishes her still how easy it was. The matrons hadn't counted the knives in the block. There was no need; she's a model prisoner.

It is dusk. The light in the window of her cell is going. She pulls back her sleeve. The scars at her wrist are old, but they gleam white in the semi-darkness, nevertheless. She thinks of the interminable lugging of thirty- and forty-pound vessels of tea and bread from the kitchens to the upper wards. She thinks of the unending washing of dishes that leave her hands peeling and raw. This is all her life is now, a drudgery only Sir Charles brightened with his zeal to see her charge expunged. And the children...

I can't think of them. I won't.

It's time to succumb and face the inevitable. It's just as she thought years ago at Walton when she awaited hanging. The freedom she craved, first to break free of William and his betrayal, then ultimately, to be free of a guilty verdict, had eluded her.

But freedom is here. It's always been a slice away. Now I shall have it on my own terms.

She rests the knife against her wrist, testing the elasticity of her skin. She makes a small swipe. Blood forms along the incision but it isn't enough.

She positions the knife again and cuts deep. A warm gush and with it, a bright burst of pain. The trickle becomes a river. It doesn't stop. The room spins and she falls, the clatter of the knife to the floor the last thing she remembers.

October 6, 1902

"You nearly bled to death, Sullivan," Mr. Brody says. "You're lucky one of the matrons found you."

The director sits on a chair beside her bed. His head is bald, smooth as an egg. The infirmary smells of carbolic and she closes her eyes. Jumbled memories: her mother's voice, the squeeze of a hand, the drift of lavender perfume.

"We sent for your mother. We thought you were dying."

Her mother had been there, and she hadn't known. The sad reality of it settles in her chest like a stone.

"When we saw you would recover, we sent her away, of course. You know the rules. No face-to-face visits without a screen between you. The doctor has released you from his care. You return to the kitchens tomorrow. I'm afraid your visiting privileges will be revoked for three months."

She breathes in sharply, his words searing into her like brands.

"It's a shame, Sullivan. The committee has agreed to release you in a year's time. You've paid your dues admirably, but for this unfortunate mistake. I was planning to tell you the morning after your," he gestures to her wrapped wrist, "attempt."

She stares at him. Can it be true? Dare she believe him?

"Unfortunately, the loss of marks will extend your stay another few months. I should hope the news of your release will bolster your spirits, to say the least. In any case, another attempt will land you in the dark cell. Do you understand?"

The dark cell. Underground, low-ceilinged, windowless. She's seen convicts return from it feeble and broken.

Brody stands and runs a hand over his pate. "Stay on good behavior, and you'll be out in a little over a year." He smiles fleetingly, squeezes her arm, and is gone.

She brings her knees to her chest and curls into a ball. Freedom. In a year. She can endure the kitchens that long. She must. She's ached to see her children, ached to know who plotted to put her here. Now, she has a chance at achieving both.

Chapter 27

Aylesbury Prison

February 20, 1903

Constance follows a matron into an oblong room and takes a seat before a screen. Three feet beyond is an identical screen behind which sits the shadow of a man. Between the screens a matron looks on.

"We have thirty minutes, Mr. Topp," Constance says. "Please make plain the reason for your visit."

She doesn't know him, but his letter had mentioned Sir Charles, and Topp had been emphatic she allow him to visit her.

"Thank you for agreeing to see me, Mrs. Sullivan. I was in the employ of Sir Charles Kent for a number of years. I know he came to visit you last spring to assure you of his continued persistence to overturn your case. His death must have been as much a shock to you as it was me."

Is his only aim to remind her of the friend, the champion, she has lost? "He never spoke of you," she says, her tone clipped. She narrows her eyes. She can see very little through the screen.

"I was not yet in his employ at the time of your trial. He hired me as an errand boy in 1891. He rescued me from the streets when he found me rooting through refuse bins. Sir Charles was a good man. He taught me how to read and write, and how to speak properly. He saw something in me, I suppose. I shall be forever in his debt." He pauses as if to compose himself. "After a few years, Sir Charles began to use me for other duties. He found I had a knack for going unseen—for finding people, locating lost things. Eventually, he tasked me with tailing witnesses, corroborating alibis, and the like. In most instances, no one looks twice at a Negro."

Her eyes sharpen. A row of perfect white teeth gleam through the screen. She sees now that Mr. Topp isn't in shadow; his skin is black as pitch.

"I owe my life to Sir Charles," Topp says, low. "I was gutted by his death. So sudden. Some sort of internal malady the doctors said." He pauses, collecting himself once more. "He spoke of you often, Mrs. Sullivan. Of the cases he lost, he always felt yours the most keenly. He believed to the end he wronged you terribly by not having your case thrown out."

His voice is as cultured and educated as a member of the upper class, with a hint of an accent she can't quite place. "Thank you for your kindness, Mr. Topp." She stands, annoyance simmering in her throat. He's come to pity her, nothing more.

"Please don't go until you've heard me out," Topp says in a rush. "He called me to his deathbed in his last days. We spoke of you and your case."

She sits slowly and brings a hand to her throat. "Very well."

"Sir Charles always hoped he would find a reprieve for you through legal means—writing to the Home Secretary, presenting errors in the case, working with the American government."

242

"If you know this, Mr. Topp, then you know nothing came of his labors, God rest his soul." Her voice cracks and she swallows. "I've been incarcerated almost fourteen years. I'll always have the highest regard for Sir Charles, a feeling we apparently share, but if there was a legal means, some judicial loophole that would have exonerated me, I'm certain Sir Charles would have found it."

"That was his mistake." His words surprise her. She cocks her head, curiosity filling her. "His words, Mrs. Sullivan, not mine. Sir Charles realized too late the courts weren't the way to vindicate you. He took my hand as he died..." Here again he halts, his voice hitching. "He confided to me he knew you were to be released next year. Is it true?"

She blinks. How could Sir Charles have known? A thought slides across her brain, clear as glass. Of course. As Lord Chief Justice, he was in a position to find out such information.

"He asked me to use my talents to help you, Mrs. Sullivan. That's what I'm offering. I can investigate the case, dig into witness testimonies. Find out who framed you and wanted you behind bars." Her heart gives an irregular beat, and she leans forward. "I don't speak of hastening your release, as wretched as it must be here."

"Watch yourself," the matron between them snaps. "Visitors and convicts ain't to speak of prison life." As if to make her point, the woman hocks up phlegm and spits on the ground.

"Forgive me, matron," Topp says. There is a beat of silence, then he resumes. "I speak of *after* your release, Mrs. Sullivan. I've studied your case. There were many who appear to have plotted against you. You must have had questions back then. Suspects. I will look into things. See what went on before, during, and after your trial. The answer is out there. Sir Charles wanted me to find it—for both of us to find it, Mrs. Sullivan."

"You would reopen the case?"

"No, nothing of that sort. This would be a private investigation. To learn what we can."

She sits back in her chair, despair flooding her chest. "I've nothing to pay you, Mr. Topp. Much of my mother's fortune went to trial costs. I myself have no funds for such a purpose."

"You misunderstand me, Mrs. Sullivan. Sir Charles left me money in his will. He hoped I would start investigative work with it. Set myself up in business. I'm not asking for money. I would take none were it offered."

She doesn't speak for some moments, afraid to trust the sudden lightness she feels, this newfound...what is it coursing through her veins? She is almost...yes. *Giddy*. "You would do this, for me?"

"With all due respect, Mrs. Sullivan, though I believe you are innocent, I would do it for Sir Charles. It was his dying wish."

Thoughts wrestle in her head. Over the years, her mind has grown sluggish. The senseless work, the dull acceptance of prison life, has rubbed her down. She doesn't know what to think, if she can believe him. Her fingers fly to her temples, vertigo swirling.

"I can understand your hesitancy," Topp says. "You don't know me. Your husband's death was over a decade ago. Perhaps you simply want to let the past go."

She wants to laugh. He doesn't understand. How could he? "Reflection has been my constant companion, the only one I've had these fourteen years. I am desperate to know, still, who put the arsenic in the bottle on the landing. Who put the cat poison —with sixty-five grams of arsenic in it—in my trunk to make it look like it was the place I kept the poison I was blamed for feeding William. I don't even know if my husband *was* murdered, Mr. Topp. Do you understand how that has plagued me, to be shut away and not even know *how* he died? I have slept fitfully for years, working over every detail I can remember, trying to figure out who put me here and why. So no, I have not let the past go." *Though I tried, once.* "I have lived and breathed it. And I have lived with rage. Rage for William's death, my conviction, being separated from my children. I used to think that rage had ruined me, but I think now it kept—*keeps* —me going."

"Your experience has been a tragic one, Mrs. Sullivan. I wish to offer you closure—if it's at all possible. Your memory of events would be enormously helpful to me. I am, perhaps, more familiar with your case than you realize. Forgive me for being so blunt, but it seems to me that all your life, you've trusted those around you. You naturally thought the best of everyone. It's an admirable quality, of course. But this...blind faith, if you will, is what made it easy for others to mislead you. Sir Charles thought the origin of everything—the suspicions, the lies—came from inside the house. From those closest to you."

She thinks of Torrence House: its darkness and mold, its unrelenting cheerlessness. She recalls the nightmare that has haunted so many of her nights in prison. In it, she walks Torrence's shadowed passages, opens its heavy doors, looks for its source of evil only to find her own face staring back in the mirror of every room.

"I will do everything in my power to find answers, Mrs. Sullivan."

"And if you find nothing, Mr. Topp? What then?"

The young man leans forward, his face inches from the screen. "Permit me to write and keep you informed of my progress. Naturally, I can't promise I'll find the culprit. But I pledge that I shall work as hard as I'm able to find what happened in those weeks surrounding your husband's death."

A thought dawns and her heart leaps. She places her palms

to the screen. "My children. I've had no news of them for years. I want...I *must* know how they fare."

"Consider it done, Mrs. Sullivan."

She feels it again, the lightness. But it's more than giddiness. It is joy.

She will learn what has become of Billy and Janie at last. She may even reconcile with them. And she could have answers to William's death. Upon her release, her destiny will finally be hers to govern.

But a thought niggles, nevertheless. That it is all too much to hope for. Too much to want.

August 2, 1903

Mr. Topp settles himself behind the screen. Papers rustle. He's found something important. He wouldn't have come unless he had. She's received two letters from him since his initial visit, informing her that Ingrid lives in the same house in Liverpool. Edward, too, remains in Liverpool, though he has married and has a daughter. Topp has been infuriatingly silent on the news of her children.

Her freedom is so close, she can almost taste it. In five months, she'll walk through the gates of Aylesbury and never look back. Yet she tosses at night, terrified when her last day dawns they'll tell her it was all a trick. That she must remain here until she dies.

Her hands lay white-knuckled in her lap, every muscle tense. "Have you discovered anything of Billy and Janie?" Even as she pronounces their names, shame fills her. They almost surely go by William and Jane now. They are not the cherub-faced children she remembers.

Mr. Topp smiles. "I have. It took me longer than expected. They left England and so the trail went cold for a bit. Don't frown, Mrs. Sullivan. I found them." He shuffles through some notes. "William is currently working for a mining company in British Columbia, near Vancouver. He graduated with an engineering degree from a university not far from there."

Canada. An engineer. She never would have thought. "And Janie—Jane?"

"She is living in California with a distant relative of Ingrid Berkshire's. I managed to track down a friend of your daughter's from her boarding school days and wrote her a letter, professing myself a distant relative of Jane's. Her friend was happy to share the information. Of course, there's always a bit of subterfuge required in cases like this, you understand."

He speaks on about the methods he'd used to locate Billy, but she isn't listening.

They're in North America. I need not remain in England to be near them.

"I thought to leave the good news for last, Mrs. Sullivan. I see now, of course, that would have been unkind."

"Thank you." She wipes her cheeks with her palms and snivels, mentally blasting the prison for its lack of handkerchiefs. "You've given me more happiness in the last minute than I've experienced in a decade."

"I regret to say I've no other pleasant news. What remains is quite the opposite. It pains me to impart it—"

"You mustn't spare me, Mr. Topp," she says. "I want the truth."

"Very well. I've learned some troubling details about the actions of Edward Sullivan in the days leading up to your trial. Something never mentioned in court. I thought it best to tell you face to face, rather than put it in a letter."

"Go on."

"I managed to locate your former servants—Delia Hunt, the cook, and Mary Cadwallader, the parlor maid. They were very much distressed by your husband's death and your conviction. They were anxious to help me in any way they could. They send heartfelt greetings to you and hope you are well."

"They were the only servants in the house faithful to me in the end."

"Then it will interest you to know that the day before your husband died, they saw Edward Sullivan come down the staircase with some papers. They distinctly recall hearing your husband shouting in his bedroom just before."

"I remember." The scene from so long ago flickers through her mind. William had been upset. She'd banged on the door and when Edward let her in, she discovered the brandy in William's hand.

"Your servants said Anne Yardley, whom they described as knowing and seeing everything, told them Edward was trying to get your husband to sign a will. I have in my possession a copy of that will. Your husband stated, should his death occur before he could prepare a regular and proper will and testament, he wished to leave all his worldly possessions in trust with his brother Edward Sullivan, and for his children, William Chandler Sullivan and Jane Evelyn Sullivan. Your annual provision of £125 from your family's trust would be the sole means of 'keeping you respectable.' The £2,500 in life insurance in your name, if legally possible, he wished to be invested in the said trustee, Edward. The will was witnessed by George Davidson and Earnest Smith, friend and clerk of William, respectively."

She begins to shake. She'd allowed Edward to stay at Torrence House, given him access to William, and all the while he'd plotted against her.

"The only mention of a will was in the transcript of the

coroner's inquest," Topp says. "While Edward was on the stand, he was asked by the coroner if William had one to which he replied in the affirmative. The coroner then asked if he was an executor. He said no, he was a beneficiary. Edward then said, and I quote, 'I would rather not have the will read unless it is material to the case.' This is most irregular, Mrs. Sullivan."

"That's a kind word for it," she retorts. Edward's face swims before her and she can't quite believe a man who'd said he loved her, a man who'd loved his only brother, would conspire in such a way.

"I'm afraid it gets worse. The servants were told to vacate the house the day you were arrested. Edward held an auction for the furnishings in the house on May 30th. Had you been found innocent of the charge, you would have had no furnishings to come home to upon your release. In fact, there would've been no home in which to return. Edward sold it some weeks later."

She swallows. Her mouth is suddenly dry, her tongue too big for her mouth. "William would never have left everything to Edward. I confessed to my husband earlier that day, before he signed those papers. We made peace. William forgave me of my affair."

"It's interesting that the will is written in a large, shaky hand. It had evidently not been prepared in a lawyer's office. It's dated December 10, 1888. William didn't get sick until spring the following year. Do you know why your husband would have made a will at that time?"

"No." She'd known about Sandra then, but December 1888 was before she and Timothy became involved.

"You should know probate wasn't granted until July 29th. By then, however, Edward had already sold everything in the house."

"The dates..." Her voice trails off and she is lost.

"Yes, it's odd. If your brother-in-law forced your husband to make a will on May 10th, how then is the will dated the previous year? It appears Edward backdated it to avoid suspicion."

That devil. "How much?" Her voice sounds far away. There's a buzzing in her ears.

"Your husband's personal estate, granted to Edward as legatee in trust, was £5,016. Net, after taxes, amounted to nearly £4,000."

Edward had taken it all. Robbed her of their belongings, every stick of furniture.

Before her trial ever began.

Chapter 28

The Anchor Saloon

Liverpool, England

January 25, 1904

Constance steps off a train in Lime Street Station and follows the crowd to the exit. It's startling, her ability to move, to go where she pleases after so many years behind bars. There are no querulous matrons, no debased women in uniforms, no echoes of cell doors slamming. It frightens her how wide the world is, how shut away from it she's been.

Frigid air hits her cheeks as soon as she's outside, and she pulls up sharp. Across the street St. George's Hall is lit in palatial splendor: its immense wall of sandstone, its columns of pillars too many to count. She can't bear to look at it. Eclipsed in its shadow, she feels deficient, overwhelmed by her inadequacy.

She gulps air, pedestrians shuffling by blurred at the edges, and walks on. The city torments like a ghost, like a lover.

Liverpool is itself, yet not. The bones of it—the theaters, the squares, the roads down which grand carriages roll—are the same, but it looms bigger than she remembers.

A thin layer of snow crusts the pavement. She passes people in shops and on street corners, heedless of the cold. There's a sense of bustle, of excitement. Carriages and omnibuses rush by, the icy slush on the streets doing little to dampen the sound. She's forgotten how beautiful Liverpool is in its evening clothes. But it's brighter now. Bulbs blaze as far as she can see. Electric current has replaced gaslight. The realization is a pricking dart, and she feels thinned with regret, for how much time has taken from her.

She walks another block and sags against a lamppost. Her body quakes, her breath smoking the air. Her legs aren't used to this. Fifteen years in prison have weakened her lungs, her very bones.

But she's determined to go on and so she does, head bent against the wind.

She continues west toward the docks, each block less grand than the last. Her fingers are frozen stiff inside her gloves by the time she takes the corner on to Vernon, a narrow road of poorly lit wooden store fronts and shuttered buildings. On the pavement ahead, a fire burns in a bin around which huddle gaunt-faced bodies in fingerless gloves.

Details leap, vivid and sharp, in the flicker of the flames. The pavement is pocked with holes. A shoddy boot lies by the roadside like a tossed toy. A rat sprawls in the street, innards bursting. Her thoughts flash. She carries a satchel that holds all she owns. If it's stolen, she'll have only the clothes on her back.

You can cling to this mortal coil all your life and still be plucked out of it in an instant.

She should've taken the train south to Newhaven and boarded a ship to France to see her mother. Instead, she'd

252

written a hasty letter informing her she was ill and confined to the prison infirmary. Her release from Aylesbury would be delayed as a result. A lie easily crafted, easily believed. Her mother would never understand her need for vengeance and so she has kept her plans to herself. Only Mr. Topp knows she's here. If she's garroted and left for dead, she'll have only herself to blame.

Poised and wary, she passes the group around the fire, her heart in her throat. To her astonishment, a few nod in acknowledgment. She wants to laugh at her own foolishness; they don't consider her a mark, but someone as downtrodden as themselves.

A pool of light shines through a window ahead. Suddenly, a door opens and vomits forth a man struggling to stay on his feet.

"Pardon me," he says, doffing his derby as he approaches. His belch steams the air, and he staggers away into the night.

Inside, the pub is full. A man in shirtsleeves mopping the bar waves her over. "Mrs. Holbrook?" He throws the rag over his shoulder and directs her to follow him through a side door. A low fire burns forgotten in the next room. Behind the counter, keys hang from hooks.

"Paid before you come," the publican says, rubbing his stubbled chin. "Don't get many of them." When she doesn't reply, he drops a key into her palm. "Put you in a room two floors above so's the din don't keep you up. You makes your own fire. Once the coal's burned, that's all you get the night."

With the aid of a lantern, she climbs the creaking stairs. She pauses to catch her breath halfway, one shoulder resting against the wall. At the top, the wallpaper is peeling in spots. The wooden floor is worn and sunken in the middle. She stops before the first door and turns the key.

The lantern reveals a sagging bed in a corner, a table and hearth in the other. She sets down her satchel and turns on the light. The room flickers to life. It's small and lacking adornment, but tidy, nevertheless.

She approaches the mirror over the dresser. It pains her to see the forty-one-year-old woman staring back. It's as if someone has hollowed her out, carved the very essence of her away. Her cheekbones are knife sharp. Her eyes, once a vivid violet, have hardened to a solemn gray. She removes her hat. The dull-brown hair beneath bears no hint of the reddish gold it had once been.

A needle of regret runs through her. She'd been beautiful in her youth. Now she's of the class she had, at one time, pitied—a female who's lost her bloom, whose best years are behind her.

A soft knock startles her awake. She lifts her head from the table, smooths her skirts, and opens the door.

He's taller than she imagined. She has only ever seen him seated, his face framed behind a screen. Twenty-seven or twenty-eight years of age perhaps, long-limbed, broad-shouldered. She is tiny beside him. He's dressed entirely in black and looks as nimble and stealthy as a cat.

"Mr. Topp. It's nice to meet you properly." She smiles and beckons him in.

The investigator sets a leather case to the floor and starts to take her hand, but she quickly places it behind her back. There was no contact in prison—not from the matrons, the convicts, not even the doctors if they could avoid it. She wasn't permitted to clutch her mother's hand or kiss her cheek when their visits ended. She is averse to touch now, and she hates this about herself, that prison has left its mark on her.

Without a hitch, Topp withdraws his hand and gives a bow. "I'm honored to meet you at last."

She gestures to the table, and they seat themselves, the fire casting a warm glow around them.

"You have the itinerary I sent?" Topp asks.

"Yes, thank you. You've been very thorough."

"A trick I learned from Sir Charles."

Their smiles widen at the mention of the former barrister's name. Constance pictures him here at the table looking between them, rubbing his hands together, eyes shining. *He would love this. He would be proud of Topp.*

"I could have done better for accommodation," he says, looking around the room.

"You forget where I've been. The fire is a delight. The bed will be softer than anything I've felt for years. Besides, we talked about the need to be elusive."

"The press has been tracking you?"

"The prison governor was good enough to allow me to evade them. I snuck out in a cart of potatoes. And you made arrangements for me here under my mother's maiden name, as I asked. They have no idea where I am. I imagine they'll be waiting for me in Newhaven to take the channel to my mother."

Topp smiles. "I'd have liked to have seen that, the cart bit."

"And I should have liked to have seen you rooting through rubbish when Sir Charles found you as a young lad."

They share a low chuckle, then Topp says, "I suppose we should get down to business." He takes a stack of folders from his case. "As you know, I communicated some of the principal information in my correspondence, but there's more here than what I could reasonably put in a letter. It's best you read through each folder to familiarize yourself with the contents." He pushes three folders across the table.

She gathers them up. Each folder is labeled with a name:

Edward Sullivan
Ingrid Berkshire
Anne Yardley

Topp withdraws a small pouch from his frock coat and sets it on the table. "Money for transportation, food, anything you require I haven't already taken care of."

"Thank you. I am in your debt, Mr. Topp."

"Not at all. This is what Sir Charles wanted." He pauses, considering her. "You must be tired, Mrs. Sullivan. It's been a long day for you. Get some sleep. Read the files. Tomorrow will be here before you know it. You'll need your wits about you."

It is an understatement and they both know it. A coil of anxiety knots in her stomach as she accompanies Topp to the door.

He looks back before he leaves, one hand on the knob. "Until tomorrow, when you give the devil her due."

Chapter 29

Outside Torrence House

January 26, 1904

Constance stands in front of Torrence House, her ragged breaths pluming the air. Her eyes rake every angle, every corner, every hip and curve. How often this ghastly haunt has filled the corridors of her mind. How many nights she lay dreaming, searching its rooms and finding nothing but herself in the shadows. Each time, she'd awakened damp and shaking, with the feeling that she'd only scratched the surface of the meaning. It eludes her still.

Has she imagined the evil that lived within it? Blamed it for William's betrayal, her rotting marriage?

No. It was wicked long before. And that wickedness grew to infect us all. How else to explain William's untimely death, the machinations of those in the house?

Most of the windows are boarded up, the roof is missing slates, the yard overrun with weeds. The house has returned to itself, as closed as the coffin it has always been. She hates it. She would light it afire had she a match.

A spike of fury unfurls in her chest. She picks up a rock and throws it. It lands shy of the porch. She picks up another and hurls it. Another miss. More rocks, more tries, and when stone at last meets stone, each resounding crack is a release. She throws until there's no strength left in her and she is panting from the exertion.

Livingston Avenue

Topp paces on a corner a block from Ingrid Berkshire's house. He stops when he spies Constance.

"You needn't look so abashed," she says, striding up. "My note was clear I'd meet you here."

"We agreed we would come together, Mrs. Sullivan. I worried you were already inside."

He doesn't ask her where she's been. It's none of his business and she doubts he would understand anyway. They fall in step together, their boots crunching on snow.

"What if it's been too long?" Her heart beats with fear now that she's close. "What if she can't remember?"

"Remind her of the facts."

She stops, her skirts swishing against her legs. "I want to see her alone, Mr. Topp. I don't want you to accompany me."

His brows lift. "You trust her?"

"She's an old woman now. What harm can she do? Besides, she'll not admit a thing in front of you."

He considers, his almond eyes roving her face. "Very well. But I'll be near at hand. In case you need me."

"I won't. I must do this on my own."

Topp positions himself across the street as she approaches

the door. Ingrid's house is shabbier than she remembers. The stoop lists to one side, the boards of the porch are warped. Paint is shedding its coat around the doorjamb.

A woman with gray hair pulled severely back from her face opens the door. She recognizes Ingrid instantly. There's a moment of silence while Ingrid appears to count the lines that age and hard living have carved into her like a knife to soft wood.

"Hello, Ingrid."

"What are you doing here?"

Settling the score, old friend. "I won't take much of your time. I promise."

Ingrid opens the door. Constance's nerves skitter. There's something too easy about Ingrid's willingness to admit her.

Inside, it's comfortably warm. She follows Ingrid to the sitting room where a fire burns in the hearth.

"You've come a long way." Ingrid seats herself in a chair facing the fire. "It seems you've slipped the press. Congratulations. I'm sure that took some clever maneuvering. You always were a cunning little thing." She reaches for a bottle on the table beside her and splashes mahogany-colored liquid into two small glasses. She hands one to her. "Sherry? You look as if you need it. To what do I owe the honor? I thought you'd be making your way to your mother in France by now."

She accepts the glass and takes a small sip. Instead of answering, she surveys the room. The furniture looks the same, if a little threadbare. The rug before the fire is worn, the curtains faded where the sun has leached them of color. There isn't a single photograph of Billy or Janie. There are no photographs at all. Though she has no permission to do so, she sets her glass on the table, removes her coat, and takes a seat in a chair beside Ingrid. "Shall we begin?"

Ingrid narrows her eyes. She was always a thin woman, but

age—she must be in her mid-sixties now—has wizened her. Her hands are canvassed with veins, her fingers gnarled. The skin around her neck hangs like a drape.

"You are changed," Ingrid says, her black-button eyes making their own assessment. "You've lost your youth and your beauty. And your health, too, if the papers are to be believed."

She doesn't miss the sound of triumph in Ingrid's voice. "Hard labor will do that."

Ingrid snorts. "If you've come for sympathy—"

"I have not."

"I see." While there is nothing friendly in Ingrid's bearing, curiosity glints in her eyes.

Constance takes another sip of the sweet, spicy liquid and squares her shoulders. "While you and others have, no doubt, tucked the inconvenient past away, it hasn't been so easy for me. When you learned Anne Yardley opened my letter to Timothy, why didn't you come to me?"

Ingrid gives a low chuckle. "That letter made you a liar, Constance. Someone not to be trusted, someone unfit for William. He married, you know, Timothy Worth. Lives in Scotland last I heard." The older woman sips her sherry and swallows, the sound somehow vulgar. "He fled the country after your trial and never came back. You ruined him."

A brief catch of her heart, but she won't be deterred. "I won't condone my affair, Ingrid. It was unwise; it was foolish. But Timothy was as complicit in it as I. That he paid publicly was not my doing. It was yours and Edward's." She rushes on, the sherry emboldening her. "I thought you, of all people, would understand how difficult marriage can be, having endured a divorce yourself."

Ingrid quirks a razor-sharp brow. "Are you going to bring up William's other family again? I don't believe a word of it. I never did. Frankly, I can't see William carrying on in such a fashion.

But even if it were true there was another woman, it gave you no right..." She closes her eyes for a moment before going on. "No right to betray him. God rest his soul."

"Your sister told me years ago you were once in love with William. I should have believed her. I'd have realized sooner you were *still* in love with him."

Ingrid rises and steps closer to the fire, arms crossed. "You never should have married him. He was more than two decades your senior. You knew *nothing* of how to run a house, and much less of how to please him. You were a mere *child*."

Constance works to control her breathing, pushing out her next words carefully. "I wager, if William had been interested in you, the two of you would have married long ago. Well before I came upon the scene. You were nothing more than a sister to him, if that."

Ingrid spins, her eyes jagged sparks. "How dare you come here and say such things to me."

She comes to her feet, her chest tight. "I felt the same fifteen years ago, when you had the gall to accuse me of poisoning him. But then, your scheming began long before William took ill, didn't it? You insisted on hiring the servants. I thought you were doing me a favor; I now know otherwise. You picked people who would have allegiance to you instead of me. You used them to spy for you and make trouble. Molly stole from me and—"

"Molly was my creature, yes, but she needed no directive from me to save the fly papers. She didn't like you and that was enough. Thank heaven she didn't destroy them like you asked."

"You cruel, heartless woman."

"And Anne." Ingrid's eyes gleam and she goes on as if she hasn't heard her. "You realize she didn't bump into Edward and me that day she took the letter to the post office? She came to me, *to this house*, with that letter. We helped her make a story up about Janie dropping it in the mud. Anne

261

was never upset by its contents. She was *excited*. She knew exactly what she was doing." Constance's mind slows, her thoughts careening. "We told everyone she bumped into us on the way back to Torrence House because if you knew Anne came to me about the letter, you'd have sacked her straightaway."

"I kept her on—I kept them all on—because they had your blessing. You hired them and I trusted you."

"Mmm. Curious, that. I didn't find Anne. That was William's doing."

"What?"

"William found Anne. Don't ask me where. He brought her to me and asked me not to mention it to you. I interviewed her and she seemed well suited enough. I did wonder all those years ago why he would've done. What man hires his children's nanny? But it's all in the past now."

Something niggles in Constance's mind, but she pushes it away. "Why? Why did you work to see that I was blamed for William's death? What had I ever done to you?"

"You married my William."

Oh, but she wants to strike her. The gall of the woman. "He wasn't yours to have."

"He'd have seen the light eventually. You were nothing but a pretty trinket. When you fled back to America—which I suspected you'd do after he gave you that horrid black eye—I would be there to console him."

A beat of silence as her words ring through the house. Ingrid turns to the fire.

Constance says, "After Molly showed you the fly papers and Anne came to you with my letter, Edward did the rest, or most of it, didn't he?"

"He took charge. Someone needed to in that house."

"I made my confession to William the day before he died,

Ingrid. I told him I had been unfaithful to him. I asked for his forgiveness, and he gave it."

Ingrid turns to her and laughs, her eyes flashing. "He couldn't have known what he was doing."

Constance takes a step toward the hearth. "You know I didn't poison him. I saw you leave the dressing room once when I was with him. I didn't think it important then—I still believed you and Edward to be decent people—but I realized the significance of it later. You planted the arsenic, didn't you? You and Edward. Then you made a show of finding it during the searches." Ingrid is silent, her lips pressed tight. "You can tell me now, or I'll get the police involved. I'm sure they'd be very interested in the events that transpired in that house."

Ingrid snorts. "After all these years? What makes you think they'll care?"

"I know Edward coerced William to sign a will that left everything to him." Ingrid doesn't flinch. Seconds stretch. The fire pops and whistles. "You knew," Constance breathes. "You knew what he was doing."

"Edward warned me of this. That you might come and try to get the truth from me." She raises her chin. "The will is in the past now and so is the arsenic we left in the dressing room. Ancient history like everything else. You'll never prove a thing."

"Perhaps I can't prove you planted the arsenic," Constance says. "But the will? That sort of maneuvering leaves a paper trail. Enough to interest the police."

Silence. She watches Ingrid weigh her words, decide how much, if anything, to reveal. For an instant, she wonders what she'll do if Ingrid refuses to talk.

Ingrid narrows her eyes. "What assurance do I have you won't go to the police anyway?"

"You don't. But would you risk calling my bluff?"

Ingrid sets her jaw, her eyes simmering with heat. "Very

well. We planted some of the arsenic, but not all of it. In the hat boxes. Once I knew William was dying..." Ingrid's voice breaks off. Her eyes are heavy and bloodshot from the sherry. "Once I knew I would lose him, I wanted you to pay."

"For marrying him."

"And running around with Timothy Worth as if William was *nothing*." She makes a shooing motion with her arms. "Get out."

"I'm not here about the will. There's something else."

"My attention is fraying, Constance."

"Tell me about the meat juice. Unless, of course, you'd rather answer the police about it." Ingrid had been about to pour herself another sherry but stops. Her brows raise. "The bottle of Valentine's Meat Juice on the landing. You told me there was arsenic in it before I was arrested."

Ingrid sighs and starts to leave the room. "I shall escort you—"

She steps in her path. "How did you know the bottle had arsenic in it?"

A scowl shadows Ingrid's face. "The doctor, whatever his name was. Hendrickson."

"You told me there was arsenic in it the day I was placed in custody at Torrence House. *Nine days before it was analyzed.* Hendrickson didn't know then."

For the second time, Ingrid looks uncertain. Her eyes flit around the room looking for a place to settle. "I hardly think it matters now. It was all so very long ago."

"If you knew there was arsenic in the bottle before it was tested, either someone told you it was there, or you put it there yourself."

Ingrid laughs, feigning indifference. "My dear Constance, you really have lost your mind." She steps to the hearth, picks up the poker, and prods the logs, sending up a shower of sparks.

"I won't leave until you tell me."

Ingrid turns and the smile slides from her face. "Do not threaten me."

"Is the truth a threat?"

Constance can feel the rapid pumping of her heart. And something else: a buoyed up feeling that she is alive.

"You paint yourself the innocent, Constance, but you made William the cuckold. You spent money that put him in debt. You brought scandal on the family."

"Tell me how you knew about the meat juice. Was it you who put the arsenic in it?"

Ingrid's hand comes up. To her horror, she's holding the poker. Her hands fly to Ingrid's and they struggle, the poker whizzing in the air. With all her strength, she manages to pry the iron rod from Ingrid's fingers and shove her to the floor. For a moment, the two stare at one another, their ragged breathing like twin bellows.

"Do you see what you are capable of, Constance?" Ingrid wipes a wisp of hair from her face, hand shaking.

"I do," she says. "Imagine what I'll do if you refuse to answer my question."

Ingrid's complexion turns from white to green. Her hands come up to shield her face and she cowers.

Still clutching the poker, Constance steps closer and holds the end inches from Ingrid's nose. "I'll ask one more time. Did you put arsenic in the Valentine's Meat Juice?"

"It wasn't me. I swear."

"Who then?"

Ingrid's eyes flick to the poker. "I don't know, but it was Edward who told me. Yes, I'm sure. He was the one who told me it was in the bottle."

The words settle in Constance's stomach like sediment. A beat passes. She wants to ask her about the children, but she doubts, under the circumstances, Ingrid will tell her the truth. And she wants very much to be rid of this ghastly woman and her house. She bends down, her face inches from Ingrid's. "I know about the children."

"They're not here."

"I know where they are. Ah, I see you're surprised. If I discover you or Edward mistreated them, sent them away to horrid schools or gave them anything less than the idyllic childhood they deserved, I shall be back across the Atlantic in a trice." With her free hand, she cups Ingrid's chin and squeezes, her fingers like a vice. *"And I shall bring my own poker."* She drops the rod and releases her. "God have mercy on you, Ingrid." She snatches her coat and exits the house, slamming the door.

On the pavement, the bracing air helps to calm her mind. Topp trots across the street and joins her, but stays silent, letting her ease her anger by attacking the pavement with the heels of her boots.

When they board the tram minutes later and are headed back to Liverpool, she tells Topp everything. She doesn't think she'll need him for her next encounters, but for now she's glad she has someone in which to confide.

Chapter 30

Anfield Cemetery

Liverpool, England

January 27, 1904

Constance walks the gravel path in Anfield Cemetery. Headstones sprawl like mismatched rows of teeth. Lichen spreads like a stain, spoiling engravings and finely chiseled flourishes. A marble urn lies in pieces, ruined from exposure. The granite slab she's looking for is unadorned and flush with the ground. Etched across it is one word: SULLIVAN.

There are no other markers belonging to the family. The dead are buried below in the family vault. She stoops and moves her fingers across the stone and places a single white rose on top. Its petals shiver in the wind.

For you, William. I'm sorry I've come so late.

She'd left the Anchor early this morning to avoid Topp. They'd planned for her to meet her next quarry at Newsham

Park with Topp looking on from a short distance, but she'd changed her mind. Yesterday's confrontation with Ingrid made her feel stronger, like she was reclaiming herself. If there is even a small possibility that Edward might glimpse Topp and clam up, it's too risky. She must manage on her own.

Her eyes land on a small chapel in the clearing, its steeple pointed to the sky. In summer, it must be beautiful here. Now, the frozen ground and lack of foliage are jarring. The crack of a twig startles her. A man slinks from behind the catacombs a short distance away.

Edward. She can tell by the set of his shoulders, the drooping mustache so like William's. She'd come early, expecting to have some time alone before their meeting. He's beat her to it. Which can only mean one thing: Edward has come to watch her.

Her brother-in-law isn't as lean as she remembers. She sees, as he nears, that he's past his peak; there's a softening around his middle, a paunch.

"Hello, Connie," he says, striding up. Edward sweeps his bowler from his head and dips before replacing it. His hair is still more brown than gray but wearing thin at the top. The way William's had been. It strikes her that Edward is the age William was when he died. She might be looking at her husband if it weren't for Edward's shorter height.

"Edward."

He smiles. "Quite a mysterious note. 'Meet me at William's grave.' Did you wonder if I'd show? I considered refusing you, but I confess, I was curious to see you."

Curious. White-hot fury courses through her. She's here to settle accounts, not satisfy his prying eyes.

"A strange place to meet, to be sure." Edward casts around the grounds. There is no one about. Low clouds the color of pewter scuttle across the sky. The black arteries of trees pitch in the wind.

"Is it? I was forbidden from attending William's funeral and his burial. I thought it was time I paid my respects."

Edward winces. "I forgot, after all these years."

She picks up a long branch and begins to walk the path, using the wood like a cane. Edward follows beside her, matching her strides. "That's the thing with prison, Edward. One gets stuck. I feel like my life, in many ways, is still fixed on the day William died." She can feel Edward's eyes roving over her and she wonders if he feels remorse for what he's done.

"You've changed, Connie. I don't know if I'd have known you." A beat of silence. "You are still beautiful though."

Her laugh splinters the air. She considers telling him that most of her molars were pulled in prison because of decay, that her lungs are weak from repeated bouts of pneumonia but decides against it. She doesn't want his pity. She only wants the truth.

"I've often wondered if I would ever see you again," he says with a half-smile and stops walking. He toes the frozen earth with his boot and then his eyes slide up to meet hers. "I never stopped loving you, you know."

"Yet you never visited. Not once. And you married a few years after I went to prison. Congratulations on your family."

"How—"

"Ingrid's been in touch, has she not? You're aware I know about the will."

"Quite a theory."

"The key you were looking for after William died. You were after his will, weren't you? You needed to destroy it and put in its place the one you made him sign while he lay dying, the one that made you the legatee. Never mind me and the children. We were expendable."

269

"Connie—"

"Tell me, Edward. Did you love me as you schemed to rid me and the children of our possessions, our home? Did you love me while I awaited the noose?"

Edward fusses with the sleeve of his coat and lets the words settle. "Do you plan to expose me, Connie? Is that why you've come? You won't be able to prove anything. It's my word against yours, and well..." He shrugs.

"I'm an ex-convict." The thought stings but she pushes it away. "You must've been terrified of what would happen to the brokerage if he died." Edward looks away. She steps around. She needs to see his face. "It's a shame, after all your craftiness, the brokerage collapsed. You never had much of a business mind. You've been in debt ever since. Pity, after all the money you stole. You changed the will's date, didn't you? You made him write it out—that, or you disguised your writing as his own, and he signed it hardly knowing what he was doing. He just wanted to die in peace. Then, once he signed, you changed the date to an earlier time, before he got sick, so there wouldn't be any question if William was of sound mind."

A corner of Edward's mouth lifts. "Nice conjecture on your part. I imagine you had loads of time to dream it up while you languished in prison."

"Not at all. I've only recently learned of the level of your duplicity. And I'm not the only one either." His pupils widen, but she talks on. "The question is, was it worth it? To send me to prison for the sake of £4,000? Assuming, of course, you got it all. Ingrid may have demanded a payoff to stay silent."

Edward's face burns. A muscle tenses in his jaw. "Tell me about Worth. Was *he* worth it? All that time I wanted you, begged you, and you spurned me. You made me believe William had your heart, bastard though he was. Did you love him, Worth?"

"I fancied I did. I wanted to divorce William. I know now, in the wisdom of hindsight, William would never have allowed it. And Timothy—"

Edward snorts. "Yes, we all got the lay of him. Spineless milksop. Not the knight in shining armor, was he?"

"Neither were you, Edward, and you were family." She wants the words to hit home, but they only stoke Edward's anger.

"Last I heard, Worth scuttled off to Scotland. Couldn't recover from the scandal."

Rapid-fire images: Timothy's smile, his lips on hers, the intense green of his eyes. She taught herself over the years to wrest him from her mind. To tuck the memories away in a place deep inside her. Gradually, when she allowed herself to think of Timothy, the agony of his desertion transformed into cold-hearted disappointment. He had never been the man she thought he was, the man she needed. She had loved Timothy the ideal, not Timothy the man.

The wind stirs the hair around her face, bringing her back to the moment. "You knew about William's mistress, didn't you?"

"Sandra? Yes, though I never met her." He watches her.

"You knew before we married? You knew of their children?"

He nods. "Do you hate me for it?"

"Why didn't you tell me?"

"Because it wouldn't have mattered." He looks away into the distance. "You'd have married William anyway and he'd have been livid that I told you. He'd have tossed me from the business like so much dross." He returns his gaze. "Why did you keep them?"

She doesn't know what he means at first and then it hits her. "Your letters? Vanity, I suppose."

"Ingrid thought it best we burn them. No need to embroil me in the mess, after all. 'I won't have another stain on the

Sullivan name' she said, like she was a Sullivan herself. She set them ablaze in the drawing-room hearth."

They've reached the middle of the cemetery where the paths converge. In the distance, down the lane, are the lodges that flank the main gate. The old clock tower rises towards the darkening sky. It's going to snow again; she can feel it in her bones.

"I never should have done it, Connie. Said I didn't know William medicated himself. It might have saved you."

"You did more than that, Edward. You threw away his written prescriptions, didn't you? Those alone might have made a difference. Tell me about the Valentine's Meat Juice."

"I wondered when you'd mention it. Ingrid came to me yesterday and told me everything. Did you really threaten to wallop her if she didn't give you a name? Bloody hell, Connie."

"I went to prison for fifteen years. I want the *truth*, Edward. I haven't seen my children since the day I was arrested. You stopped sending pictures of them." *They were all I had to live for, and you didn't even give me that.*

"We sent the children to good schools, Connie. They were loved. They never went without."

"Mark my words, if they tell me otherwise, I'll do what I told Ingrid. I will return for vengeance. See if I don't." She grabs his arm, her fingers biting through his coat. "Tell me the truth! Did you poison the meat juice?"

Edward glances down at her hand. "You really believe I would do that, poison my own brother? It was you and Worth I was angry at, not William."

"Do you think me a fool, Edward? You stood to gain from his death. You plotted to make it so. Who had a better motive than you?"

"I didn't poison him."

"Yet you knew the meat juice had arsenic in it before it was tested. Days before."

"I meant no harm to William, Connie. I swear. I admit to the will business, if you must know, though I'll deny it to anyone else. It's true; Ingrid and I planted arsenic in the dressing room. Not much, but enough. And I destroyed his prescriptions, but as God is my witness, I didn't think you'd hang for any of it. It was all just a way to get back at you and Worth. I was relieved when your sentence was commuted."

She steps closer, dares him to look away. "Who told you the meat juice was poisoned?"

"What difference does it make now?"

"I sent the note asking you to meet me here for a reason, Edward. I didn't want to show up on your doorstep and surprise your wife. I knew it would only cause questions you wouldn't want to answer. And you might've refused to tell me the truth with your wife in the next room." She tightens her grip on the branch, wonders if she has the strength to use it. "But perhaps I should have knocked on your door and introduced myself to the lovely Lisette. Discussed you over tea and crumpets. Does she know of your lies? The will, the planting of evidence? What would she think if she knew you sent me to the gallows to die?"

Edward's face blooms red, his rage flaring like a lit match. "Don't you go near her, don't you—" He steps closer. He looks so like William the day he struck her long ago, she fights the urge to recoil.

"Tell me, Edward, or I'll do it. I'll lie in wait until you leave the house, and then I'll knock and tell her everything."

His hand clamps so suddenly around her throat she doesn't have time to raise the branch. She doesn't move. Instead, she pins him with her eyes. *This is it*, she thinks. *He'll kill me now and no one will ever know.* Suddenly, with a grimace, Edward

273

drops his hand. "Blast it. Very well. It was that horrid nanny. The one who was always snooping about. Anne."

The name is like a slap and yet, she isn't surprised. She takes a few steps back, repulsed by Edward's nearness.

"I've told you," he says, his eyes murderous. "Now go. I don't want to see you again. If I find you've approached my wife, I'll, I'll—" His face contorts in rage again.

"Ah," she says, raising her chin. "It's the real Edward Sullivan now." She turns and heads for the front gate, swinging the branch and calling over her shoulder, "He should watch himself. Lies are dangerous things."

The Anchor Saloon

Constance walks down the street, her steps purposeful. Her mind fizzes with Edward's plotting, his lies. She casts back and realizes she remembers nothing of the tram ride. Edward's cunning has consumed her. Deep within her a fire burns and she feels in control, as if her body is her own again. There's a spring in her step, a vitality she's long missed.

She's turning into the entrance when a dark shadow presses in.

"We must speak, Mrs. Sullivan." Topp takes her elbow and leads her to a quiet corner of the saloon. He presses her into a seat and sits down across the table from her. "You met Edward Sullivan, didn't you?" His voice is calm but beneath is a steeliness that belies it.

"He admitted he and Ingrid planted arsenic in the dressing room, just as Ingrid said," she replies. "He confessed to faking the will and throwing out William's prescriptions. He might not have done if he'd seen you in the cemetery."

Her words give him pause, but only for a second. "Is that where you met, a boneyard? He could have attacked you, for heaven's sake. I don't like this, Mrs. Sullivan. You're taking unnecessary risks."

"Edward is a coward."

"If he confessed as you say, you're a danger to him. Did he admit to telling Ingrid there was arsenic in the meat juice?"

"Not exactly." Two men wander in and take seats before the hearth. She lowers her voice. "I am very close to answers. I can feel it. Your presence is a hindrance to learning the truth."

"My presence is required for your safety. That's always been the plan."

"Do you have family, Mr. Topp?"

The question surprises him. "I have a brother. But I fail to see—"

"Has he ever betrayed you? Did you ever have to fight to clear your name because of his lies?"

Topp's eyes travel over her. "You look feverish, Mrs. Sullivan. Frenzied. In such a state, I fear you will make rash decisions. You have already."

"Forgive me for my lack of decorum as I work to solve who put me in prison for fifteen years."

Topp replies as if he hasn't heard. "What is your plan, Mrs. Sullivan? What is it you wish to accomplish? My assistance was always about getting answers, yes. But for your own peace of mind, not reckless accusations that could get you killed."

"It is accusations that will lead to the truth, Mr. Topp. Either someone will admit to wrongdoing, as Edward has done already, or one of them will point the finger at the other."

Topp clasps his hands together on the table and leans forward.

"Had you allowed me to accompany you when you confronted Edward, I would have tailed him. I might have learned something. His state of mind, who he met afterwards. Now, we know nothing."

"You didn't tell me you planned to follow Edward."

"How could I have done when you evaded me this morning?" Topp says. "We've only Anne left. You cannot approach her alone. It's madness."

"Madness? You believe her the weakest suspect of the three. If that's true, I have nothing to fear." She doesn't dare tell him that Edward learned of the arsenic in the meat juice from Anne. It will only agitate him further.

"It's Anne's neighborhood I fear, Mrs. Sullivan. It isn't safe."

"You forget I lived with convicts every bit as coarse and cruel as those who live in the docks."

"You cannot go to the docks without an escort."

"I'm perfectly capable of managing myself. I've survived prison riots, Mr. Topp. Dangerous convicts."

"There were guards in prison. Those to come to your aid if violence broke out."

She leans back in her chair and laughs, a short trill that has no levity. "How naive you are. I suppose if I told you the guards were often the reason for the violence, you'd call me a liar." Topp looks away and she can see his uncertainty. "You told me once my naive belief in others, 'blind faith' you called it, was my Achilles' heel. You were right. For the first time in my life, Mr. Topp, I'm relying on *myself* to learn the truth. This is my battle, not yours." With the unfurling of the words, she feels a soundness of mind she hasn't felt for years.

The moment stretches. Topp rubs the bottom of his lip with a finger then says, "Sir Charles would be disappointed, not to mention alarmed, to see you doing this on your own. You're making a mistake, Mrs. Sullivan. I won't allow it."

A rush of anger and she knows what she must do. She hates

herself for it, but she won't have whatever information might be forthcoming from Anne stymied by Topp's presence. She'll never get to the truth. Hasn't she learned that those she believed good, those she trusted—William, Edward, Ingrid, Timothy— betrayed her in the end? While a little voice inside her says *Topp would never do that*, another one says *there's too much at stake*.

She raises her chin. "If you don't leave now, I shall tell the manager you're harassing me. I'll have you thrown out."

The words hit with the force of a punch. The tall black man who has been nothing but a friendly ally to her pushes back his chair and rises. "Very well." He straightens his frock coat, shoots his cuffs. "I shall take leave of the city at once." He bows his head with a quick jerk and exits the saloon.

Chapter 31

Chisenhale Street

Liverpool, England

January 27, 1904

C onstance rounds the corner onto Tithebarn. Carriages and wagons roll by, filling the air with the clamor of hoofs and wheels. The farther north she walks, the grittier the scene, the blacker the snow. She passes under railway bridges. Brick warehouses run entire blocks, their surfaces smothered in soot.

There's no sign of Topp. She feels a tremor of shame for her ugly words to him and squelches it.

Above, a train roars past. The breeze in its wake whips the air: a mixture of oil and coal smoke. She walks faster. The northern slums were notorious for crime, poverty, and infectious disease when she was living the high life in Aigburth. She recalls William talking of thefts and slayings around the pubs, gin palaces, and brothels along Scotland Road that attracted the lowest ruffians of the city. Nothing seems to have changed.

She's relieved to turn right onto Chisenhale, where the overhead trestles don't blot the sun. The road rises almost immediately to form a bridge over a narrow canal. Below, brown water lies partially frozen and reeks of sewage.

Terraced homes flank the street. The houses are filthy—brick facades begrimed, angles warped and listing, as if the weight of destitution is sinking them ever lower into the earth. The blind eyes of boarded-up windows stare vacantly onto a street of pocked cement where rubbish lies scattered, baking in the winter sun.

A child squats with a tin cup by the curb, packing dirty snow into it, humming to himself. An older girl with only a thin shawl for warmth sits on a stoop watching him.

"Excuse me," Constance calls. "Do you know where Anne Murrin lives?"

The girl points across the street. "Alley. Green door. She ain't in. Don't get home til 'bout now. But she won't like you waitin'."

Constance enters the alley, so thin she has to edge through sideways. It opens into a small courtyard with several doors. The flags are uneven, pitching the walls at odd angles. The air is thick with the stench of excrement coming from a pail beside a stoop. There is only one green door.

She knocks in the chance Anne is in or has a flatmate. To her surprise, the door creaks open as soon as her knuckles hit it. She pushes it farther open. To the right is a small passage. To the left, a narrow stair climbs to the next floor. An old woman is coming from a door in the passage. A baby's cry from somewhere within is silenced by a woman's shout.

"I'm looking for Anne."

The old woman's cheeks are scored leather. A milky film

covers one eye. Thin lips bow in; the crone has no teeth. She points to the top of the stairs with a filthy fingerless glove. Pungent body odor wafts to Constance and she resists the urge to shrink back.

"Thank you." She climbs the stairs. There is only one door above. She knocks once, twice. No response.

She bites her lip. She doesn't want to come back. It's another mile's walk back to the Anchor. Behind her is an alcove just dark enough to conceal herself. She steps back and waits, hopes the girl on the street and the old woman won't betray her presence.

Twenty minutes later, she hears footsteps on the stairs. A hatless woman clad in a beige coat steps onto the landing and inserts a key in the lock. As she opens the door, Constance steps forward and plants a boot over the threshold.

The woman shrieks, raises her fists, leaps back. "What the devil!"

"I won't hurt you, Anne. It *is* Anne, isn't it?"

Constance pushes the door the rest of the way open and steps inside. The room is small and filthy, crammed with a bed, table, and chair. Plaster has flaked from the walls where damp has seeped through. Clothes litter the floor. The air is heavy with the smell of damp wool and unclean linen.

Anne steps over the threshold. Time has not been kind to her. Her eyes are the haunted, sunken orbs of want and strife. Her hair, gathered into an unkempt bun, needs washing. But there's no mistaking that she is Anne. It's the same tiny face, the same blue eyes, the same thin frame. She may be seven or eight years younger than Constance, but she's just as diminished by hard living.

"What the hell do you think you're about? I'll call a rozzer if you don't hike it."

"You don't recognize me, Anne?"

The former nanny raises her chin. Recognition flickers, cold and brazen. "Prison spit you out, did it? You look a right mess."

"I could say the same of you."

"Except the prison part." Anne snickers. She kicks the door closed and shrugs off her coat, throwing it on the table. Her shirtwaist and skirt are reasonably clean, but they're threadbare at the cuffs and hem. She's all angles and points.

"I'd congratulate you on your marriage, but as you've been estranged from your husband a good while, I hardly think it appropriate," Constance says.

Anne's eyes widen just enough to show she's surprised she knows this, then she flops into the chair and looks daggers at her. "How did you find me?"

Constance looks around the room again, taking in new details. The window that looks out to the courtyard provides the only natural light. No sign of food, only empty bottles. The bed is unmade.

"Don't you go thinking I'm a doxy up Scotland Road. I have a respectable job working behind the bar at a pub."

"I don't care what you do, Anne. It's no business of mine. What I want to know is why you helped work up a case against me for a crime I didn't commit."

Anne pads her coat and pulls out a half-empty bottle of gin. Realization dawns. Now the empty bottles make sense, as do Anne's red nose and ruddy cheeks.

She twists open the bottle, hands quivering, and takes a long pull. When she sets the bottle down, one hand wraps around it, as if she's loath to part with it. "The police worked up a case against you, not me."

"You started it. The suspicions were borne by you."

"The fly papers were Molly. She's the one who saved those."

"And the letter I asked you to post? I know you went to

Ingrid after you read it. She didn't just happen upon you on the street and notice how upset you were. It never fell in the mud, did it?" Anne chuckles and takes another drink, more gulp than sip. The sharp punch of the gin drifts to her. "The world hasn't been kind to you, has it? You were never able to get a nanny position again. What woman would employ you when you'd betrayed your mistress by opening her private letter?"

"I've done well enough." Anne's eyes are already turning glassy. "Still cutting yourself, are you?"

"Not for a very long time."

"I imagine the lock-up doesn't allow much in the way of sharp things round the likes of you."

"Why did you do it?" Constance says. *Who are you? What became of sweet Anne?*

"I didn't do anything."

Constance won't be swayed. "Why did you testify about how I cut myself? You could have easily left it, but you didn't. You told the court that if I could do that to myself, I could *murder*. It was so unlike you, all of it. I believed you were devoted to me, devoted to the children."

"If you've come for a confession, you'll not get one."

"Was it the fly papers that first put the idea in your head to make it look like I killed my husband?"

"Your husband." Anne wipes her lips with the back of her hand and laughs, her shoulders moving up and down with mirth. "How you hated him."

"William was unfaithful to me. I learned he had children by another woman. I despised him at times, yes, but I didn't poison him." Anne continues to chortle, and she has the sense she's missing something. "You'll have to let me in on your joke, Anne. Fifteen years have dampened my humor."

Anne looks at her, eyes twinkling. "You still don't get it. That's the best joke of all. The fly papers, that was just good timing. But the love letter to that man, what was his name? Worth. Perfection. I couldn't have made up a better opportunity to throw suspicion on you if I'd invented it myself."

"Someone wanted to blame me for William's death, Anne. Was it Edward Sullivan? Or perhaps it was you. Perhaps it was always you and you worked Ingrid and Edward like puppets to see me hanged." Anne takes another swig of gin. Constance steps to the table. "Ingrid said when you came to her with my letter, you were excited. Why?"

"You were always high and mighty. Thought you were better than everyone else."

"I've had a chat with Edward. He said you were the one who told him there was arsenic in the meat juice before it was tested." Anne's sly grin is back and with it the odd sensation once more that she's missing something. "How did you know?"

"I'll not tell you a bloody thing." Anne rises unsteadily, her words slurred. "Get out, or else I'll tell the papers you've been here. They've been looking for you. I'll talk to reporters, tell them you've been here to harass me."

Dread pools in Constance's stomach. The papers are what frighten her most, the dogged determination of men who have nothing to lose by retrying her in the press. Ruining her life all over again. She considers Anne. She's taking another gulp, swaying on her feet. She should have taken the gin, refused to give it back until Anne spilled the truth. Now she's drunk enough to cause trouble.

"I'll find out," Constance says, walking to the door, "and when I do, perhaps it's you who'll go to prison. Wouldn't *that* be a lovely turn of events."

She slams the door behind her just as Anne's bottle hits the other side.

"Bitch! Burn in hell!"

Constance sprints down the steps to the courtyard. Behind

her, another bottle shatters against Anne's door. The old woman is sitting on a stoop, her good eye trailing her as she slips into the alley. She walks to the street. Stops.

Anne knows something. She's certain of it. Her mind has sharpened over the past few days, her thoughts razor-pointed on the events of William's death. But now she feels as if they've slipped and scattered, like marbles from a bag.

Behind her, Anne emerges from the alley, her shoes slapping the pavement. She knocks her shoulder against the corner of the building and rights herself. Oblivious to her, Anne stumbles down the street in the other direction.

Chapter 32

The Anchor Saloon

January 27, 1904

Constance's booted foot rests upon a chair, her skirts hiked to reveal her thigh. It would be easy. So easy. She catches herself in the mirror: the knife, her leg. There's something in her face, too. Her eyes dance with vitality, there is color in her cheeks. The food she's eaten since her release is already adding pounds, filling in the hollowed-out emptiness of her. The hunger for the blade, the searing want of it, withers within her. How could she have ever believed that taking pieces of her made her whole?

I am strong. I am worthy. I will know the truth.

She drops her leg, straightens her shoulders, and sends the knife across the room. It hits the wall, falls to the floor, and skitters under the bed.

She paces and bites her thumbnail. What has she accomplished tracking down the three? Edward admitted throwing away William's prescriptions to conceal his brother's medicinal habits. He forged a will, forced William to sign it, and inherited his assets. She can lay perjury, fraud, and theft at his door, though proving them is another matter.

Both Edward and Ingrid planted arsenic in the dressing room. Ingrid burned Edward's love letters to protect his reputation. Anne opened her letter to Timothy, then went straight to Ingrid. The story of dropping the letter in the mud was pure fiction, designed to expose her affair.

None confessed to adding the arsenic to the meat juice on the landing. Was it meant to kill William or incriminate her? The culprit couldn't have known she would touch it on the landing, much less that a nurse would see her do so.

The poison must have been meant for William.

Except half a grain wasn't enough to finish him. A lethal dose, according to the doctors, was somewhere between two and three grains. Was the culprit planning for more doses to come—administered by an unknowing nurse—or was the amount of a lethal dose simply unknown to him or her?

She stops suddenly, her skirts swishing. Had the three plotted *together*? Ingrid and Edward worked to bring her down, united in their jealousy—Ingrid resentful of her marriage to William, Edward envious of her affair with Timothy. But where did Anne fit in? What had motivated her to open the letter and paint her capable of murder on the witness stand?

Her heart races. She wants to scream. The answer is there, hovering just out of reach.

Where had Anne come from? A memory bubbles up, something Ingrid said yesterday. *"William found Anne. Don't ask me where. He brought her to me and asked me not to mention it to you."*

If William hired Anne without Ingrid's approval, her interview was merely a ruse. William must've known Anne before.

But where? The answer is the key to everything, she's certain. She must see Anne again, refuse to leave until she has answers. What would make her talk? She bites her lip. There must be something...and then the answer is there.

So simple. Of course.

Chisenhale Street

A smudge of clouds has moved in off the River Mersey by the time Constance hails a carriage. The temperature has dropped, and the sun is sinking fast. She tells the driver the street and sits back, her mind unsettled. She pats the bottle of gin in her coat pocket. It's her security, as good as payment in coin.

Or so she hopes.

Her thoughts focus inward. Anne's words play again in her head. *"You still don't get it. That's the best joke of all."*

What does Anne know? Whatever it is, she's been hiding it for years. Topp was right. She'd put her trust in people who'd pulled the wool over her eyes and betrayed her. She hadn't seen any of it coming until it was too late.

She sighs, her impatience flaring. Why is the carriage moving so slowly? Her eyes dart to the window. To her dismay, fog is rolling in off the river. The cab slows to a crawl. It's eerily quiet. No sounds of other traffic, just the slow plod of the horse. With every step, they're nearer the slums. No sensible pedestrian would risk being ambushed in this fog.

She recalls Topp's warning: *"It's Anne's neighborhood I fear, Mrs. Sullivan. It isn't safe."*

The carriage turns right, then lifts to cross the canal bridge.

When they're over, she tells the driver to stop and she gets out. Darkness is coming down quickly; soon there will be no light left.

"You sure you want me to leave you 'ere, miss?" The driver scans what little of the street is visible, his eyes wary.

"I'm sure."

He shrugs and moves off, swallowed by the fog. The muffled steps of the horse die away, and she's alone. She follows the pavement, moving in the direction where she knows the alley to be. The brick facade comes into view and then the alley itself. She turns sideways and crabs her way through, placing her hands on the filthy bricks to edge down it. The fog is so dense, she can barely see the other side of the courtyard. The green door is open. This time, the passage is empty.

She takes the stairs, her heart in her throat. She knocks once. Nothing. She knocks again. No response. She curses under her breath. Where had Anne run off to? To a newspaper office to alert reporters that the woman who's dodged them for days is in Liverpool? A sharp coil of fear knots in her gut. She presses her forehead against the door, her chest tight with dread.

The door gives a little with her weight. To her surprise, the knob turns. It's unlocked.

She steps into Anne's flat. Wan light streams through the courtyard window. She blinks, waits for her eyes to adjust. She can't imagine Anne would leave the door unlocked. *She must be passed out drunk.*

Her gaze flickers to the bed. The bedclothes are still in disarray. Anne isn't among them. She closes the door and starts forward, heading toward the hearth. Her boots crunch on the glass Anne shattered earlier. Wherever she went, it must have been urgent. She fled without locking the door.

She'll wait for Anne again. With the help of the gin she

brought, she will learn the truth. She positions herself beside the threshold so she'll be hidden behind the door when Anne arrives. Beside her is a small chest of drawers. Its surface is littered with clothes. Something peeks from under the pile of soiled linen: the corner of a book. Her curiosity piqued, she pulls it out. It's not a book at all, but a photograph album. Her scalp prickles. She opens it to the first page. To her dismay, it's too dark to make sense of the images.

She moves to the fireplace, album in hand. There's just enough light left to see the candle on the mantle and beside it, the box of Lucifers. She takes one out and strikes it along the hearth once, twice. On the third try, the match ignites.

In the dance of the candle flame, pictures reveal themselves. In the first, three children pose together. The eldest, a blond boy of perhaps six years, stands next to a girl with similar features seated in a chair. A large, jaunty bow perches on her head, her locks ending in fat sausage curls. On her lap, a baby lies in swaddling clothes, its tiny fists raised.

She flips the page. The three in the first photo have aged and are joined by two younger boys in knee breeches. Another photograph of the five a few years advanced, this time posing before a faux backdrop of bucolic fields. She's certain the girl in each photograph is Anne. The next page confirms it. Anne smiles for the camera in a solo shot. She's only a year or so younger than she was when she'd come to work for them. On the facing page is a family picture: the same five children with two adults that can only be their parents. A tall willowy woman in a white dress smiles beside a man with pale hair and a drooping mustache.

Her breath catches. Details shift, fall into place like the gears and levers of a clock. From the catacombs of her mind leak horrors: Billy on the landing when William lay sick, a bruise on

289

his arm, eyes round with fear. *"She said she'd put me in the Witch Orchard if I didn't behave."* His odd tantrums that had perplexed her for months. *"I hate Nanny! She lies! I shan't do a thing she says!"* The summer day long ago at the pond. Coming from the orchard, she'd seen the children playing with Anne from a distance. *Three flaxen heads spinning like tops.* Minutes later, she pulled her son from the water, saved him from certain death, while Anne looked on.

When the shock subsides, the anger arrives in its place. Her mind fizzes, her thoughts so whip-fast she sees stars. She'd trusted Anne with the children. And William. He'd allowed Anne into their home, saw to it that she was hired to look after Billy and Janie. Anne had been a ruse from the beginning. A pretender with dark motives who—

The creak of a door startles her back to the present. Boots climb the stairs.

When Anne enters, Constance is still standing at the mantle with the candle. It only takes a second for the younger woman to see what else she's holding. "I understand now," she says, low. "What did you call it? The 'best joke of all.'" She wants to run at her, scratch her eyes out. How could she have been so stupid? Anne's eyes scan the shadows. "We're alone. I didn't bring help, though I should have. I did bring this."

She places the album on the mantle and pulls out the bottle of gin. She holds it aloft, doesn't miss the hungry eyes that take it in.

"Thought you'd get me talking, did you?" Anne says. "I brought a little something too." She bends and withdraws something from her boot. When she straightens, the blade of a knife glints in the candlelight. "That's the problem with the slums. You live in hell, you learn to protect yourself." She takes a step toward her. "You were an intruder, I'll tell them. A thief ransacking my room. They won't blink an eye that I gutted you like a fish."

There's nowhere for her to go. The only way out is through Anne. With the candle in one hand, the gin in the other, she can't even defend herself. In a flash, she has an idea. It's the only thing that might work. "That's the problem with the slums," she says, "they go up like a tinderbox."

She drops the candle and flings the gin down, hard, at the same time. The bottle breaks with a satisfying crash. As Anne bends to snatch the candle, the flame flickers, then roars as it meets the spilled gin. This is her chance. She launches herself through the open door and shoots down the steps so quickly, one foot misses a step. She falls back and slides down several steps on her rear. She lands heavily at the bottom, scrambles to her feet, and tears out the door. There's no one in the courtyard, but the fog is too thick to be certain. She heads for the alley, heart knocking in her chest.

By the time she clears the passage, her breaths are coming in deep gasps, but she doesn't stop. She runs, stumbles once, sinks into cold mud, and rights herself. She hears a horse whinny, the sound of carriage wheels. As she's crossing the bridge, a man's cry punctures the night.

"Fire! Fire!"

Shouts. Running feet. The street is coming alive. Neighbors are rushing to Anne's flat. She may already be engulfed in flames.

Constance clears the bridge, her thoughts coming fast. The girl and the old woman saw her earlier. They'll be able to identify her, a stranger in the neighborhood. Anne may have tipped off reporters she's in Liverpool. She can't be caught, can't be blamed. She won't let it happen again. She'll never survive another trial, another prison sentence.

She stops to rest against a lamppost. The yellow cone of

light doesn't dispel the fog but illuminates it. It's dense, almost solid. So thick she can taste it.

And then she hears them: footsteps. Slow, measured.

"Constance." A man's voice. Husky, low.

Fear pushes through her, turning her blood to ice.

She pitches herself across the street, toward the docks. To the water.

Chapter 33

The North Docks

January 27, 1904

Vague shapes slip into focus only to melt away as she runs. Iron bridge supports and stone pilings swim into view. She's passing under railway bridges, but the vapor is so thick, she can't see the tracks above. There's no traffic, no carriages. Only a strange quiet. The fog has shuttered the world.

A hitch in her side forces her to stop, and she bends to pull air into her lungs. The footsteps behind her cease. Her pursuer is tracking her by the sound of her steps. And then, in the other direction, a faint moving glow too high for street level. A train on the overhead track. It rumbles like a beast, its *chuff chuff* quickening in her chest. She dashes down the street, under the bridge, using the train's roar to cover her steps. It passes, whistle shrieking, light hazing the vapor, and is gone.

Keeping clear of the light cast from a streetlamp, she crosses another intersection and keeps going. The smell of the sea hits like a clout: brine and decaying fish. Two stone pillars rise up. Placards announce the Victoria and Trafalgar Docks. Between them is an iron gate secured with a lock dangling from a fat metal chain.

A dead end.

She can go left or right along the road that borders the docks. Which way will her pursuer expect her to go? Left. Toward the city. Right leads to she knows not where. She considers the gate. She doesn't know what's beyond it, but her stalker is less likely to think she'll take the time to climb over it.

Constance grips the bars and hauls herself up. The gate makes a faint metallic clank. She's got to be careful, go slow enough to keep the gate from swaying. Another crossbar, another step. Her arms shake from supporting her weight and a wave of desperation passes over her. Pain sings through her muscles, her chest. She isn't strong enough. She's high enough to swing over, but what if her arms give out?

The prospect of being sliced to ribbons sends a bolt of terror through her. She bunches up her skirts and lifts her right leg over but the hem catches and rips as her leg finds footing on the other side. She's straddling the gate when she hears footsteps again. She removes her left hand from its hold on the bars and fumbles frantically with her trapped skirts. It seems an eternity before they're clear. She swings the other leg over and scrambles down. As one foot taps the pavement the gate clanks again, louder this time. She prays it's too low to reveal her presence and steps away.

A breeze from the Mersey glides in, whispering through her hair. There's a break in the fog. Two warehouses loom at right angles to each other, their upper stories disappearing into the mist. A glow wavers in the space between them.

"*Connn-staaance.*"

A chill moves through her. The way the word is stretched out. Like it's a taunt.

It sounds as if it's coming from the other side of the gate.

This time, the voice is unmistakably a woman's. Is she hearing things? Is more than one person following her?

She slips between the warehouses. The light is coming from the left, a story above perhaps. Probably attached to an upper section of the warehouse. It illuminates the fog but nothing else. The sea is straight ahead in the near distance: she can smell the salt, hear the faint crash of waves against the pier. Lights glow there. Probably the lanterns along the pier's edge to warn ships of the approach of the docks.

Her limbs shake. The sea air is freezing. She's wondering where to hide when a metallic clank slices through the fog, followed by the scrape of heels landing on pavement.

She bolts a few steps forward and then lurches back, arms windmilling for balance. She's at the lip of one of the enclosed pools where boats anchor to unload cargo. In her panic, she'd almost stepped off the edge into the icy water.

Footsteps. The air is charged; she can feel it. She spins.

Anne emerges from the mist, knife poised.

Tempus omnia revelat. Time reveals all.

"You, all this time," Constance breathes. "You're his daughter."

Anne's hair hangs damp against her cheeks. Her face is leached of color. But it's her eyes that alarm her most: two dark voids.

Anne advances one step, then another. "We were a family. He was everything to us. Everything. And then he married *you*. When Mama found out, she didn't get out of bed for months. He tried to make it up to her, like he always did." Anne scrapes hair from her eyes. Her voice is matter-of-fact, betraying no emotion. "He gave her money, spoiled us, told us how much we meant to him and that you were 'for show,' a way to bring up his social standing for his business. He got Mama with child again. It was the last thing she needed. Another mouth to feed."

She envisions a bawling baby, hears William tell her he didn't know if Sandra's children were his own. "You never left Liverpool."

"No. Mama agreed to move so you wouldn't find us on Old Hall Street, but only because he gave her twenty-five pounds for the trouble."

Constance takes a careful step back. The toe of her boot drops over the edge of the pool, and she sidesteps a few paces, careful to stay clear of the water.

"Move like that again and I'll stick you," Anne snaps, then her thoughts turn inward. "Papa stopped supporting us regularly soon after he married you. Do you know how difficult it was for Mama to put food on the table? We had no help, no other family. A hundred pounds a year was all she asked, but he always had an excuse: the cotton season was poor, the market was down, he had expenses. The money was coming, it was always coming, we just had to be patient. I went to Torrence House one day to see for myself where he lived. I saw the house, the grounds. You wanted for *nothing*."

Anne swipes the air with the knife, and she flinches. "I told him if he wouldn't give us money, I'd go to you. You should have seen his face. He told me your brats needed a nanny and he would give me the job if I kept my mouth shut."

Bile chases up her throat. She swallows it down, resisting the urge to be sick. "He brought you to Ingrid."

"I told her I was Anne Yardley, not Anne Sullivan. She hired me without a single reference because Papa wanted it so. Then I met you and made sure you trusted me." Anne bats her lashes, affects a look of innocence. "*Yes, Mrs. Sullivan. Anything you want, Mrs. Sullivan.*" She laughs, the sound cruel in her throat. "You fell for it all."

Constance begins to shake. "That day at the pond—"

"My torture of Billy started long before that. I told him he was good for nothing, that he was simple. I filled his mind with the most horrid stories about the house. He thought it was haunted, did you know? I demanded he do my work—clean up after our meals, scrub the nursery, wash my linens—and if he refused, I'd stick him with pins. Smart boy. After a few stabs, he learned."

Constance fizzes with rage. She wants to run at Anne, but her adversary is stronger. To act is to die.

"Of course, part of the game was that he was never to tell anyone, because if he did the witch in the orchard would eat him." Anne's expression sobers. "With Janie, it was different. I grew up with only brothers. They treated me awful—always playing pranks, frightening me. Once I grew of age, they told me I could help the family by earning wages on my back, so to speak. That if I didn't have so much *pride*, I could feed us. No, I was good to Janie. She was special."

"You meant to drown him," Constance says, eyes welling. "My boy."

Anne licks dry lips and shrugs. "I told him to fetch his sailboat, or else I'd smash it to pieces. If he drowned, what of it? I certainly couldn't have saved him. I don't swim. Of course, you came and spoiled *everything*."

"William resented you after that." She remembers his moods, the way he bristled in front of Anne, and feels ashamed. *I missed what was staring me in the face. I misjudged them all —Ingrid, Edward, Anne. I believed them good.*

"Papa couldn't sack me because he knew I'd go to you. But he told me if anything like it ever happened again, he'd kill me and have no regrets." Another limp shrug. "I had other ways to take my revenge. I stole from you, you know. Jewelry, ribbons, combs. Nothing too flashy. I didn't want you or Molly to get suspicious."

"Anne," she says, her palms splaying the air. "I never would have married your papa had I known about your family. Please believe—"

"You didn't leave him when you learned of us."

"He told me he wasn't married to your mother."

Anne's eyes narrow. "What difference does a piece of paper make saying two people are wed? They were married in every way but that one and the paper, he said, mattered least of all."

She feels queasy, flattened by disgust. William and Sandra had never married, but William had manipulated Sandra and the children for years. A legal union might have protected Sandra from desertion. She could've appealed to the courts. "Why did your mother never come to me?"

"You think Papa would've given her another shilling if she did? If it weren't for you, we'd have had a life. We wouldn't have *starved*."

The knife is inches from her upraised palms. She senses Anne's story is winding down. When she's said all she has to say, she will kill her and no one will ever know. *Keep her talking*. "You poisoned the meat juice." One tiny side-step, another.

Anne follows apace. "When Papa got sick, I wanted to poison him—give him more of what he was already taking to speed things up and finish him. I was tired of his promises. Then Molly showed me the fly papers. She wondered if you were soaking them for the arsenic."

"Not for the reason the two of you thought."

"Oh, I never thought you were poisoning Papa. I only wanted it to *look* like you were. When you asked me to mail the letter that day, I saw it was addressed to the same man you and Papa had quarreled over."

"And you used it to bring suspicion on me. You wanted my affair to look like it was motive for me to murder him."

"But it wasn't murder, was it? Papa poisoned himself. *For*

298

years. Sooner or later, arsenic or the strychnine were going to do him in. He died by his own ends."

Slow suicide. Hadn't she thought the same over the course of their marriage?

"It was all so easy," Anne snarls. "Ingrid and Edward needed no convincing of your guilt, not after I showed them your letter to Worth. I added common Fowler's solution to the bottle of Valentine's on the landing. Available at any chemist." Anne juts out her chin and Constance sees a flash of the young girl she'd once been, a girl who'd appeared like she only wanted to please. "The nurse seeing you pick it up off the table was a stroke of luck. You do realize things would've been better if you'd died with him?"

Constance's heart scuds. "What?"

"The tea. Don't you remember?"

A memory swims. Constance is once again in the guest room. A flicker of lightning, a cup steaming beside the bed. She sees herself take the tea, taste it. It was too strong. Mrs. Hunt forgot to add the milk. She was ill after. Yes, she'd fainted at William's bedside and laid for days, gripped with nausea and diarrhea. "You poisoned me," she breathes.

"I wanted you to die with him. I added arsenic to your cup and carried it to the guest room. But you didn't drink all of it and I didn't get another opportunity. I was quite beside myself. I vented my rage on the peacocks."

Anne grins and Constance sees again the hacked bodies of the birds, the bloodied axe, and wants to retch.

"I let things take their course after that. My attempt to poison you to death failed, but Papa was dead, and you were already suspected of taking his life. I put the packet of arsenic for cats in your trunk, along with the morphia and your hand-kerchief. Then I pretended to find them in the closet. The day you were found guilty was one of the best of my life." Anne's smile fades and her mouth hardens. "You should never have come back."

Anne lunges. Constance screams and pitches right, just missing the blade. She moves in the direction of the warehouse, away from the water. She doesn't dare turn and run. If she loses Anne in the fog, she could come at her from anywhere.

Anne pitches forward again and the knife comes a hair's breadth from her neck. She screams again and veers, darting left. She runs another ten feet or so, then trips over a pile of wooden planks, landing on her side.

Anne steps to her and raises the knife. "Your time is up, Constance."

Constance's heart scampers in her ribcage, beats a wild pulse in her ears. She's on her back now. She braces herself for the fall of the knife, hopes it's quick and clean.

"Enough, Anne."

The voice startles them both. A woman steps from the fog.

She is tall, thin, and hatless, her hair streaming from its bun. Even in the hazy murk, it's evident she isn't young. Mid-sixties perhaps. It's been sixteen years since Constance first laid eyes on her, but there's no mistaking who she is.

"Mama?" Anne straightens. "I said I would handle this."

"I told you," Sandra replies, her tone firm. "This isn't the way." She makes a motion for Constance to stand. "Release her. She's done nothing to you. This is about Papa and his choices."

"No," Anne says, her forehead creasing. "This is for you, Mama. For all of us. Don't you see?"

"You will not hurt her, Anne. Do you hear? I forbid it. Give me the knife."

Anne's face crumples. For a moment Constance, who's come to her feet, thinks Anne will fall into her mother's arms. Instead, the former nanny's head snaps up and she runs at her. Constance pitches left and almost falls into the water. She rights herself, her hands coming up to fend off the knife that's now clasped in both of Anne's hands. With all her strength, she struggles to prevent the knife's descent. To her horror, it comes ever closer, the tip piercing her coat.

"Anne, *stop!*"

Sandra tries to wrench her daughter away, but with one savage thrust, Anne drives the knife into her upper arm. Pain radiates and shoots through her body. She screams again, buckles, and sinks to her knees. Anne is there, reaching to drive the knife further, but Sandra bellows and pushes Anne.

A splash as something hits the water. Running steps. Someone calls Constance's name. The scene fuzzes then clears. The fog swirls and Sandra is huddled at the edge.

Turbulence in the water. "Mama!"

Sandra's arm stretches out. "Come to me, Anne! *Anne!*"

Constance concentrates all her strength on the water, her breaths ragged. Anne goes under and her words play back: *I don't swim.* She can save her. She can. She tries to move, but the world spins. The pain, the *pain.* She looks down. To her horror, the knife is still embedded in her arm.

As she collapses to her back, Sandra keens at the edge, a high-pitched wail that enters her bones.

A shout. Running steps.

All goes black.

Chapter 34

Northern Hospital

Liverpool, England

February 7, 1904

Her children walk among a field of daisies, fingers skimming the blooms. The day is golden, the air laced with dandelion clocks. Janie is in a butter-yellow dress, ringlets bouncing. She cups her hands and whispers into Billy's ear. They turn together, find her watching. Billy takes his sister's hand and they run to her, twin conspirators flushed with sun. Below his short trousers, Billy's knees are dimpled and dirty. Janie's mouth is smudged with jam. From behind him, Billy reveals a peacock feather. He lays it in her palm as if he has bestowed upon her the greatest of treasures. When his eyes meet hers, they are the same violet blue as her own.

The scene darkens. Black swirls of fog and water invade her senses. Her children recede to pinpoints and are gone. There is only darkness and cold. She floats, suspended in the black. Her strength is ebbing, but she manages to lift her head. Light glows above, at the surface. It streams through the water like bands of silk. Air bubbles float from her mouth like translucent pearls. Her legs kick and she finds she can rise a little. Her arms reach but fall short of the light. Her limbs are burdens now, not her salvation.

She must leave the children. She can't protect them as she vowed, and the knowledge of it breaks her into pieces. But she doesn't want to die. She can't end, not like this. As long as there is a seed of possibility that she will see them again, there is something to live for.

She surges up, up, legs kicking. Her head crowns the surface.

Constance opens her eyes with a gasp. Bright light. Blurred, indistinct shapes. A white blot moves closer.

"Miss?"

A face swims into focus. A woman in a nurse's cap. One of her front teeth is crooked. There is something splendid about it. Precious.

She lies in bed, tucked into a blanket like a sausage in a casing. Late afternoon light spills through the window, the dying sun a bright orange lozenge. It dapples the blanket covering her.

"Can you sit up, miss?"

The nurse fusses with pillows and she lifts her shoulders. Pain explodes through her body—limbs, ribs, every muscle cramping, twinging, stinging. Her left arm is wrapped with gauze to the elbow. Her nails are broken. Blood has dried along her cuticles. Her arm throbs when she tries to move it and for a moment, she sees stars.

"Best keep it still for now, if you can manage it." The nurse helps back her up against the headboard. By the time it is done, she's exhausted. The nurse pours water from a pitcher and brings the glass to her with a smile.

"Thank you." The water is an oasis to her throat. She drinks and drinks. When she's finished, her lungs ache. "Where am I?"

"Northern Hospital on Great Howard Street. You were brought in several days ago. Seems you were a victim of a mugging down in the North Docks, miss. That awful fog didn't help a bit, but there's nothing for it now. You'll be as good as new in no time. I'll tell the doctor you're awake. There's a gentleman waiting to see you. Do you feel up to talking?"

She nods, not quite certain why she is here. The reason floats at the edge of her senses, but she's not ready to grasp it. The sun is too pretty on the blanket. She wants to look and look, absorb it. It's like the nurse's tooth. Beautiful. Something to be wondered at, cherished.

The nurse leads a man into the room and closes the door halfway, leaving the two of them alone.

As soon as Constance sees him, memories collide: her race through the fog, the struggle with Anne and the knife, Sandra appearing from nowhere. The image of Anne fighting to stay afloat in the water and Sandra's cries bring tears to her eyes.

Topp's eyes are watchful as he takes her in. He removes his hat and dips his head. She reaches her good arm out to him. He takes her hand, his smile transforming his face.

"It's good to see you, Mr. Topp, but how..." Her voice trails off. She doesn't understand.

"May I?" Topp indicates a chair across the room. He scoots it to the bed and takes a seat. "I warned you about the docks."

She nods, chastened. "I should have listened."

"I packed my bags and made my way to the train station after we argued," Topp says. "I felt I'd done all I could for you. But in the end, I couldn't leave. As angry as I was, it didn't feel right to desert you. I've learned in this business to trust my gut,

304

Mrs. Sullivan. I realized your desire to talk to Edward and Anne alone was you trusting yours. Though it was damned foolish."

"You came back for me," she says. For a moment, it is everything. It's been a long time since anyone showed regard for her. She looks down at their clasped hands. She couldn't bear to be touched days ago, couldn't bear the feel of skin against her own. Already she is changing, warming to things long denied her.

"Good thing I did." If his words are meant to chastise her, they fall short of the mark. "I'll tell you my end of the story, but you'll have to fill me in on yours. I'm still trying to piece together what happened." Topp places an elbow on his thigh and leans forward. "You are well enough for this?" At her nod, he continues. "By the time I left the station, it was getting late. I inquired at the Anchor if you were in and when the clerk said you'd gone out, I took a cab to Chisenhale Street. There was quite a disturbance going on due to a fire."

"That was my doing." She tells him of her first visit to Anne, and that she decided to return. "I waited for her in her flat. She'd left the door open. When she arrived, she drew a knife. The only way I was getting out of that flat was to drop the candle I was holding, along with the bottle of gin I brought to loosen her tongue."

"The gin helped fuel the fire," Topp says, musing.

"Yes." She looks at him. "Was...did anyone..." Her eyes fill. She can't say it.

"No victims, Mrs. Sullivan. I confirmed it later after I brought you here. Everyone got out. There was considerable damage to the building, but no real injuries to speak of."

Thank heaven. "I rushed to the street after that. I don't know what I feared most—that Anne was burning to death, or she was coming after me. It was you, Mr. Topp. You were the man who called my name. It must have been your carriage I heard."

"Yes. But I also thought I heard someone else. I was afraid to

call after you again and betray my presence—and yours. I didn't
know what exactly happened in that flat, but I knew it wasn't
good. Of course, I hoped you would make your way back to the
Anchor, but someone was heading down the street ahead of me
and appeared to be following someone else—possibly you. The
problem was the train. I lost the trail after that. I went south
down Pall Mall, but there was nothing, no one. I was frantic. I
retraced my steps and heard someone call your name. A woman.
It was coming from the water, or near it."

She shivers, recalling the slithery way the sound had crept
through the fog, how frightened she'd been.

"I waited, listening for anything that might tell me where
you were. Presently, I heard a scream. It helped me pinpoint
your location, but it wasn't until the second scream that I
jumped the gate. I knew I was close. I heard voices and crept
closer to the water. Then someone shouted for Anne and there
was another scream and what sounded like a skirmish.
Someone, or something, hit the water and I heard the most
awful wailing. By the time I came upon you, you were lying on
your back with a blasted knife in you. Anne—if she was the one
who followed you—was gone."

"Do you mean to say Sandra wasn't there when you
found me?"

"Sandra?" Topp shakes his head, thoroughly perplexed. "No
one was there. It was just you."

A memory unfurls. "When my husband said his goodbyes to
the children before he died, I should've known then, if not
before," she says, more to herself than Topp. "Anne was in the
doorway looking on and he called her to the bed. I thought he
meant to apologize. William had been unkind to her since the
day my son went into the pond. She was supposed to be
watching the children that day but Billy almost drowned." She
recalls Billy's strange behavior on the landing, the bruise she'd

seen on his arm. "Anne was unkind to Billy. It was all right there. My son tried to tell me, but I wasn't paying attention. Anne despised us."

She remembers coming upon Anne in William's room, her odd look as she stared down at him sleeping. She had believed Anne wasn't herself, that she was in some sort of fugue. How wrong she'd been. The girl she'd seen was the real Anne, unmasked. A daughter looking down at the father she'd come to loathe and wanted dead.

Constance's vision blurs as her eyes fill. Topp reaches in his breast pocket and hands her a handkerchief. He stares at her as if she might disintegrate if he speaks.

"I shouldn't have trusted what anyone told me," she says between sobs. "Had I relied on myself, my own intuition, none of it would've happened." She takes a deep breath and says slowly, "Anne was my husband's daughter by his longtime mistress. I should've known, but I didn't see it. Now she's dead." She can't quite grasp it. The woman who had brought so much chaos to her life is gone. Then she pours it out, all of it: William's other family, his desertion of them, Anne's position as nanny, her wish to see her father dead and her with him. She explains the picture album she found in Anne's flat, seeing William smiling from its pages.

"And Sandra? She was your husband's mistress?"

Constance had never told him. It hadn't seemed important. "Yes, Anne's mother." Topp's eyes widen. "I believed she and the children left town years ago—another of my husband's lies. I thought I saw her at trial one day."

"I remember reading in the trial notes that Ingrid mentioned another family of William's," Topp says. "She testified you made the whole thing up so she'd help you get a divorce as I recall."

"Yes."

"Forgive me, Mrs. Sullivan. I never dreamed they were

connected to this. I should have asked you more about them. I could have searched for Sandra. Discovered she and Anne were related."

"I doubt it. Anne changed her surname when she became our nanny." She pauses, sifting details. "Anne must've gone to Sandra after my first visit to her flat. I threatened to find the truth. She was probably scared I'd discover her link to William and stir the whole thing up again. Sandra must've followed Anne after she left her. She must've been worried Anne might seek to harm me. Sandra came upon us at the dock, just like you did. She told Anne to leave me be. That Anne's anger was misplaced."

"Indeed it was."

Her throat tightens. "She tried to pull Anne away from me. She might've stabbed me through the heart if it wasn't for Sandra." She worries the handkerchief. Her fingers smart with the effort. Every part of her aches. "Anne wouldn't stop attacking me with the knife and Sandra pushed her. She went into the water. It was an accident. She only wanted...Anne couldn't swim."

The words settle in the room, their implication clear. "I see," he says. "The wail I heard..."

"Sandra." She stares at Topp. "She must have heard you coming and slipped away into the fog."

She tells him of Anne's attempt to poison her the day William died. She feels strangely detached from the memory, as if it happened to someone else.

"Anne wanted to do to you what she'd done to her father."

"That's the thing," she says, frowning. "Anne didn't poison him, though she tried. She told me that, once William got sick, she wanted to quicken the process. She added the arsenic to the Valentine's Meat Juice, hoping the nurse would give him some of it. She must have heard Edward tell the nurse he'd put the bottle on the landing for William. The nurse seeing me touch the bottle played right into Anne's hands. But he never had anything from it; the nurse removed it from the table. In the end, it was clear he would die anyway. His habitual dosing caught up with him."

"So he wasn't murdered," Topp muses. "He died from years of arsenic abuse. I suppose that explains why the doctors didn't find a fatal dose in him." There's a tick of silence, then he says, "The police will hear nothing of this. Not from me."

Her head snaps up and she searches his eyes. "But I should go to them. I must tell them about Anne—"

"To what end? It's a nasty business, but no good will come of her drowning being connected to you. You're not to blame. You've been punished enough, Mrs. Sullivan."

She wipes her eyes and squeezes his hand again. "I owe you an apology, Mr. Topp. Please forgive me for sending you away, for saying the ugly words I did. This was something I wanted to do alone, and I was frightened that if Anne saw you, I'd learn nothing."

"I have already forgiven you, Mrs. Sullivan. I only wish I'd followed you straightaway instead of going to the station first."

"You were angry." She smiles through her tears. "You saved my life, and I don't even know your first name."

He smiles, the pearls of his teeth flashing white. "Tipp."

"How lovely and unique." She blinks. "Wait a second..."

A corner of Topp's mouth lifts and then they are both laughing.

"One of the things Sir Charles insisted when I began to work for him was my anonymity," Topp says. "He wanted to make sure my privacy, and my safety, were always protected. I feel so different from the boy he rescued from the streets. I suppose I've become my alter ego."

"Sir Charles was a very wise man."

They speak a few more minutes. Topp promises to visit in the morning when he will say his final goodbye.

A quarter of an hour later, the doctor arrives, fussing over her with his stethoscope and taking her pulse. "How are you feeling?"

She feels the peace of a stilled moment, perfect and golden. "Alive. Very much alive."

Chapter 35

The East Wharf

Newhaven, England

February 11, 1904

Constance narrows her eyes at the afternoon sun as she emerges from the dining room of the London & Paris Hotel. The wharf bustles. Sailors lash a tugboat to the quay. Seamen stack crates onto horse-drawn carts. The odor of seawater and rope hemp hangs heavy, mingled with the smell of pasties a vendor hawks from a rickety wooden cart. A dog dances around him, barking at the gulls wheeling above for a stray piece of meat.

She settles on a bench, her attention directed south where the ships roll in from the channel. Light dances on the water like molten gold and it's as if the sun has come out just for her. There is not a single press agent in sight. According to the *Liverpool Daily Post*, an anonymous tip that one Constance

Sullivan, late of Aylesbury Prison, was seen in Liverpool at Pier Head purchasing an ocean liner ticket to New York sent reporters scrambling to follow. The edges of her mouth lift. The paper printed the tip in full. It was signed cryptically 'T.T.'

While her body mended in hospital, her mind spooled back to the past—to the mistakes she made, the wrongs done her. She hadn't known in prison what to do with the weight. The past was a burden so great, it threatened to mince her in its claws. And so she lived with the rage for years, and it had kept her alive.

Then Topp appeared like a mirage, willing to help her learn what she'd ached to know for so long.

Her thoughts tick to William. If he were living now, would they be happy? Would they have worked through the troubles of their marriage? He was irascible, a firebrand, but kind-hearted and passionate, too. He had loved her, and she him. As for his longtime relationship with Sandra, what man would criticize him for it? What man would point a finger? Women have never been judged by the same standards as men. Perhaps one day they will be considered on equal terms. But that day, she fears, is far in the future.

She thinks, too, of Anne. That she is here, her lungs filling, her heart pumping, and Anne is not. She feels no anger, no contempt for William's daughter, only a deep sadness for the life Anne might have led. While she floats somewhere in the velvet black, Constance has taken measure of her life. Laid it out and tried to fit the pieces of herself, and the crime against her, together.

The greatest realization, the one that bewildered her as she lay healing in hospital, is that Sandra—the woman she'd hated for years, the woman who'd curdled her marriage—saved her life. She could not have intended to pitch Anne into the water. It was a mistake in the heat of the moment, and Sandra will live

312

with it for the rest of her life. It can never be undone, but she hopes Sandra will heal and the pang of loss will ease with time.

As for her own children, she is pulsing with anticipation for their reunion. Snug inside her bag is a folder with details she'll need to contact them, courtesy of Topp. "A parting gift," he'd said, and she'd cried so hard at the kindness of it, he'd left her with his handkerchief. Her darling Janie will know her. She will learn her daughter all over again—every trait, every mood, every longing. She will stroke her hair, cup her cheek, embrace her. Drink her in. They will laugh, they will sing, they will cry together. Billy is already a man. She has missed his childhood. She has missed the boy. But his life is ahead of him, and she will be there, part of his future.

It's not too late.

The doctor said she must mind her health, that her lungs are weak. She must rest. Recuperate. Paris will be good for her. She will walk with her mother down its streets with greedy eyes, eager for fresh experiences, hungry to make new memories. When her health is restored, she'll return to America. After she reconciles with her children, perhaps she will write her memoirs. Campaign for prison reform.

The SS *Arundel* slides up the river. Her mother is aboard, too impatient for Constance to come to her. Instead, she boarded at Dieppe to take the steam packet over so they can cross the Channel to France. Together.

She comes to her feet. Imaginings swirl. She envisions her mother on deck waving a white handkerchief, the glisten of tears on her cheeks. She will see, once she steps from the ship, that her daughter hums with well-being, that her life sings with possibility.

THE END

Author's Note

The Arsenic Eater's Wife is inspired by the 1889 court case of Florence Elizabeth Chandler Maybrick, the first American woman sentenced to hang in England. My version of events closely follows her marriage, her husband's sickness, Florence's affair, trial, conviction, sentence commutation, and incarceration. However, my story diverts from the historical record from the point that she's released from prison (more on that below). For this reason, I decided to change the names of the characters in the book. If I was going to give the players alternate 'endings,' I needed to make them truly fictional.

When Florence was released from prison in 1904, she was broken in body and spirit, having endured fifteen years of hard labor. After returning to America, she wrote her memoirs and went on a lucrative five-year lecture tour, campaigning for prison reform. After that, interest in her waned. She began to recede from public life. She eventually ended up in a small two-room cottage in Connecticut in the woods. As the years passed, she became increasingly more reclusive. She stopped bathing and began to take in cats. She was by then relying on charity for food and fuel. Her health declined swiftly.

In 1941, she was found dead inside her home dressed in filthy rags, surrounded by cats, her mattress teeming with insects, her front teeth held together with a piece of string. She was seventy-nine years old.

Tragically, Florence never saw her children again. In 1911, two months before his wedding, Florence's son died in a freak accidental poisoning (he swallowed potassium cyanide mistaking it for drinking water). Her daughter would go on to marry a navy lieutenant in London, but her husband's family disowned him when they learned his wife was the daughter of a convicted murderer. She refused every appeal Florence made to see her, an outcome Florence described as 'a bitterness worse than death.'

So much *tragedy*. I wanted more for Florence. She deserved better.

As mentioned, my character, Constance Sullivan, follows Florence's story until the time of the latter's release from prison fifteen years later. Constance's tale is my re-imagining of what *might* have happened if Florence had had the energy and assistance to go after those who'd wronged her. The inimitable Mr. Topp, Constance's stalwart ally, is my invention. In my version of events, Constance's insistence on finding the truth was paramount to everything else when she was released. She burned to know how her husband died and, if he'd been murdered, who was to blame. I answered these questions by going back to the roots of the original case.

It was rumored that Florence and her brother-in-law, Edwin Maybrick (my Edward Sullivan), had been having an affair. There were whispers of love letters. However, none of them ever came to light during or after trial. Could it have been because the family destroyed them to avoid further scandal? In the days following her husband's death and later, when Edwin testified for the prosecution, he was bitter and outraged at

Florence. I believe, in part, it was because she'd spurned him and chosen Alfred Brierley (my Timothy Worth) instead.

Timothy's actions very closely match his alter ego, Alfred's. He abandoned Florence as soon as the scandal broke. He appeared in the gallery at court a few times but was never called for questioning. Just like the original case, while Constance's infidelity was on trial, neither her husband's nor her lover's conduct, extramarital or otherwise, had any bearing on the case.

When Florence's closest friend, Matilda Briggs (my Ingrid Berkshire), testified at trial, it was clear from the outset she was in the Maybrick camp. She adored Florence's husband, James. It was easy to cast her alter ego, Ingrid, as a jealous woman who despised Constance from the beginning. Hiring the servants and enticing Constance into writing to Timothy for help, then handing that note directly to the police, were facts I lifted from the original case. Such a devious woman!

And what of the children's nanny, Alice Yapp (my Anne Yardley)? This is where the Maybrick saga gets *really* interesting. The nanny was described at the time as 'a very efficient, capable woman but a most deceitful and treacherous one.' For all her shadiness, she might have been conjured from a Dickens' novel. There are accounts of Florence scolding Alice for her cruel treatment of the children. Her testimony about the fly papers and reading her mistress's love letter (she really did open it and tell the jury that one of the children had dropped it in the mud) were the beginning of the end for Florence. But where did all that spite come from? I decided that the source of her alter ego's maliciousness would be rooted in her blood relation to the master of the house. Was Alice really the daughter of James Maybrick? No. Her decline into alcoholism and financial strife are also my invention.

Sarah Robertson (my Sandra Roberts) was and remains an elusive character. She was mentioned at the inquest and trial only in passing. No evidence has surfaced that she and James Maybrick ever married, but I did wonder. Years after the trial, a Bible came to light handed down in Sarah's family that James gifted Sarah on her birthday in 1865. 'To my darling Piggy,' it read. He signed it, 'your affectionate husband, J.M.' While the record is clear that Florence knew about Sarah and her children, I could find no reference as to *how* she learned of them. Therefore, Constance's stealthy tail of her husband to Sandra's home on Old Hall Street is my creation, as is Sandra's maternal relationship to Anne.

By narrowing the charge so definitively to arsenic poisoning, the cause of James Maybrick's demise will be forever shrouded in mystery. No tests were ever conducted that might have revealed other poisons in his system, poisons that James was known to have self-administered regularly (such as strychnine). For this reason, I chose for Anne to assume her father's long addiction to arsenic was what killed him. In other words, slow suicide. In the weeks he lay languishing, it exited his system, leaving only a trace. For me, the big question wasn't who killed William. It was who wanted Constance blamed for it.

As if adultery wasn't enough to make Constance look guilty, there is that mysterious bottle of Valentine's Meat Juice. It is a fact of the original case that *someone* added half a grain of arsenic to it. While Constance had motive and opportunity, so too did Edward, Ingrid, and Anne.

I took much of Justice Stevenson's final address to the jury from the court record. The real judge, Justice James Fitzjames Stephen, was blatantly against Florence in his closing statements. He would later be called 'Mad Judge Stephen' due to some erratic behavior which began in 1885 when he apparently suffered his first stroke. During Florence's trial, he was often confused, uttering strange statements, and needing clarification from the barristers on details of the case. This mental decline led to his retirement a few years after the trial. He died in 1894 in an asylum—just five years after Florence's conviction.

It is true that, with the exception of the judge, every legal man at St. George's the day Florence was found guilty immediately signed a petition against the verdict. This included the counsel for the prosecution, who was heard to say as the jury was being led out to deliberate, "Well, they can't convict her on that evidence." That half a million American and British citizens would later sign a petition for her release is a testament not only to the popularity of the trial, but the outrage it garnered.

The Maybrick trial is often cited as one of the cases that led to two important changes in English law. At the time, a defendant indicted for murder couldn't testify on his or her own behalf. It wasn't until the enactment of the Criminal Evidence Act of 1898 that a person accused of murder was allowed to give evidence. For Florence, it came nine years too late.

The second change was the creation of England's Court of Appeal in 1907. At the time of Florence's trial, there was no legal framework upon which to propose a criminal appeal. One wonders how her story might have differed had she been granted one.

"A time will come," Florence wrote prophetically in her memoirs, "when the world will acknowledge that the verdict which was passed upon me is absolutely untenable. But what then? Who shall give back the years I have spent within prison walls; the friends by whom I am forgotten; the children to whom I am dead; sunshine; the winds of heaven; my woman's life, and all I have lost by this terrible injustice?"

I like to think *The Arsenic Eater's Wife* as my justice for Florence. The alternate course her life might have taken.

Author's Note

Further Reading on the Maybrick Case*

Blake, Victoria. *Mrs. Maybrick*. Surry, UK: Crime Archive, 2008.

Gordon, Dee. *Bad Girls from History: Wicked or Misunderstood?* Yorkshire, England: Pen & Sword Books, 2017.

Hutto, Richard Jay. *A Poisoned Life*. McFarland & Company, Inc. Jefferson, NC:, Publishers, 2018

Jones, Christopher. *The Maybrick A to Z*. Countyvise, 2008.

MacDougall, Alexander William. *The Maybrick Case*. London, England, Bailliere, Tindall and Cox, 1891.

Maybrick, Florence Elizabeth. *Mrs. Maybrick's Own Story: My Fifteen Lost Years*. Big Byte Books, 1905

*Note: There is some (admittedly *very* inconclusive) evidence that James Maybrick may have been Jack the Ripper, the infamous serial killer who terrorized London in the late 19th century (to be fair, there are *a lot* of suspects on that list!). James wasn't fingered for the murders of the five prostitutes until 1992 when a diary surfaced purportedly written by him. Whether the diary is a hoax is a subject of debate. It was a rabbit hole I chose not to go down. For more, you can read *The Last Victim: The Extraordinary Life of Florence Maybrick, the Wife of Jack the Ripper*. Or take the plunge on numerous Ripper sites and forums online.

Acknowledgments

I owe a huge debt of gratitude to Kim Taylor Blakemore, my first reader and earliest champion of the book. Kim, your attention to detail and suggestions helped the story shine. Thank you for talking me back from the ledge with the "instead of 'based on', how about 'inspired by?'" conversation that turned the book around for the better. Your genius and editing expertise are much appreciated. I'd also like to thank my early beta readers, some of whom read the manuscript *twice*! Pam Lecky, Tonya Ulynn Brown, Maryka Biaggio, and Jenny Graman, you are my heroes. I am always happy to return the favor.

A happy accident along the way of researching this book was my discovery of the UK podcast, *The Poisoners' Cabinet*. To my delight, episode 47, *Florence Maybrick & the Endless Accusations*, was every bit as dark and intriguing as I'd hoped. Those fifty-three minutes were yet another sign this story needed to be written. Sinead Hanna and Nick Gordon, thank you for your comedy and brilliance, and bringing this feast for the ears to weekly listeners. You're an addiction, and my liquor cabinet proves it (every episode features a cocktail themed to the story!).

Huge thanks to the folks at Bloodhound Books who believed in me and my manuscript. Betsy, your initial email was the stuff of dreams. I read it in an office supply store while I was shopping for printer paper. That Office Depot will always hold a special place in my heart. Thank you for walking me through Bloodhound's process and the elements of the contract. Tara,

Abbie, and Vicky thank you for your patience and putting up with my endless questions. Your professional expertise is first class.

To Connie Murphy, my sister and early reader, I thank you. You always drop everything and buckle down with what I send, whenever I send it—even when your day is full. Your opinion means everything to me, big Sis.

Without the patience and understanding of my family, this book wouldn't exist. To my boys, Thomas, Nicholas, and Christopher: thank you for putting up with my endless hours at the kitchen table and for allowing me to disappear into my office for authory stuff. This one didn't take as long as the first! I'm getting better!

And as always, thank you to my husband, Ron. My biggest fan and the one whose own hard work allows me to do this tricky thing called writing. I love you.

About the Author

Tonya Mitchell's debut historical novel, *A Feigned Madness,* won the Reader Views Reviewers Choice Award and the Kops-Fetherling International Book Award for Best New Voice in Historical Fiction. She is a member of the Women Fiction Writers Association and the Historical Novel Society. She lives in the US with her husband, three boys, and an overweight golden doodle.

For more: https://www.tonyamitchellauthor.com

Book Club Guide

1. In the beginning chapters, what were your first impressions of Constance's illness and her being shut away in her home?

2. What were the early indications that Constance's marriage wasn't a happy one?

3. Have you ever heard of an 'arsenic eater'? How might William's addiction compare (or not) to an addiction today? Do you think his hypochondria played into his addiction?

4. In chapter seven, the reader learns of Constance's history of cutting herself. What other ways might women in her era have dealt with the pressures of society? Do women today have better outlets for dealing with societal expectations?

5. The judge's final statements to the jury were extremely biased against Constance. In the original 1889 case upon which the book is based, there was no criminal court of appeal, therefore there was no legal framework to retry the case. If a new trial had

been possible, do you think the verdict would have been different? Why or why not?

6. Did Timothy Worth's behavior surprise you? Do you think the trial would have gone differently if he had openly supported Constance?

7. The behavior of those in the house against Constance was in many ways a 'perfect storm.' She had many enemies working against her. Why do you think this was? Was Constance simply too trusting or was she just a victim of bad luck?

8. Was Constance's plan to confront Ingrid, Edward, and Anne a good or bad idea? What would you have done in her shoes?

A note from the publisher

Thank you for reading this book. If you enjoyed it please do consider leaving a review on Amazon to help others find it too.

We hate typos. All of our books have been rigorously edited and proofread, but sometimes mistakes do slip through. If you have spotted a typo, please do let us know and we can get it amended within hours.

info@bloodhoundbooks.com

Printed in Great Britain
by Amazon